DOCTOR WHO

IMPERIAL MOON
CHRISTOPHER BULIS

Published by BBC Worldwide Ltd,
Woodlands, 80 Wood Lane
London W12 0TT

First published 2000
Copyright © Christopher Bulis 2000
The moral right of the author has been asserted

Original series broadcast on the BBC
Format copyright © BBC 1963
Doctor Who and TARDIS are trademarks of the BBC

ISBN 0 563 53801 5
Imaging by Black Sheep, copyright © BBC 2000

Printed and bound in Great Britain by Mackays of Chatham
Cover printed by Belmont Press Ltd, Northampton

Prologue

The Queen Empress herself came to see the expedition depart.

As guards patrolled the rugged heather-lapped cliff walls above, the small black-clad figure, accompanied by Commodore Bristow and her loyal attendant, inspected the three ships and the crews assembled before them. The Queen Empress had taken a keen interest in the project and it was only natural that she should be there to witness the culmination of so many months of work.

With final words of encouragement and wishes of Godspeed on their voyage, she was escorted to a small viewing platform. The crews entered their ships and the hatches were sealed.

For a minute all was quiet. Every eye was fixed upon the silvery hulls of the ships as they rested on their splayed support struts. A low hum emanating from each of the vessels became noticeable, gradually rising in pitch until it passed beyond the range of hearing. The ships rocked slightly as though swayed by the wind, and then, with only the slightest sigh of displaced air, they lifted clear of the ground.

A hundred feet up, their support legs retracted, folding inwards into their tail sections. Like great silver bullets they hurtled skyward, gaining speed every second. By the time they had vanished from sight in the clouds they were travelling faster than the sounds of cheering that echoed up from the glen below.

Supported by her attendant, the Queen Empress made her way back to her waiting transport. As they proceeded she heard the man muttering under his breath.

'Whatever is the matter, John?' she asked.

'I dinnae hold with this.' He gestured at the sky with his free arm. 'The heavens are nae for men to roam in. Yon machines are nae natural.'

'We live in an age of change, of scientific and mechanical marvels. We cannot pretend otherwise.'

'Mark my words: nae good will come of this.'

Her steps faltered. 'Do you have a vision?'

'Just a bad feeling in me bones.'

And so, wrapped in thoughtful silence, John Brown helped Queen Victoria into her carriage then took his seat on the box by the coachman.

As they drove back to Balmoral, Victoria mused over Brown's gloomy premonition. For years she had suspected him of having second sight after he had seemed to foretell the death of her dear Albert. But even she was powerless to change things now, she reminded herself. The future was taking its, no doubt predestined, course.

It was 3 September 1878, and the first ships of the Imperial British Space Fleet were on their way to the Moon.

Chapter One
Time Wake

Turlough would never have chosen to talk over his problems with Kamelion, had his current circumstances been anything approaching normal. But as he was travelling in a space-time ship beyond what most people would consider the accepted boundaries of reality, his options were somewhat restricted. In fact, since Tegan had left the TARDIS's crew, his possible confidants were limited to either Kamelion or the Doctor.

He had to talk to somebody, that was certain. Muttering angrily to himself, he had decided, was proving unproductive and was also meant to be, he recalled, the first sign of madness.

Turlough was not sure he completely trusted Kamelion; the shape-shifting android had been a tool of an enemy of the Doctor's when they had first met him, and he was still an unsettling companion. But at least it wouldn't look at him with too-deep eyes as the Doctor did, or give that slight knowing smile that had been shaped by centuries of experience and which made Turlough, though he never liked to admit it, feel like a callow youth.

He hesitated at the entrance to Kamelion's room. It was hardly more than an alcove furnished with a single chair, but it seemed to be all Kamelion required. Unless called for, he would sometimes sit there motionless for days at a time. Turlough realised, with a rare pang of guilt, that until now he had not considered whether Kamelion was content with his situation. Perhaps he was meditating – always assuming androids could meditate.

Turlough cleared his throat as he stepped inside. Kamelion's silver mask of a face, with its permanent expression of mild interest, turned towards him. Through it shone two disconcertingly human blue eyes.

'Er… hi, Kamelion,' Turlough said. 'How're you doing?'

'I am functioning within my specified parameters, if that is what you mean, Mister Turlough,' Kamelion replied in his smooth, perfectly modulated voice.

'Good… fine…' Turlough said, thrusting his hands into his pockets and beginning to feel embarrassed.

Kamelion observed him for a moment.'Is there any service I can perform for you?'

'Well, if you're not busy…' Turlough's words sounded foolish even as he said them. What was the matter with him?

'I am only listening to the TARDIS,' Kamelion said.

Despite his own preoccupations Turlough hesitated, suddenly curious:'Listening to the TARDIS? You mean it talks to you?'

'In a manner of speaking. Our data-stream rhythms are compatible, so I can access its memory banks and experience something of its travels. They are most enlightening. We have much in common, you know. We both are shape-shifters… and both serve the same master.'

His words made Turlough feel uncomfortable. Of course it was only the way the android was programmed to respond, automatically giving allegiance to the strongest mind in his vicinity. Doubt assailed Turlough once more. What use would it be, confessing his problems to such a creature? Still, it was better than talking to himself.

'Well, can you listen to me for a while?'

'Of course.'

Turlough began pacing up and down. 'Look, there's something missing in my life but I don't know what it is,' he said in a rush.

'You lack some material possession which you cannot name?'

'No, I mean metaphorically, emotionally, that sort of thing. I should be having a great time. I've got away from school, I've had some fantastic adventures in wild places… but where has it all got me?'

'I regret I am not an expert in humanoid psychology.'

'I thought you read the minds of the people you copied. Didn't you learn anything about them?'

'I cannot read every detail of a being's mind. Whatever knowledge I acquire is only applied to the behaviour of the

4

particular life form I have assumed. I was not designed to interpolate the data into generalisations of a psychological nature.'

Turlough's shoulders slumped. 'OK, well, it was worth trying.' He stepped to the doorway then hesitated. 'Are you happy, Kamelion?'

'I am not designed to be "happy", but I experience what you might call contentment knowing I am fulfilling the purpose for which I was created.'

Purpose, Turlough thought, turning the word over in his mind. Was that the key? Did he have so much trouble getting on with other people because they had purpose and he didn't? Was that the cause of his ambiguous feelings about the Doctor, who had more sense of purpose than anybody he'd ever met? Why? Because he had a past – centuries of past! Even Kamelion had his programming. But Turlough only had a blank space where his past should be. He knew he wasn't Earthborn, but he had no idea where his homeworld lay or why he had been exiled from it. No past, no purpose... no sense of belonging.

'Kamelion. Copy me right now!' he snapped.

Kamelion's outline shimmered, was enveloped for a moment in sparkling points of light, then solidified into a new form.

Turlough's breath caught in his throat as he saw his own face staring up at him. This was not like looking in the mirror. He forced himself to walk around his doppelgänger, examining it intently. Did he really have quite that bitter, preoccupied expression? Then a blindingly obvious fact struck him.

Why was he still wearing his old Brendon school uniform? He was never going back there and the TARDIS had a store of clothes he could have borrowed from. He must have kept it because, subconsciously, it provided some sense of continuity despite the generally miserable memories that clung to it.

Right, he couldn't begin to find out where he really belonged in the universe while he still wore that thing.

'Thanks, Kamelion,' he called out over his shoulder.

'You are welcome,' Kamelion replied.

Turlough was halfway down the corridor that led to the

wardrobe room when the floor under him shuddered. He grabbed a wall to steady himself. The ship began rocking to and fro.

'Uh, oh,' he muttered, 'here we go again.'

He turned about and headed up the corridor instead.

The Doctor was bent over the main console when Turlough ran into the control room.

'Another time corridor?' Turlough asked anxiously.

Without looking up from the controls the Doctor said: 'No, we're merely crossing our own temporal wake. It'll only last a few seconds more.'

Even as he spoke the wallowing sensation died away, leaving the floor steady underfoot again.

'What's a temporal wake?' Turlough demanded. 'A funeral party for time past?'

The Doctor beamed brightly at him. 'That's very good. I must remember that one.' Sometimes he behaves more like a schoolboy than I ever did, Turlough thought.

'Actually,' the Doctor continued, 'I was using the term in its nautical sense. We crossed a part of the hyperspace vôrtex that relates to a time and place in the past that we will obviously be visiting at some future date. Fortunately there was adequate temporal separation otherwise we might have met our future selves coming in the other direction, which could be very embarrassing. Still, it's all over now.'

Even as he spoke a pulsating whirring sound, rapidly descending in pitch, filled the room. The Doctor frowned and scanned the controls, punching buttons. 'That's very odd. We seem to be...' The whirring ended in a dull thud followed by silence. '... materialising,' he finished lamely.

'I take it this wasn't planned,' Turlough said.

'Not by me – at least I don't think so.' The Doctor touched the controls and the scanner screen came to life, revealing a grey, pitted and hummocked landscape starkly lit by a brilliant sun burning out of a black sky. The ground seemed to fall away before them, while a line of rounded mountains rose at their backs.

'Very uninviting,' Turlough said. 'Where are we?'

The Doctor was checking coordinates. 'On the far side of the Moon, apparently. The crater basin of Tsiolkovskii some time in the early twenty-first century. We were heading back to Earth and the twentieth century but seem to have stopped a little short.'

'Because of this temporal wake thing?'

'Perhaps, but by itself it shouldn't have triggered materialisation. However, this is the wake's physical, if not temporal, point of origin. We will have been here before – I'm afraid the English language doesn't really have the correct tenses for time travel.'

'So now what do we do?'

An urgent beeping filled the room. It was a sound Turlough had not heard before.

'Ah, the time safe,' the Doctor said. 'That might explain it.'

He crossed to the nearest wall and tugged at one of the recessed roundels. It hinged back to reveal a perfect mirror-like surface within.

'Stasis effect,' said the Doctor. 'It should shut off in a moment.'

'A time safe?' Turlough demanded. 'Wait, let me guess. In an ordinary safe you put valuables away for later use… so, in a time safe, you put things away later for prior use. Right?'

'Correct. It's a permitted temporal paradox, but it must be used sparingly. Whatever's in there has to be important.'

The mirror surface faded to reveal a dark cavity. The Doctor reached cautiously inside and withdrew a battered leather-bound pocketbook, much stained around the edges. He turned back the cover and read aloud the inscription, written in a neat copperplate hand, on the first page:

The personal diary of Captain Richard Haliwell, RN,
commanding Her Majesty's Astral Ship 'Cygnus'.
A record of her trip to the Moon in the Year of Our Lord 1878.

'1878?' Turlough exclaimed. 'Nobody had spaceships on Earth then. It's a joke!'

The Doctor was frowning thoughtfully.'Then why did I put it in the safe? I don't usually play tricks on myself.'

'Well, what else does it say? Read some more.'

Chapter Two
Diary: The Secret Mission

I am making this personal account of our remarkable journey in the hope that one day, when the necessary vale of secrecy surrounding our endeavours is lifted, it may be published in a suitably edited form as a supplement to the official record. It is my contention that our undertaking will have a profound effect upon mankind's appreciation of his place in creation, and that such small but telling observations may well be passed over by logbooks containing only facts and figures and scientific observations. At some future date I may recount in greater detail the preparations for the journey, but for now I shall only relate them briefly in the interests of completeness.

I was, then, early in the year 1878, one of the newest captains in Her Majesty's navy, having acquitted myself passably well off the South American Pacific coast the previous year, and now somewhat impatiently awaiting word on what ship would be my first command. The summons to the Admiralty was then not unexpected. It was only when I was shown into the presence of a Board of such distinguished members, headed by the first sea lord himself, the whole representing far greater seniority than would ordinarily be required to assign a captain to his ship, that I realised something singular was taking place.

This was confirmed when I was informed that the, as yet unspecified, posting was offered on a volunteer basis, and that I could decline without any adverse comment being entered upon my service record. During the course of the close questioning that followed, it became evident that they were looking for younger men in good health, who were also unmarried and preferably without close dependants. Also, that time spent at sea was not in itself their first consideration, rather evidence of an ability to think for oneself in circumstances beyond the scope of the naval manual. This at once suggested an unusual mission of some danger, which aroused both a thrill of excitement and trepidation within me. When the interrogation had finished and it was apparent that the Board were satisfied, I at once accepted my advancement and the mysterious assignment associated with it. Only then was I given the full details of the incredible undertaking to which I was now committed. Had my informants been men of any lesser standing I think I would have doubted their sanity.

Within a week I had arrived at the secluded base in which the great expedition was being prepared. Not one of the navy's home ports or even some outpost of the empire, but tiny Glen Marg, lying between the Cairngorms and Grampians, some twenty miles from Braemar. Such a remote site was chosen not only to reduce the chances of the aerial manoeuvres of the ships being witnessed, but in case of some accident occurring during ascent which might precipitate many tons of metal out of the sky.

The base comprised many wooden buildings, evidently erected in some haste, topped with shingled roofs and sided with lapped boards. These provided the somewhat spartan living quarters, mess halls and workshops. The only brick and tile buildings were those that housed the boilers and generators that supplied the considerable quantities of electrical power the base required. Only the final stages of assembly took place on the base. The numerous sections of the ships' hulls, internal frames and working components were built to precise specifications by many firms across the country, who had no conception of to what use they were to be put. These items were brought in by sea and rail and finally cart, to be checked over and then assembled with the aid of a mobile gantry running on rails, and a steam winch. When I arrived the three hulls were almost completed and work on their interior fittings was well under way.

The astral ships themselves were both extraordinary and yet oddly familiar, resembling gigantic artillery shells dotted with shuttered portholes and standing over a hundred feet high and

*perhaps fifty feet wide. Each vessel rested on four sturdy
latticework legs extending from a conical structure, tapering
downwards from the base of their main hulls, which housed a
double airtight hatch assembly.*

*I shall explain the ships' functions further as they become
relevant to my narrative. For now I only want to provide an
impression of the remarkable vessels as I saw them that first
day. In the same way, I must comment only in passing on the
three-hundred-odd persons who made up the strange little
community of Glen Marg. From the contingent of marine
guards that patrolled the surrounding hills and ensured no
stranger should disturb our labours, to the officers and ratings
who would serve as crew, to the riveters, instrument men and
hauliers; all played their part in our venture and will I trust one
day be able to publicly receive due credit. I may mention only
that the entirety of our efforts were ably co-ordinated by
Commodore Bristow, who ran the base with a strict but fair
hand.*

*One person I must single out for special mention is Professor
Boyes-Dennison FRS, without whose remarkable invention of
the impeller engine none of this would have been possible. He
divided his time between Glen Marg where he supervised the
installation of his engines in the ships, and London where
modifications to certain of its more delicate components were
being made. In this task he was assisted by his daughter Emily,
who was perhaps twenty-one or twenty-two years of age, and
who had his full confidence in all things.*

*Her presence as the only woman on a military base was,
needless to say, somewhat irksome to the commodore. However,
since the professor's continuing co-operation was essential to
the venture and he would not work without his daughter at his
side, there was no recourse but to accept Miss B-D's presence,
even as far as allowing her to participate in the journey itself.
I should have thought no father would have allowed his
daughter to undertake such a trip, considering the unknown
dangers involved, but it seemed that since the death of his wife*

he had become totally absorbed in his work, and appeared to view her as more a working assistant than his kin. I realised, as I came to know him better, that this was quite in keeping with the professor's character. Though perfectly amiable in an absent-minded way, he could also be selfish and short-tempered. There was a certain secretive side to his character, as though he was constantly afraid he might lose due credit for his invention.

I will say that Miss B-D performed her duties with every sign of efficiency and never complained about the lack of modern amenities in our isolated situation. However, on the occasions we talked of matters beyond the preparations of the ships, I found her more forthright in expressing her views than I personally feel is fitting for a lady.

As the ships were taking shape we had to train ourselves and our crews to man them. Officers and ratings alike had been selected as had I, namely that we had few dependants and all showed some aptitude above and beyond the ordinary in our various skills. However, the unusual nature of our commands required many modifications to standard naval procedure which have taxed both myself and my fellow commanders, Captains Sinclair and Green (who would command respectively the astral ships Lynx *and* Draco. *My ship would be the* Cygnus). *As steam power has introduced the engineer into the navy, now the possibilities opened up by the impeller device have brought the scientist and the specialist mechanical artisan on board ship. One day, no doubt, their presence will be taken for granted, but judging by the lessons of steam such acceptance will be both grudging and protracted. Meanwhile it fell to us to integrate these civilians, capable men but hardly versed in the ways of service life, with our regular crews.*

Finally we arrived at the following disposition of personnel to form the complement of each ship:

Officers:
Captain   *1*
Lieutenant   *1*

Sub-Lieutenant	1
Navigator	1
Engineers	2
Surgeon	1

Ratings:	
Bosun	1
Cook	1
Helmsmen	2
Surgeon's assistant	1
Cook's assistant	1
Signallers	2
Engine room assistants	6
Astral ship maintainers	6
Watchmen and general duties	10

Civilian special advisers:	
Mathematician	1
Electrical engineers	2

Civilian scientists/observers (2 from the following per ship):
Astronomer, Geologist, Cartographer, Chemist, Professor B-D and Daughter.

| Total complement per ship: | 42 |

And an odd list it must appear to those familiar with standard shipboard practice. But then so many normal seagoing functions would be absent in our ships, while other completely novel tasks would take their places. For example, we could think of no better general description for those men detailed to tend the devices that circulated and replenished the atmosphere, and also fed the electrical lighting and heating supply within the ships, than 'maintainers', but obviously their duties were vital ones.

These and numerous other matters were worked through and

solutions found. By the summer the impellers were fully installed and a few cautious tests confirmed they could raise the ships clear of the ground and support them there as long as their supply of electrical power lasted. Propulsive force, duration of lift and steering controls could now be adjusted and calibrated.

The question which must be taxing my reader by now is: how could such devices possibly function without the displacement of air or by the thrust of a rocket? Regretfully I cannot say. I requested the same explanation from the professor but simply could not understand his reply. Indeed he seemed to find himself at a loss for words at times, as though the concepts were clear in his own mind but science had not yet provided him with adequate terms for their communication with others. Neither could he explain the peculiar effect that limited the size and hence the lifting power of a single impeller device, and also why each of two units in some way interfered with the function of the other and so could not be placed inside the same hull. This restricted the tonnage of the astral ships and was the reason why we could not install the devices in a battleship, for instance. All I can say of them is that they were composed in part of evacuated glass tubes with strangely shaped wires mounted within that glowed brightly when operating, drawing considerable quantities of electrical power from great banks of batteries in the process. Loops of cable ran from them up through the inside of the ship's hull to which they were firmly secured.

Be that as it may, they functioned as the professor had promised. I do not say that the thought of trusting my life to whatever intangible forces they generated did not trouble me - indeed impeller tubes sometimes burnt out under heavy power - but provisions had been made for all foreseeable emergencies, and I believed we had a better than sporting chance of success.

The testing continued. For several days each ship was sealed, simulating an astral voyage. This was primarily to confirm that the automatic chemical devices for removing excess carbon dioxide from the air were functioning properly. The consumption of oxygen by a full crew was measured and adequate supplies of the gas, contained within pressurised bottles, were placed aboard.

At the end of July, while the Moon was near new, the first true flights were made to test the airtightness of the ships. With powerful but carefully shielded arc lights pointing skyward from our base to guide our return, over successive nights each ship was taken up to greater altitudes, making rapid 'hops' skyward that soon exceeded the maximum height so far attained by man – that of the 1875 ascent by the hydrogen balloon Zenith, launched from Paris, which reached 27,950 feet. By 4 August we had achieved the astounding altitude of one hundred miles. With essentially all Earth's atmosphere below us visibility was unimpeded. Had it been daylight or even moonlight the panorama laid out below us would have been no doubt spectacular. As it was we could observe the great black mass of the globe resting in a bowl of unwinking stars, and pinpricked by the lights of cities. Our altitude gave us a theoretical horizon of over 1,300 miles, which would include most of Europe! The great conurbation of London seemed almost at our feet, while the faint firefly flicker on the very limb of the world might well have been the lights of Rome.

At the top of these narrow ellipses we cut into space, and as our inertial motion diminished and before braking power was employed we experienced for the first time the predicted phenomenon of the apparent absence of all weight. Though we had taken precautions against this with straps on chairs and numerous handrails about the ship's interiors, some of our crew were so disturbed by the experience that they were physically sick. It was certainly disconcerting to see men and loose objects floating freely in mid-air, and I do not pretend that I enjoyed the sensation myself. Upon returning to Earth it was evident that a few could not face the like again, and had to be replaced by those men we held in reserve against such contingencies.

The professor seemed unaffected by our 'weightless' experiences, being preoccupied with the performance of his engines and other ship's devices, many of which he had designed himself.

Miss B-D was evidently more troubled by the experience, but continued stoically at her task. She was an amateur photographer and intended to record the expedition in pictures, setting up her camera opposite one of the portholes. I might add that for these ascents she wore jackets and riding britches; skirts, as she pointed out, being neither practical nor proper dress for such conditions. One could not argue with her reasoning, but I can foresee that this necessity will inevitably limit the number of female passengers who would undertake astral voyages in future if impeller propulsion ever enters the civilian sphere, since few ladies would be willing to don such attire.

After our sequence of experimental flights came a space of a few weeks when minor modifications and improvements were made to the ships, based upon the practical knowledge we had obtained, and provisions for the voyage were obtained and loaded. Meanwhile we waited for the Moon to enter its correct phase. It was planned to launch when it was in its waxing crescent so that when we arrived it would be half full and part of both its Earthside face and the mysterious far side would therefore be illuminated. The first date that would fulfil our requirements was 3 September.

And so I have made use of my relatively free time in the intervening period to set down the above. I will now make entries as events unfold in the manner of a normal diary and as an aide-mémoire, *to be further enlarged upon when time permits. I feel certain that whatever adventures or hardships lie before us, they will be of a most sensational nature.*

Chapter Three
Interruption

'Hold it!' Turlough said.

The Doctor lifted his eyes from the diary. 'What's the matter?'

'Come on, Doctor, who's writing this… H. G. Wells or Jules Verne? It's fiction. A secret navy base in a highland glen in 1878, a space-drive built by an eccentric scientist – with a beautiful daughter as an assistant.'

'The writer doesn't mention her looks.'

'Well, I bet she is.'

'Oh, so you agree she's real then?'

Turlough gritted his teeth. The Doctor could play very childish games at times. 'I mean it's too good to be true. A token woman along for the ride to provide love interest for Haliwell, but a proto-feminist rather than a shrinking violet just to make it interesting.'

'If she was a "shrinking violet" she would be unlikely to be part of the crew,' the Doctor pointed out. 'Nor were "proto-feminists" unknown at the time. There were several notable Victorian women explorers, and daughters have been known to help their scientist fathers before now, you know.' A wistful smile came to his lips. 'Sometimes even granddaughters. Never try to put limits on what people will do out of love or loyalty.'

'Well, I can't believe the Victorians could build working spaceships,' Turlough persisted. 'They just didn't have the technology. This has got to be a put-on.'

The Doctor looked thoughtful for a moment. 'By 1878 British engineering – especially shipbuilding – was about the best in the world. They could certainly have built a sound, airtight hull, which is the basic requirement of a spaceship. Captain Haliwell mentions testing that, also a chemical system for purifying the air. They could guard against the extremes of heat and cold they would encounter easily enough. They wouldn't know about the dangers of exposure to solar or cosmic radiation, of course, but

17

for a short trip to the Moon that wouldn't be much of a problem. The only thing completely beyond them would have been a conventional propulsion system…'

'Exactly!'

'But evidently Professor Boyes-Dennison's impeller device is *not* conventional. I admit it's the one detail that doesn't fit with the rest, but huge advances have sometimes occurred before their predicted time through one person's insight and intuition. It's not impossible that a crude form of reactionless drive could have been invented about two hundred years early.'

'But have you ever heard of this Boyes-Dennison?'

'No, I can't say the name's familiar, but then even I don't know every Earthly scientist who ever lived.'

'Maybe because he never existed! And isn't it convenient that, according to Haliwell, this professor can't explain how his impeller works?'

The Doctor smiled gently. 'Would you understand how the TARDIS works if I tried to explain it to you in detail?'

'Of course not.'

'But you still accept that it exists.'

'But that's because I've travelled in it and seen it work. That diary's just words on a page, not hard evidence.'

'My dear Turlough, you're quite right to be sceptical,' the Doctor said. 'But you must also keep an open mind when faced with the unexpected.'

'Can you do both at the same time?'

The Doctor smiled. 'I didn't say it was easy.'

Chapter Four
Diary: Circum Luna

3 September

The day and then the hour arrived, by which time we were all impatient to make that great leap out across the void and into the unknown. We planned to launch in daylight for convenience, since we were now confident that our ships would ascend so rapidly there would be little chance of them being seen. From the closest point to Glen Marg from which an outsider might observe us, we would appear no larger than birds and be visible for only a few seconds before passing into the clouds.

Her Majesty, who has shown a keen interest in the progress of the venture, graciously made the journey from Balmoral to witness our departure. With her kind wishes for a successful voyage and a safe return in our minds, we sealed the ships and settled ourselves in our padded chairs which tilted back on gimbal mounts. Controls were positioned so they could be operated from a reclining position.

Experiments had shown these fittings were essential to preserve consciousness when the effects of acceleration multiplied our apparent body weights by more than three times. Had we a means of storing an infinite supply of electrical power we could have made the ascent through the atmosphere at a more leisurely pace. But since every second of motion required energy simply to support the ships and combat the resistance of the air, the first stage of our flight had to be made as rapidly as possible. Unfortunately, the mysterious impeller effect does not move us along with the coils secured to the hull of the ship so we have to suffer the full force of our motion.

I watched the chronometer ticking off the seconds until the moment determined for launch. At my command the power flowed into the impeller and set its coils vibrating. A resonant hum sounded through the hull. Then the ship rose smoothly and inexorably upwards. There was a clank as the landing struts were retracted. Now we could feel the pressure growing and the distant howl of air passing over our hull. According to the calculated plan, I gave the helmsman the command to tilt the ship, judged by a pendulum hanging over a graduated scale. We made a long arc through the thinning atmosphere. When our rate of acceleration reached its predetermined maximum it was automatically limited by a preset spring weight actuating a rheostat control. At 120 miles altitude and travelling parallel with the Earth's surface, I ordered the power to the impellers cut and a state of weightlessness overcame us. We were in orbit about the Earth like a tiny moon.

We had our first sight of the sunlit globe of the Earth. Such was our velocity that, though we had only been in flight for a few minutes, we were already passing over central Asia. Great tracts of brown and green land were overlain with a thin haze of blue, supporting strikingly brilliant white spirals of cloud, each individual mass with its attendant shadow. Miss B-D was, needless to say, already working her camera to record the scene. If her pictures come out they will tell better than I can of the wonder of the sight.

We spotted our sister ships floating freely within a few miles of us and made contact by heliograph to confirm all was well. By synchronising all our manoeuvres we intend to stay within communications range throughout the voyage and thereby be ready to render mutual assistance should it be needed. Meanwhile we checked our course and position while recharging our batteries for the second stage of our journey.

To accomplish this, four parabolic mirror panels, which had been folded flat against the hull during our ascent, were released and cranked into an extended position so that they faced the Sun. At the focus of each mirror was a pipe containing mercury, which the concentrated solar rays boiled into a vapour.

This was channelled into the engine room where it drove a dynamo coupled to the batteries. Condensing the vapour in the cool shadow of the reflector panels returned it to its liquid state and so the cycle could be maintained. Meanwhile our navigators took sights through the domed glass portals set in the nose of the ship to confirm our course and speed, and to determine the optimum moment of our departure from orbit towards the Moon.

After three circuits of the globe our batteries had sufficient charge for the next stage of our journey. This was much easier than our launch, since we were in no danger of falling back to Earth and so we could increase our velocity gradually. The manoeuvre began on the far side of the Earth from the Moon so we climbed in a slow spiral. After the initial impulse the power of the drive was reduced to a constant acceleration rate of eight inches per second, the equivalent of one-fiftieth of gravity, which we calculate we can maintain whilst still keeping the batteries adequately charged. Not only is this steady acceleration less wearing on the impeller tubes, it also gave us an illusion of weight, even if it was only a couple of pounds or so. If this speed seems too slight to achieve our goal, then I should point out that after twelve hours we would be travelling at almost five and a half miles a second, and be about halfway to the Moon. At this point we would turn the ship about and apply the same acceleration to slow us down, so we should arrive with a manageable velocity.

And so, in company with our sister ships, we set out across a quarter of a million miles of void towards the Moon.

To the credit of her builders the Cygnus is functioning perfectly, except that after a few hours the side of the hull facing the Sun became uncomfortably warm, while the shadowed side became bitterly cold. The same problem has arisen on her sister ships. However, by rotating the ships every hour this disparity was equalised, though it required realigning the solar reflectors after each adjustment.

Despite our strange circumstances, I was determined that we should maintain a routine as close as possible to that which we would follow were we at sea. To this end we had meals in the small cabin that did dual service as wardroom and officers' mess, which the Boyes-Dennisons and whoever of our civilian specialist crew were off duty attended.

Unfortunately, it was during our first dinner that Miss B-D made some comment about utilitarianism and the work of John Stuart Mill which I felt compelled to disagree with. As a consequence we became embroiled in an intense debate concerning universal suffrage, which soon showed signs of embarrassing our fellow diners, especially Simon Granby, our eager young sub-lieutenant. Therefore I attempted to let the matter drop and withdraw gracefully. However, Miss B-D seemed to take this action as misplaced deference based upon the presumption that she would be unable to hold her own ground in the argument. The meal was concluded in stony silence.

I fear I shall never understand the female mind. Perhaps this explains my continuing bachelor status. The professor has perhaps been too liberal in his upbringing of her and one wonders what would happen to the country if the views Miss B-D espoused ever became widespread. On reflection, her forthrightness seems to have grown as the project progressed. Can this be an unexpected consequence of proximity to the machinery of astral travel? As we break the bonds of Earth perhaps she feels other conventions may also be broken?

The Moon gradually fills our forward portholes. Its stark beauty is remarkable. Miss B-D is taking many photographs. She seems to have put our disagreement out of her thoughts, which is probably for the best. After consultation with our astral navigators the fleet made a small alteration to its course, refining our angle of approach. Our projected path is intended to take us over the Moon's darkened hemisphere at an altitude low enough that we might be swung around by its gravity and *pass over the unseen far side. At this point we will use the engines to reduce our speed still further so that we fall into an orbit approximately over the Moon's equator. We should then witness dawn over half of a world never before seen by human eyes.*

4 September
As the Moon's bulk eclipsed the Sun and we passed into its cone of shadow, we were alert for any atmospheric refraction or distortion of the Sun's disc, but we saw none. This confirmed that the Moon lacked any significant free atmosphere. Shortly afterwards the Earth also vanished below the lunar horizon. I think we all felt a pang of disquiet at the sight, realising how totally isolated we were from all humanity.

Some three hundred miles above the darkened far side of the Moon we reduced our speed. The ragged line that marked the division between night and day slowly rolled beneath us and we looked down upon a landscape far more rugged than the familiar face of the Moon and, as far as we could see, without any of its dark-floored and distinctive maria, *or lunar seas. It was all rolling cratered upland tinted in greys and faded browns. An almost monochromatic landscape, save for one striking point of contrasting colour.*

Lying about twenty degrees south of the lunar equator was a shallow dome of misty azure blue. It was like a smooth, clouded sapphire lying half-buried on some bleak grey beach.

Signals exchanged with the other ships proved that they had seen this curious formation as well, and all telescopes were trained upon it as we made our closest approach. The dome appeared to sit over a large crater, capping it like a lid. Dimensions were hard to determine accurately, but I judge that the crater was perhaps a hundred miles across, with a prominent central peak. As we continued our observations it became clear that its floor was covered in a carpet of some mottled green substance. We watched until the strange feature fell below the horizon and we were passing over the familiar hemisphere of the Moon, with the welcome sight of the Earth hanging in the void before us once again.

After a further exchange of signals with my fellow commanders I determined we should make a closer inspection of the mysterious dome. I directed our navigators to calculate the necessary application of power that would not only reduce our altitude but change the plane of our orbit with respect to the Moon's equator, so that we should pass directly over the dome on our next orbit. As we rounded the Moon for a second time we swung the ships about and power was fed to the engines. We descended until we reached a height of approximately seventy miles, moving at a velocity which would carry us round the Moon every two hours.

Our calculations had been true, and we passed almost exactly over the dome. Though we still could not tell of what it was composed, from this lower altitude we could see through its misty substance that the green areas were vegetation, most probably the tree tops of some vast forest. There were even fleeting sparkles from within this greenery suggesting that sunlight was being reflected off the surface of rivers or lakes. But how could such things exist on a world which every other indication showed was quite dead?

Even as we pondered this, a signal was passed from one of the observers on the Draco drawing our attention to the central peak of the crater. Looking closely, we saw that the forms of the very topmost ramparts were far too regular to be natural. By straining our eyes we made out what appeared to be a stretch of levelled ground and at least one dome flanked by several towers. There was intelligent life in the crater!

It was while we were coming to terms with this startling discovery that Professor B-D suddenly exclaimed 'Air!' very loudly. He had noticed that the boundary of the crater dome was not sharp, as it would be if it were formed of some solid material, but quite tenuous. We were seeing a 'bubble' of air sitting over the crater and it looked unnaturally substantial simply by contrast with the absolute clarity of its surroundings.

As to why this bubble had not dispersed into the vacuum of space, the professor proposed that there was some force at work, perhaps related to static electricity, that was retarding the normal motion of the air molecules at the dome's boundary. But was this a natural phenomenon, or in some way associated with the citadel on the central peak? If the dome's boundary was not solid we could pass through it and discover the truth.

We spent the next three orbits mapping the crater as best we could, but added nothing substantial to our original findings. I decided that we should wait until the morrow to make the landing attempt so that the crew should be fully rested. At least our dinner that evening was a more cheerful affair. All thoughts of Mr John Stuart Mill's philosophy had apparently been wiped from Miss B-D's mind by speculations as to what we might find within the crater. Was the citadel and the crater it commanded the last vestige of some lunar civilisation? How would their physical forms differ from our own?

For my part I was sensible of a great responsibility looming before me. Naval history holds many instances of captains making contact with inhabitants of other lands for the first time, but to me might fall the task of being the first to meet beings from another world.

5 September
It was morning as reckoned by the Greenwich meridian, though it had little meaning here. The Sun would remain in the sky over our objective for several days. Long before lunar nightfall we should have learnt at least some of the Moon's secrets.

At the calculated moment, I gave the order to my little fleet to begin our descent. The rolling, pitted moonscape passed beneath us with increasing rapidity. The improbable dome rose steadily over the sharply curved horizon. Fifty miles from its misty wall I gave the command and we swung about, losing speed and making an arc about the dome that would allow us to approach it from the western side.

Landing on the very rim of the crater to which the dome seemed to cling would be a dangerous affair, yet neither did we wish to be so bold as to attempt to set down on the central peak within the grounds of the citadel itself until we knew a great deal more about its inhabitants, if any. However, we had observed a stretch of higher, shelving land inside the western wall of the crater which seemed to be less densely covered in forest and which sported many substantial clearings. This seemed an ideal compromise as a landing site as it would allow us to penetrate the mysteries of the place in our own time.

When the dome filled our portholes as a wall of hazy blue I ordered forward speed cut to dead slow while holding constant height. The impeller coils hummed as the bow lifted until the ship was standing on its tail with supporting legs extended in preparation for landing. The ship drifted sideways over the mountains of the crater rim. The navigator gave an exclamation of surprise. The compass, which until that moment had shown no response, suggesting the lunar magnetic field was feeble at best, had suddenly begun gyrating wildly. There came an anxious moment as the ship touched the tenuous dome, but there was only the slightest sensation of resistance and a whisper of air washing over the hull, then we were through. The airless void and the bleak wastes were retreating behind us, rapidly softened by the intervening air. We signalled it was safe and the Draco and the Lynx followed after us. We passed through a thin layer of cloud and suddenly the crater lay before us, a great bowl of life and colour stretching away over the curve of the shrunken horizon. In the distance, rising above the steaming forest, was the peak of the central mountain.

But we had little time to take in the vista. We had to find a safe landing site. The lower gravity of the Moon extended the time we could stay aloft supported by our impellers, but only by minutes.

We increased our speed until we had left the jagged slopes of the inner crater walls behind us, and glided over the expanse of shelving upland dotted with stands of strangely formed trees, low scrub or grassy pasture and the occasional rocky outcrop. At my direction the helmsman steered us lower, looking at the ground immediately below the ship through an ingenious periscope system, devised by Professor B-D, which extended through the hull.

I saw an open glade cut through by a small stream that ran down from the highlands at our backs which seemed to suit our purposes admirably. I gave the command to land. The ships descended together. Through a speaking tube we could hear the voice of a lookout stationed over the porthole set in the stern calling our height above ground. 'Twenty feet... ten... five...' There was a creak from the supporting legs, the ship swayed and settled. I ordered the power to the impellers cut. All was still.

We had landed on the Moon.

Chapter Five
Fragile History

The Doctor paused, put down the diary and crossed over to the food machine. He dialled up a cup of cold water and sipped.

'Thirsty work, reading aloud,' he commented.

'So they're supposed to have landed here over a hundred years ago,' Turlough said.

'If not on this very spot then somewhere close by, I should imagine,' the Doctor agreed. 'There is only one deep basin like Tsiolkovskii on the Moon. That much about the diary is accurate, and no Victorian could have known it was here.'

'Then it was written later.' Turlough gestured at the bleak image on the scanner again. 'See for yourself. Where's the blue dome of air and all that vegetation?'

'Perhaps it depends on what reality this diary comes from.'

'What do you mean?'

The Doctor sighed. 'The diary may come from the Earth's past that you are familiar with, but for some reason these events were never made public knowledge. Or else it comes from an alternative timeline where there was life here and this landing was the start of humanity's exploration of space...' He hesitated. 'Or perhaps the diary comes from a point somewhere in between the two possibilities. A potential bifurcation in the time stream where history divides.'

The Doctor's eyes were staring into eternity, his face a mask of concentration. He seemed to have forgotten Turlough's presence. His voice fell almost to a whisper.

'If I sent the diary back to myself and also retrospectively programmed the TARDIS to materialise after crossing its future-past time wake, then it's a sign that I must decide which alternative shall occur. To judge if an entirely new temporal worldline should come into existence! It's an awesome prospect... I'm not sure if I'm worthy.'

Turlough grinned. 'Maybe you left a note for yourself to tell you which one to pick?'

The Doctor turned an implacably stern face to him. 'Don't joke! I must not be influenced in any way! Don't you understand how serious this is?'

Turlough shrank back. The force of will behind the Doctor's words was almost palpable. 'No... obviously I don't... I'm sorry.'

The Doctor seemed to gather himself. He took a deep breath and his face relaxed. 'No, of course you don't understand. I'm sorry I snapped at you, Turlough. Only a Time Lord could understand the choice I'm facing. There's no power without responsibility, and sometimes it falls to my kind to decide the fate of untold millions as yet unborn.'

The words could have sounded pompous, except that Turlough knew the Doctor meant them as the literal truth.

'Do you have to make the choice?' he asked hopefully. 'Can't you just let it work itself out?'

'No. I've become involved already. The crossing time paths, the diary. I can't pretend it isn't happening.'

'Well, then let the new worldline start up. It'll be a laugh... Victorians on the Moon a century before the Americans. Good luck to them.'

The Doctor shook his head sadly.

'It's true that alternative universes can exist in parallel with each other, separated only by a millisecond of time and a nanometre of space, without ever having any contact. But there is a danger, at the point of divergence, that one reality will wipe out another instead of splitting from it cleanly. If that happens you probably won't have been at Brendon where we met, or on Earth at all. Your personal timeline would be rewritten. Possibly for the better... possibly not.'

Turlough gulped, feeling suddenly queasy. He forced a smile. 'Well, you'd better get it right then.'

The faraway look returned to the Doctor's eyes. 'I'll know the moment when it comes. Everything will focus on one object or person, and the slightest word or touch will decide matters one way or the other. That's when I'll have to choose.'

Then the look was gone and he shrugged and smiled easily. 'Meanwhile, let's see what happened after they landed.'

He picked up the diary once again.

Chapter Six
Diary: First Men on the Moon

There was a slight delay after landing while Professor B-D improvised a means of testing the outside air. Having assumed the Moon would be without any atmosphere, we have brought along no materials to perform gaseous analysis. I have therefore taken the opportunity to bring the ship's logbook and this diary up-to-date. I shall continue to make entries when circumstances permit so that all is recorded, as far as may be possible, when still fresh in my mind and may serve as both a personal and scientific record.

Signals from the Draco *and* Lynx, *which both set down within a hundred yards of us, report all is well with them. The return of weight after almost a day in orbit is very welcome, even if it is only a fraction of that on Earth. Actually this lower gravity gives one a pleasant sense of vitality and, in rather a childlike manner, I find myself secretly speculating how high I will be able to jump once I am beyond the confines of the ship. Is this odd digression due simply to relief at our safe landfall or some characteristic of our surroundings? For the moment I must content myself with the view from the ports.*

The glade is ringed with the tallest trees I have ever seen – at least three hundred feet high with spindly trunks that would be quite inadequate to support their weight on Earth. My vantage point is too high to determine any peculiarities about the sward on which we are resting or the clumps of reddish ferns scattered across it. The open end of the glade looks out across falling ground to the great forest basin and the central mountain. What strange life forms may await us there? I realise we have been guilty of an understandable omission in our planning of the expedition as we have neither a botanist nor zoologist.

Professor B-D has prepared his equipment and wishes to leave the ship to make his tests, wearing an atmosphere suit. These garments are modified Siebe, Gorman and Co. closed diving suits, including H. A. Fleuss's recently developed self-contained air-regeneration apparatus, built up with additional layers of insulation. They were intended to allow expeditions outside the ship on the airless surface of the Moon. It may now be that they will not be required should the outside air prove breathable.

I detailed the bosun to break out a rifle from the arms locker, don a second suit and accompany the professor. We have not had any indication that danger exists outside, but it is well to be prepared. For the same reason I have ordered the solar reflectors, folded back to the side of the ship during landing, to be extended once more. I wish the batteries to be fully charged at all times while we are on the surface, in case there should be need of a hasty departure.

We watched the two men emerge from under the ship and make their way a few yards out on to the grass. The professor struck a match and watched it burn, then opened his test tubes to the air and examined the results on the reagents within them. Finally he waved up at us and removed his helmet. I saw concern written on the face of Miss B-D who was standing at my side, but her father appeared to be breathing normally. The bosun also took off his helmet and signalled all was well.

Within a quarter hour the first exploration parties descended from the ships, and I took my first breath of lunar air, which seems perfectly fresh and wholesome though mingled with many strange scents. I noted in passing that the thermometer in the airlock compartment reads seventy-three degrees Fahrenheit, while the barometer shows a pressure equivalent of 27.21 inches of mercury.

What I took to be grass I find on closer inspection to be a kind of thick dense moss with tints of green, yellow and even blue, here and there dotted with small patches of many-coloured flowers that seem strangely formed to my eyes, though I am not an expert in such matters. Around the edge of the glade are flashes of light where the Sun reflects off the wings of what I assume to be large darting insects. For the moment they are keeping their distance, no doubt disturbed by our arrival. I trust we shall be able to secure some specimens of them soon, though we may have to fashion a butterfly net first!

Walking carefully, for in these conditions there is a tendency to skip and bound like a newborn lamb with each step, I met my fellow commanders on the open ground between our ships where we solemnly shook hands. Here also we planted the Union Flag and I took possession of the Moon in the name of Her Majesty. Miss B-D recorded the scene with her camera. I venture to suggest, in all modesty, that it will eventually become one of the most famous photographs in the world.

I admit some private apprehension over the ceremony as it had originally, of course, been intended for a lifeless world. What will the inhabitants of the citadel, if any exist, make of it?

We then decided our strategy of exploration. Leaving a watch on the ships we would form two exploratory parties. One would investigate the immediate area about the landing site, taking mineralogical samples of upland terrain. Meanwhile the second smaller party would reconnoitre the route down to the floor of the crater and the forest proper. Naturally Professor and Miss B-D wish to be part of this group. I forebore to argue.

The party consisted of myself, the B-Ds, the bosun and half a dozen ratings, and young Granby, who is desperate for adventure and fervently requested he be included. In case the forest held dangerous animals we were armed, Granby and myself with revolvers, the men with rifles. We had never thought when we set out that there would be any need for weapons on the Moon, but as commissioned ships in Her Majesty's service, properly stocked small-arms lockers were installed as a matter of course. In addition we took provisions for twenty-four hours, though we did not expect to be away more than ten at the most. At least we do not have to worry about the approach of night. The Sun will not set over the crater for more than four Earth days.

One observation of interest: the compass has settled down to

35

point directly to the mountains, suggesting they contain an attractive source of considerable power.

Leaving my second, Forrester, in charge of the Cygnus *we started off, moving in long bounding strides which take little exertion and seem the easiest form of locomotion. As we progressed we naturally kept alert for all signs of life, but apart from the darting flying insects we saw none. Perhaps no larger forms live in these highlands. In the distance, wheeling over both the forest and the peaks behind us, we saw bird-like shapes, but even with my glasses focused upon them I could make out little detail. I could only say that their wingspans could scarcely be less than twenty feet.*

   We came across one curious feature of the landscape. An area of ground perhaps thirty feet across had risen into a cone some twenty feet high, which was devoid of all plant growth. With a scramble we reached the top to find it was the mouth of a volcanic vent. The shaft descended into blackness and seemed quite cold. I now recalled seeing several other similar structures from above as we searched for a landing site. Professor B-D theorises that heat from such vents might help keep the crater at a tolerable temperature through the long lunar night.

   After an hour we reached the edge of the great terrace on which we had landed. Here the ground fell away in a series of slopes and ledges to the forest below, a total distance of perhaps two thousand feet. The way looked steep in places, but not unduly arduous under the lesser gravity.

   As we descended, both the heat and humidity rose markedly and we were soon perspiring freely. Perhaps it was due to this change in conditions, but I gradually began to imagine we were being watched. Several times I turned my head sharply expecting to see something, but there was only the shelving cliffside with its clinging moss and clumps of reddish ferns.

   Eventually we came level with the forest canopy, but still we descended. Only gradually did the slope of the ground lessen and we passed into the green-tinted twilight of the forest floor.

I had thought the trees on the higher ground were tall, but they were mere saplings in comparison with the giants that now surrounded us. Monstrous boles rose fully five hundred feet above our heads, laced about with shaggy coated vines and decorated with huge dangling aerial blossoms. For the first time we heard unmistakable animal sounds all about us. Whoops and chittering cries, and the distant crash of some larger beast plunging through the undergrowth. We soon noticed distinct game paths running between the trees, marked where the ground was soft by the spores of many strange creatures. I could not help but think what a terrible place this would be to traverse at night, and resolved that our first excursion into this wonderful but ominous forest would not be overlong. However, we would make a survey of the area immediately about the base of the cliff path so that we would be prepared when we returned later with a larger party.

Our first find was another of the volcanic vents, almost identical with the one we had seen on the upland. It was situated in a gap between the great trees and must recently have been producing considerable heat, for some of the overhanging foliage was brown and shrivelled. Yet there is no sign of any material discharged from the cone. Professor B-D is clearly puzzled by this absence.

Shortly afterwards we had an altogether less pleasing encounter. Leading Seaman Davis, wandering a little way off the path, gave a cry of pain. To our horror we saw that a plant some five feet across, lying half-buried in the leaf litter like a rotting lily pad, had suddenly sprung to life and closed itself about his legs, holding him fast with an array of long and viciously hooked thorns. The other ratings beat at the base of the dreadful plant with their rifle butts, then levered the thing's jaws apart so we could drag Davis clear. At the centre of the plant's leaf ring was revealed a thorn-ringed hole, doubtless leading to some buried digestive chamber. The bosun thrust his rifle barrel into this maw and fired three rapid rounds. The thorned leaf pad thrashed convulsively then collapsed into a trembling heap.

Breaking out the medical kit we treated and bound Davis's wounds. He has many deep slashes about his legs and has lost some blood, but unless there is some poison in those thorns I think he will recover. Miss B-D helped most efficiently with the bandaging, which did much for Davis's morale, then took a photograph of the plant thing that had almost claimed him. She is a little cold-blooded at times, I fear. We shall give Davis a short while to regain his strength, then start back.

Events both tragic and remarkable have occurred! I shall try to set them down while they are fresh in my mind.

I was just bringing this record up-to-date. A couple of ratings were seated by Davis while the bosun and the others kept watch on the forest about us. The B-Ds had been examining the foliage, taking care where they placed their feet. Miss B-D was operating her camera equipment and Granby was standing just a few feet from her.

Without warning there was a rush and swish of leaves. Granby gave a cry of alarm, and was gone before we could turn our heads. It was quick almost beyond belief.

We all snatched up our guns and plunged after him, but the underbrush was very thick at that point and we could hardly see five feet before us. There was no visible trail and, strain our ears though we might, there was no sound that might tell us which way he had been taken. Already the forest seemed to have swallowed him. We stumbled back into the glade to see Miss B-D's face blanched white.

'I caught a glimpse out of the corner of my eye,' she said. 'It was something dark that moved like a shadow.' I had never seen her so discomposed.

We could not abandon Granby, but equally there were too few of us to mount a proper search, already burdened as we were with an injured man. We would have to send back to the ships for help. Davis gamely insisted he could walk with support, so I *detailed two men to help him back up the cliff. In the lesser lunar gravity they could take turns to carry him and still make good time. They set off while we continued to look for any trace of Granby or his abductors, circling the spot where he had vanished and calling out in the hope he might be able to reply.*

And it was while we were so engaged that we had our most unexpected encounter yet. Two figures stood on the path before us. Not alien beings in keeping with our surroundings, but human-looking men dressed in Earthly clothes. Before we could recover our wits one hailed us.

'Hallo,' he said, 'I'm the Doctor and this is my assistant, Turlough...'

Chapter Seven
Predestination

The Doctor snapped the diary shut.

'And that's as far as we can go,' he said.

Turlough felt dizzy and struggled to speak through lips that had suddenly gone dry. 'But… that was us!'

'Apparently so.'

'We're actually inside the diary!'

'In a manner of speaking. Unless there is a very elaborate hoax under way, I think we can now assume it's an accurate record of events.'

'But what happened next? You can't just stop.'

'Turlough, that's exactly what I must do,' the Doctor said firmly. 'Otherwise we'd be reading about our own future actions, which is rather a dangerous thing.'

'It can't be worse than not knowing if something unpleasant's going to happen to us.'

'Really? Suppose you did learn of some event you wished to avoid and acted on the information so it never came to pass. Either the timeline would divide, sending you into an entirely new future to which the information did not apply and so was useless, or else the event would never come to pass. Then what would happen to the words you'd read describing the event?'

Turlough frowned. 'Well… I suppose they'd change.'

'Or perhaps vanish altogether. Either way, you couldn't have read them, so you wouldn't have the knowledge to take avoiding action, so the event you were trying to avoid could now happen, so you could be warned about it through the diary… and so on. You'd be locked inside a transcendental self-negating cyclical paradox for eternity.'

He held up the diary in emphasis and, as he did so, a thin slip of paper fell out of it.

Turlough picked it up curiously. On it was written: *Believe me, you don't want to know!* He felt the hair rise on the back of his neck. The handwriting was unmistakably his own.

The Doctor took the message from his numbed fingers and read it with a smile of satisfaction. 'Ah, so it seems you will agree with me.'

Turlough saw a glimmer of hope. 'But if I wrote... will write... that, then it means I get through whatever's to come OK.'

'At least up until you wrote it, always assuming it's not from an alternative timeline, or its existence isn't negated by our own actions in the meantime, or...'

'All right, Doctor, you've made your point!' Turlough sighed. 'It seems like we don't have any free will in this at all. We have to meet these people or else we get caught in a time paradox.'

'Now you begin to understand why I didn't want to read any further. Once the meeting has taken place as described, we will be free to act as we wish once more.' The Doctor crossed to the control console and began entering coordinates. 'Meanwhile the diary has served its purpose. We know a good deal about the situation and we have a specific time to aim for – the morning of 5 September 1878. We only need to take a short hop backwards.'

The TARDIS ground into life, the time rotor rose and fell a few times then settled into quiescence once more. The image on the scanner now showed a stretch of moss-covered ground dotted with spinneys of impossibly slender trees lifting towards a deep blue sky.

'Here we are,' the Doctor continued brightly, 'and in the process we're creating the time wake we have already experienced. Best not to start these affairs leaving loose ends about the place.'

He busied himself with the long-range scanning controls for a few moments. 'I can detect a sizeable concentration of metal a few miles north of us. That will be the British ships. There's also a fair amount of energy being radiated from the direction of the central mountains – no doubt causing the magnetic anomaly they observed.'

Turlough was scowling unhappily. 'Look, are you sure about this? We know it's dangerous out there.'

'The diary shows we'll reach Haliwell's party safely,' the Doctor reassured him. 'Then we'll have stalwart British sailors at our shoulders.'

'Yeah, and look what's happened to them already. One half-eaten by a plant, another missing. At least let's take Kamelion along. He might frighten off whatever snatched that lieutenant.'

'There's no mention of Kamelion.'

'Give it a chance. Maybe he'd turned himself into a bush or something so they didn't notice him. Come on. What's the point in having a shape-shifting android around if you don't make use of him?'

'Kamelion's not here to be used.'

'But you know he'll do what you tell him – that's how he's made.'

'I'll ask him, nothing more,' the Doctor said firmly. 'If he decides to accompany us, it'll be his free choice.'

Kamelion was quite agreeable, once the situation had been explained to him.

'Certainly I shall be pleased to accompany you, Doctor. Especially if my presence may ensure your safety.'

'Only if you're quite certain,' the Doctor said.

'You heard him,' Turlough said impatiently. 'Come on, let's get it over with.'

The TARDIS's stores provided two old-fashioned canvas rucksacks, which they packed with provisions for two days since they had no idea how long they would be. When they were ready the Doctor opened the main doors and, putting on his hat, strode briskly outside.

Turlough followed more cautiously, peering round the doorframe. The TARDIS had materialised in the middle of a small copse of the reddish fern plants. Their tops wavered slightly in the gentle breeze, but he couldn't see anything immediately threatening. He took a step on to the mossy ground and almost fell over.

'Mind the change in gravity,' the Doctor said over his shoulder as he looked about him with interest. 'The transition can be quite disorientating.'

'Thanks for the warning,' said Turlough heavily, steadying himself.

Kamelion emerged from the TARDIS. He took two steps forward, gave a very human groan of pain and sank to his knees, clasping his head.

The Doctor was by his side in a moment, catching the android before he could topple over. 'Help me get him back inside!' he snapped.

They dragged Kamelion back through the doorway, his head jerking and rolling from side to side. Turlough could feel the synthetic body rippling in his hands as though it was about to transform, and he had to nerve himself to keep his hold.

But as soon as they were within the control room once more all signs of Kamelion's distress vanished. He gently shrugged off their support and stood upright, somehow managing to convey a sense of acute embarrassment.

'I must apologise,' he said. 'Some form of external interference affected my neural circuitry. I... lost control of my functions.'

The Doctor was checking instruments on the console. 'Yes, there it is. A faint but complex resonant energy wave associated with the dampening field that holds the air over the crater.'

'Is it artificial?' Turlough asked.

'Oh yes, no doubt about it. Though whether the interference is deliberate or merely a side effect, I couldn't say.'

The Doctor turned to Kamelion. 'Sorry, old chap, but it looks as though you'll have to stay in here where you're shielded. The dome field might change its characteristics when the Sun goes down, so the interference could lessen then.'

'I understand, Doctor. I shall check the field strength regularly. Meanwhile, do not concern yourself any further with me.'

Turlough was not concerned about Kamelion. Kamelion would be safe inside the TARDIS while he and the Doctor had to continue unaccompanied. It seemed that destiny was not to be evaded so easily. He scowled at the diary still lying innocently on the console. His whole future might lie within those pages – and apparently he could do nothing about it.

At least, once they'd set off for the second time, Turlough found the low gravity a novel distraction. Their surroundings were just as Haliwell had described and close enough to a stretch of Earthly grassland for Turlough to imagine he had been endowed with a dream-like ability to walk in slow-motion ten-foot strides. Meanwhile the Doctor moved sedately with a poise and economy of movement that suggested long experience with such conditions.

In less than an hour they reached the edge of the highlands and stared out over the great forest to the central peaks that seemed to float above it. It was a breathtaking spectacle.

Turlough narrowed his eyes, trying to pierce the haze. 'Do you think that citadel they saw on the top of those mountains is the source of the energy field that keeps the air in place?'

'I'd be most surprised if it wasn't,' the Doctor said brightly. 'This is all too perfect to be a natural phenomenon. That's something we'll have to find out in due course.'

They started down the escarpment, dropping lightly from switchback inclines to ledges and back. The forest seemed to rise to meet them.

'How do we find the British once we're down there?' Turlough wondered.

'It's predestined, so we can almost leave it to chance. As long as we head north once we reach the ground we're bound to bump into them.'

'As long as we don't bump into anything else along the way.'

They negotiated a jumble of fallen boulders at the base of the cliff and entered the forest.

It was as magnificent as Haliwell had described, but Turlough found it hard to appreciate the experience. He was too preoccupied with watching where he put his feet and keeping well clear of the thicker undergrowth.

Then came a reminder that they were not alone. The distant

crack of three rapid rifle shots filtered between the huge trees, sending bird-like shapes flying through the branches with protesting cries. Turlough started before he realised what the sound was. The bosun had just shot the plant that had attacked Davis.

'Everything seems to be proceeding as the diary said,' the Doctor observed.

'And in a minute something will take Granby. We can't do anything to stop it, can we?'

'No, I'm afraid not.'

It was an uncanny feeling, Turlough thought, knowing what was going to happen, like reading the script of a play before seeing it acted out. He shuddered. Would he also become an actor in the strange story, helplessly following the directions of fate?

Sudden cries of alarm floated through the trees. Granby had been taken.

'We'd better move away from the cliffside and circle round,' the Doctor said, 'otherwise we might meet the men going back to the ships for help.'

They made their way deeper into the forest. Turlough found his voice falling to a whisper, hushed by the overwhelming presence of the great trees. 'When we meet them, do you have to introduce me as your assistant?'

'I think it makes sense in the circumstances,' the Doctor said. 'Remember the century we're in and who we're dealing with. We'll have to have a story they'll accept, since they won't believe we arrived here by chance and we can't tell them about the diary.'

From ahead came the sounds of bushes being beaten and Granby's name being called out at regular intervals. The remainder of the party were searching for their missing comrade.

'Come on,' said the Doctor.

They rounded a bend in the track and suddenly the British party was right in front of them; real people, no longer characters from a century-old diary.

Leading the group was a man who had to be Captain Haliwell; full side-whiskered, holding a pistol, and wearing a dark blue tail coat with braided epaulettes, and a peaked cap. The white-haired man in a faded black frock coat was obviously Professor Boyes-Dennison, and the young woman at his side his daughter Emily – a fellow redhead, Turlough noticed. Ranged about them were blue-jacketed sailors carrying heavy bolt-action rifles.

As the Victorians gaped at them in astonishment, the Doctor raised his hat politely.

'Hallo, I'm the Doctor and this is my assistant, Turlough…' There was the slightest pause then he continued smoothly: 'Captain Haliwell, I presume.'

Chapter Eight
Pursuit

Of all the things he could have imagined encountering in the unearthly forest, Haliwell thought, the very last would have been the two strangers who now stood before them. Until that moment he had assumed that the nearest human beings apart from the men in the ships were almost a quarter of a million miles away. With an effort he recovered his composure and addressed the man calling himself the Doctor.

'You seem to have the advantage of me, sir. I must ask you to account for your presence here.'

'Why should we?' the Doctor's companion retorted. 'It's a free moon.'

'This world has been claimed for the British Empire,' Haliwell said. 'As a representative of the crown I am entitled to demand such information from you both.'

'They're spies!' Professor Boyes-Dennison interjected sharply. 'The government assured me our work would be carried out in the strictest secrecy, but clearly details of my impeller have been stolen. How else could they have come here? No doubt they now intend to sabotage our mission.' Anger seeming to crackle off him, he glared at the man who called himself the Doctor. 'Who do you serve, sir? The French or the Prussians, maybe?'

Then his daughter laid a restraining hand on his arm. 'Hush, Father. Let us hear what they have to say. I do not believe spies would announce themselves in quite such an open manner.'

The Doctor bowed to her slightly. 'Thank you, Miss Boyes-Dennison. Let me assure you, Professor, that we are not spies, nor have we stolen any particulars of your most remarkable invention. My own transport does not operate on the same principle as your ships. But I do have an interest in scientific advances, especially where they relate to the exploration of space. I was sent details of your expedition by, shall we say, a like-minded acquaintance and have been following your progress with interest ever since.'

'That is a very incomplete explanation,' said Haliwell. 'As the professor said, this voyage was mounted in the strictest secrecy, yet you contrive a meeting in the middle of this forest and even know our names. Who told you, sir?'

The Doctor smiled. 'If you knew the name of my ultimate source of information, Captain, I know you would trust him.' Then the lightness was gone from his manner to be replaced by a tone of compelling sobriety. 'For now all I can say is that we mean you no harm. Indeed, you may need our help. This place, as I believe you have already discovered, can be dangerous.'

'We are quite capable of taking care of ourselves, young man,' Boyes-Dennison said. 'If you truly wish us no harm as you say, then good day to you!'

'Father!' Emily said.

'Come on, Doctor,' said his assistant. 'We've done what we had to. Leave the rest to chance. Obviously we're not wanted here.'

'Turlough!' the Doctor said in exasperated tones.

The professor held up a finger. 'Wait one moment. Do you intend to dispute our achievement in landing first on the Moon when you return to Earth?'

'Not at all,' the Doctor said. 'You undoubtedly landed here before we did.' Then again his face darkened as he turned to Haliwell. 'But whoever built that structure on the central mountains might not be so understanding of your claiming the Moon as your own, since they clearly arrived here before either of us. I suspect that possibility troubles you as well, Captain.'

Haliwell wondered how the strange man had discerned his innermost concerns so accurately. Before he could frame a reply the Doctor continued.

'But that can wait. We heard you calling out for somebody before we met. I take it you've lost a member of your party.'

'Sub-Lieutenant Granby,' Haliwell replied automatically. 'No more than a quarter-hour past. Something took him from our very midst.'

'Then you must continue looking for him. Can we help? Two more pairs of eyes, you know.'

Do I trust them? Haliwell wondered. They were certainly not telling the whole truth, yet there was something sincere in the depths of the Doctor's eyes. Besides, he could not delay the search for Granby any further and if the two men did mean them any harm it might be best to have them in sight.

'Thank you, Doctor. We shall be glad of any assistance you can offer us.'

For half an hour they pressed on, their search carrying them deeper into the forest. The bosun blazed trail markers so they would not lose their way. Then, just as Haliwell was beginning to give up hope, the Doctor found the first clue.

Even when the signs were pointed out to him Haliwell marvelled at the sharpness of the Doctor's eyes, for they were no more than a scrape in the moss, such as might have been made by a dragging heel, then a little way from it a broken fern frond and a turned stone. But the Doctor seemed certain that they proved a body had been carried past the spot recently.

His assistant, the dour-faced Turlough, said: 'You'd better believe him. He's good at this Sherlock Holmes stuff when he puts his mind to it.'

Who was Sherlock Holmes? Haliwell wondered.

They followed the direction indicated by the traces, the Doctor in the lead with his head bent low, his keen eyes darting from side to side. Haliwell found himself wanting to trust the strange man and thought he read the same sentiment in the expression of Emily Boyes-Dennison. Her father, however, retained a frown of displeasure which finally moved him to edge over to Haliwell's side and speak to him in low tones.

'I'm sorry about Granby, Captain, but I think we must give him up for lost. We should return to the ships to avoid any further delays.' He glanced meaningfully at the Doctor and his assistant. 'Circumstances here are obviously more complex than we imagined. Now we have proven my impeller engine, we can return to Earth with news of the success of our mission.'

'Professor, I will not abandon a missing man until I am sure he is beyond help. You and your daughter may return to the ships when the relief party arrives. Until then we shall continue the search.'

Just then they came upon a slight rise of harder-packed ground where several game paths crossed between clumps of bamboo-like growths. The great trees about them were smothered in trailing arm-thick vines that tangled with the bamboos so that fallen twigs and leafs formed solid masses suspended between them like huge crudely made nests. It was gloomy in the shadow of this natural awning and the Doctor had to pause in his tracking.

'The trail seems to peter out here,' he said after a moment. He bent down and touched a dark stain on the ground. 'There's fresh blood. Can anybody see any more?'

Stephens, one of the ratings, called out: 'I think there's some over here, sir…' He was cautiously probing amongst the ferns with the barrel of his rifle. Before the Doctor could reach him he had parted the fronds. 'It's the lieutenant! He's… Oh, God save us!'

The Doctor pulled the horrified man away and carefully spread out the tangled stems. Haliwell peered over his shoulder.

Granby's pale, blood-splattered face stared up at him, a look of utter horror frozen on his fine features. He was hatless, and where his thick crown of blonde hair should have been there was only a distorted pulpy mass.

Haliwell had to avert his eyes for a moment. Behind him he could hear the bosun saying, 'Steady, lad. Keep a grip,' to a still-trembling Stephens.

Turlough had put out a warning arm to hold Emily Boyes-Dennison back. 'I wouldn't get any closer unless you've got a strong stomach,' he said.

The Doctor seemed to have that necessary strength of constitution and, as they looked on, he examined the remains of Granby's head. Only the rigid flatness of his voice betrayed his true emotions.

'The skull has been punched right through… it must have taken considerable force… a disc of bone about three inches across has been displaced. The interior of the cranium… seems quite empty of grey matter.' He turned bleak eyes to Haliwell. 'The poor fellow appears literally to have had his brains sucked out!'

One of the other ratings was murmuring a prayer and even the professor looked suitably appalled at the Doctor's pronouncement.

'Bosun,' Haliwell said quietly. 'Break out a blanket and cover Mister Granby. Then cut some of these bamboos for a stretcher.'

'Aye, sir.'

The first man I have lost under my command, Haliwell thought bleakly. Why did it have to be in such a terrible fashion? Perhaps I was too eager to explore this place, carried away by the success of our voyage. Well, the forest had taught him a bitter lesson in humility. He would not attempt such a thing again without being far better prepared.

He saw the Doctor looking at him closely and once again felt his thoughts were being read. 'Don't judge yourself too harshly,' the strange man said.

'I'm afraid that is a matter for my Maker, Doctor. But thank you. And for tracking him down. We might have wandered about for hours otherwise… and clearly we can't afford to spend one minute more than we have to down here…'

His voice trailed away as he caught sight of Emily Boyes-Dennison. She had her head tilted back and was staring up at the tangle of branches and creepers above.

'Is something wrong?' he asked.

'Those vines,' she said curiously. 'I thought they were higher just a moment ago.'

Haliwell followed her gaze. Silently, almost imperceptibly, shaggy tendrils were uncoiling from the undersides of the nest-like masses over their heads.

'Run!' the Doctor shouted.

His cry galvanised them. Earthly reserves of strength that had been held in check by hours of walking in the lesser gravity now sent them leaping aside in huge bounds, even as the clearing was filled with lashing tentacles questing for prey. Stephens cried out, twisting and jerking at the end of a tendril that had fastened about his arm. The bosun leapt to his side and swung his cutlass, slicing clean through the tentacle. Sticky green fluid sprayed from the severed end as it recoiled. Dragging Stephens with him, the bosun bounded clear after the others.

They halted some fifty yards from the deadly glade. Stephens was moaning and clutching his arm. 'It's burning…!' he gasped. There were ugly red blotches where the tentacle had touched his exposed flesh.

Haliwell felt cruelly cheated. They would not even be able to give Granby a decent burial. He glared angrily back at the glade only to see it apparently begin shaking itself apart. Lengths of vine were thrashing and falling aside, carrying the tangled nests with them….

Then he felt the breath catch in his throat as he realised the vines were not vines at all. His incoherent gasp alerted the others, and for a moment they were all transfixed by the sight that met their eyes.

From out of the shadowed glade, picking their way with improbably dainty steps, came half a dozen monstrous creatures. Haliwell could only think of twenty-five-foot high spiders, their legs and spherical bodies covered with a shaggy growth that resembled trailing moss, while from their undersides hung the coiled tentacles that had so nearly snared them. They had actually walked between the creatures' legs as they searched for Granby without realising the horror that was all about them.

Then Turlough broke the spell that held them in its thrall. 'I think they're coming this way,' he said.

'Aim at their bodies and fire at will!' Haliwell ordered, drawing his pistol.

At thirty yards range the sailors emptied their weapons into the monstrous things. Two of the beasts staggered slightly as bullets tore into them, but the wounds were apparently not fatal for they recovered in seconds and continued their remorseless advance.

'It's no good!' the Doctor shouted. 'Run!'

They did so, bounding between the trees in fifteen-foot fear-driven strides. At their heels came the spiders, moving with silent, terrible purpose, the length of their legs giving each step they took a dream-like illusion of slowness, but in fact covering considerable ground. On Earth such legs would have been too thin to support their weight, but here they were clearly perfectly adapted to the creatures' needs.

Haliwell and his companions covered half a mile before they halted again. For a moment all was still behind them. Then the spiders emerged from the trees, still moving at the same relentless pace.

'Keep moving!' Haliwell shouted.

As they bounded on he wondered how the creatures were following their trail. He'd seen no sign of eyes or any recognisable sense organs on their bodies. And who would tire of the pursuit first? In the confusion they had lost sight of the trail markers they had blazed earlier. He had to hope they were travelling in approximately the right direction to strike the path back up to the highlands.

'This is abnormal behaviour in predators,' the Doctor said, synchronising his strides with Haliwell's. 'They not only lie in wait and try to trap prey subtly, but they then give chase in a pack. Two different hunting strategies. And they should not have pursued us this far in any case. The energy they expend will exceed our food value.'

'Perhaps they're feeling really hungry,' his assistant, running at his side, said with a distinct edge of sarcasm. Fleetingly Haliwell wondered why the Doctor tolerated such rudeness.

'Then why didn't they consume Granby?' the Doctor continued. 'They must have had time enough before we arrived. They weren't the same creatures that took your man?'

'No, it was something much smaller,' Haliwell said.

'Then perhaps whatever it was frightened our friends into temporary quiescence.'

His assistant looked aghast. 'What could frighten those things?' he panted.

Professor Boyes-Dennison was beginning to falter. Haliwell called: 'Professor… discard your pack. Bosun… help the professor along!'

He realised Emily was also visibly tiring. 'Miss Boyes-Dennison… throw away your pack as well, and the camera apparatus – it's slowing you down.'

Emily shook her head. She had insisted on carrying the camera equipment herself throughout their journey. In the lesser gravity it was no great burden, though the sight of a lady portering such baggage had discomforted Haliwell. But now she must give it up for they could not delay even seconds while it was handed to one of the men.

'I cannot,' she panted. 'The pictures…'

'That is an order… for all our sakes. Otherwise we shall be compelled to reduce our own pace to match yours.'

Finally she saw sense and shrugged the straps from her shoulders. The camera case and folded tripod fell to the ground with a crash. The group bounded onwards.

'I think we're nearly there!' the Doctor said.

The ground was rising slightly and the trees ahead were visibly thinner. Then they burst through the last of the ferns and the cliff face rose before them.

It was a sheer wall of rock without any sign of the easy slopes they had descended.

'Which way do we turn?' Haliwell asked.

The Doctor was feverishly looking left and right. 'I think we're too far south,' he gasped.

The spiders stalked out of the trees, maintaining the pace of their relentless pursuit. They cut off the way to the north and the fugitives had no choice. Firing a volley over their shoulders, for what little good it might do, they headed south.

Haliwell ran with his neck craned, desperately looking for some place where they could ascend the cliff face. He prayed that the spiders, with their great bulk, could not climb as well as their smaller cousins even in this lesser gravity. There were places where the rock was rougher and might offer a way up to a careful climber, but with the horror that was at their backs they could not afford to spend even half a minute searching for footholds.

Then he became aware that the rock wall at their side was curving. The mouth of a narrow dark gorge opened before them, with a stream running out of it into the forest.

'There might be a cleft or cave too small for them to get into down there,' the Doctor said. 'Or perhaps a ledge they can't scale.'

Haliwell nodded. They certainly could not risk plunging into the forest again. In seconds the gorge had swallowed both them and their pursuers.

Along its shadowed floor they ran. Jumbles of fallen rock narrowed it to a matter of feet in places, but they could find nowhere safe from those poisonous probing tentacles.

Exhaustion was taking its toll. Only the bosun and the Doctor looked capable of maintaining the pace they had set. Two men were helping the professor now. Emily was stumbling. How long they had been running? Haliwell wondered. The almost stationary Sun had distorted his sense of time and the strange motion of their flight made it hard to judge their speed. He guessed it was about that of a cantering horse; remarkable on Earth but it seemed not quite fast enough on the Moon.

He snatched a glance over his shoulder once again and felt a thrill of hope. Their lead had opened to two hundred yards. As the gorge narrowed the spiders were having to pause while they gathered in their legs to pass through clefts and between larger boulders.

Haliwell had reloaded his revolver as he ran. He shouted to the others to press on while he halted, wiping the sweat from his eyes and trying to steady his heaving chest. As the leading spider emerged round a shoulder of rock he fired six shots into it as rapidly as he could pull the trigger. The beast staggered and its fellows, following close behind, crashed into it in a confusion of flailing legs. Haliwell did not wait to see the outcome but ran on to rejoin the others.

He had bought them a little more time, but would it be enough? The ground under them had been rising steadily – the upper reaches of the gorge were filled with an ancient accumulation of fallen rock and smaller detritus washed down from the mountains. The stream, which must have been fed by meltwater from the high peaks, leapt down shelves and drops in spectacular cascades that threw up clouds of misty spray. Now the clifftops were only a couple of hundred feet above their heads and he could see the tops of trees overhanging the chasm. He saw a mound of fractured rocks that seemed to reach to the cliff edge, and came to a decision.

'We climb here. It's our only hope.'

Gasping for breath they started to ascend, hauling themselves up like human flies, climbing at a speed impossible on Earth.

They managed fifty feet before the spiders reached the base of the mound. Five spiders only! He had stopped one at least.

For a moment the creatures hesitated, their ridiculously slender legs reaching upward, tentatively probing for firm footholds. And then they began to climb; steadily, remorselessly.

And Haliwell knew they could not possibly reach the top of the cliffs before the beasts were upon them.

Chapter Nine
Artefact

Turlough desperately tried to force his way into a cleft in the rocky slope, but it was too narrow even for his thin frame. There was nowhere to hide.

Choking with fear and exhaustion he twisted about to kick at the tip of a spider leg that was probing around his ankles for a new foothold. All about him he heard rifle hammers clicking on empty chambers as the sailors expended the last of their ammunition. The bosun was swinging his cutlass, but he could only postpone the inevitable. The Boyes-Dennisons were clinging together, the professor looking as though he was already finished.

'Doctor!' Turlough said, trying not to let fear crack his voice. 'What do we do?'

But for once the Doctor looked as helpless as the rest of them. 'I'm sorry, Turlough, but right now –'

A fresh volley of shots rang out to become a steady stream of gunfire. Fragments of stone and dust exploded from the rocks about the spiders, whose shaggy bodies shivered as round after round struck home. For a moment Turlough could not make out where the fusillade was coming from. Then he twisted his head about and looked up. A dozen sailors lined the cliff edge pouring fire down as fast as they could pull the triggers.

'Get to the top now, while they're distracted!' he heard Haliwell shout.

They scrambled on up the cliffside, the spiders still clawing their way after them as though the hail of bullets was no more than a shower of rain. What keeps them going? Turlough wondered incredulously. Bullets tore away two adjacent legs on the leading spider. Unbalanced, it scrabbled vainly for new footholds, then tumbled over backwards, bouncing down the cliffside in a tangle of flailing legs. But the four remaining beasts continued on, apparently undeterred.

The explorers reached the cliff edge and strong hands hauled them over on to level ground. As Turlough lay on his back gasping for air, his limbs trembling from effort and nervous shock, he heard the Doctor shouting: 'Your guns won't stop them – use rocks.'

Haliwell added: 'Push everything you can over the side!'

Shouted orders and grunts of effort mingled with the grinding of stone against stone. With a crash and rumble loose boulders tumbled over. Other men were kicking at the crumbling edge of the cliff itself with their heavy boots until a whole slab of rock fell away. Turlough saw two sailors staggering past him carrying a dead tree-branch between them that would have weighed half a ton on Earth. With a heave it went over. A few seconds later a great cheer went up from the men.

Rolling on to his hands and knees, Turlough crawled to the cliff edge and looked down. At the foot of the cliff the dust was swirling about a mound of shattered rock from which a single broken spider leg protruded, twitching feebly.

'Good!' he said aloud to nobody in particular, and sank slowly down again.

The Doctor came over and knelt by his side. 'Are you all right?' he asked anxiously.

'Never better,' Turlough assured him without looking up.

When he started taking notice of his surroundings once more, Haliwell was conversing with the officer leading their rescuers, a man similar to the captain in stature but with jet-black hair.

'... we had reached the top of the cliffs when we heard shots from below,' he was saying in a clear Scottish accent. 'Unfortunately we couldn't see what was going on but I supposed it was your party. Since you seemed to be moving pretty rapidly, I thought we should best follow on until we found a way down to you. Some rough ground held us up so we didn't strike the mouth of the canyon until after you'd passed. I wasn't certain whether you had turned up it or gone by until we heard more shots. Then we simply headed this way as fast as we could.'

'Well, it was a timely piece of work, Sinclair,' Haliwell said.

'A minute later and those things would have had us.' He hesitated. 'I'm afraid we lost Granby in the forest.'

Sinclair's lips tightened. 'Your men said he was missing. Are you certain he's... gone?'

'Quite certain,' Haliwell said.

'That's a great shame. He was a bright young fellow.'

Turlough wanted to say to them: come on, don't be so stiff-upper-lipped, the man's dead! But at the same time he had to admire their self-control.

Sinclair turned to look curiously at the Doctor and Turlough. 'But you seem to have found some unexpected guests.'

Wearily Turlough got to his feet and dusted himself off as Haliwell made the introductions. Their recent shared adversity seemed to have dispelled his doubts, and they were accepted as fellow travellers from contemporary Earth.

Haliwell decided they should rest for half an hour before setting off back to the ships, which was fine by Turlough. The Doctor looked perfectly fresh, having recovered from his exertions with his customary annoying ease. A man from the rescue party whom Turlough took to be one of the expedition surgeons was applying salve and bandages to Stephens's arm. Emily was tending her father who was sitting with his back to a rock taking a drink from a flask and looking very pale. Nobody seemed to be paying Turlough much attention, being only the Doctor's 'assistant', so he had a chance to study Emily more closely. She wasn't exactly the beauty he had assumed, with rather too strong a nose for ideal proportions, but she was far from plain and certainly possessed a strong character. He wondered idly how she and Tegan would have got along. Of course, the way it should work out in the end was that she and Haliwell would get together and...

He blinked. This is not fiction, he reminded himself, and these are real people. But at the same time it was hard to believe this because the words of the diary, which had seemed so fantastic only hours earlier, were fixed in his mind.

Turlough glanced across at Haliwell and felt the hairs rise on the back of his neck. Before his very eyes he was making an entry in the

61

diary, presumably bringing it up-to-date with an account of their escape from the spiders. But the diary was back in the TARDIS... Turlough pinched the bridge of his nose. There were two diaries, of course; or rather one diary temporarily doubled in time.

So everything that had happened to them, including his part in it, really was recorded on those pages. If only he'd been able to read them he'd have made sure they'd kept well clear of the spiders' lair. But then that was the very thing the Doctor had warned him he could not do. Was his future really immutable? What part did free will play in events? Was he trapped in the diary with the rest of them?

When he looked up again Haliwell was talking to Sinclair. The Doctor, in his usual deceptive manner, had insinuated himself into their discussions.

'What were those creatures?' Sinclair wondered aloud. 'There was the work of the devil in them.'

'Merely predators of a kind new to you,' the Doctor said mildly. 'Best not confuse the strange with the supernatural.'

'Well, whatever they were,' Haliwell said, 'we cannot risk another trip into the forest unless we discover some more immediate means of dealing with them, since clearly nothing less than death will cause them to break off their pursuit. How did they track us? I could not see any signs of eyes or ears.'

'Perhaps by our scent or the vibrations of our footsteps,' the Doctor said. 'Or even the electrical fields of our bodies. There are many senses apart from the five you are familiar with.'

Sinclair was looking at him curiously. 'And just how, Doctor, do you explain their ability to take a score of rifle rounds without apparent harm? Is that not unnatural?'

'Not at all. They probably have limited nervous systems and few specialised internal organs. If they breathe by direct diffusion of air to the tissues there would be no vulnerable vital centres such as a heart or lungs. It's their behaviour that puzzles me. As I mentioned to Haliwell during our little run, it's not common for animals to pursue their prey with such determination. Usually only intelligent creatures behave so irrationally, and I don't think these spiders were intelligent in any meaningful sense. They should have given up sooner and looked for easier prey. As it is, all their persistence did was get them killed.'

'Well, you won't find me regretting that,' said Haliwell.

Once Professor Boyes-Dennison had recovered sufficiently, the party prepared to move off. The Doctor, however, seemed to have taken an interest in the mountains on the rim, and was studying them through a small pocket telescope.

'What is it?' Turlough asked.

The Doctor handed him the telescope and pointed. 'Look at the cleft the stream has cut in the mountainside.'

Their route up the canyon had brought them close to the foothills where the canyon dwindled to a gully and continued upwards into the mountains proper. It was overhung by fern bushes for some of the way, but these were gradually replaced by bare rock and pockets of snow that thickened until they merged with the white-capped summits. For a moment Turlough could see nothing strange, then he spotted it.

'Looks like someone's laid a thick pipe along the side of the stream. It's obscured in places, but it seems to run all the way up to the snow line.'

'Yes, now why do you suppose they did that? You might feed water in at the top of a stream or extract it from the bottom, but you rarely need to lay pipes along its length. Assuming it is a water pipe, of course.'

'Well, what else might it be?'

'I don't know, but it might be interesting to find out.'

'Can't we just get back to the TARDIS? Haven't we had enough excitement for one day?'

The Doctor grinned. 'Ah, but remember this is the Moon where the days are fourteen times as long. It takes a lot of "excitement" to fill them. Besides, the pipe might tell us something about the intelligent beings who live here.'

Turlough sighed. 'Go on. I suppose it can't be worse than the forest.'

The Doctor went over to Haliwell. After a short debate the captain agreed they should make a detour to investigate.

They set off towards the hills. In fact it was only about half a mile to the gully and Turlough took heart from the fact that the intervening ground was open enough for it to be unlikely that they would to be taken by surprise. He kept glancing anxiously at the distant bird-like shapes wheeling in the sky, but they showed no sign of coming any closer.

The foot of the gully was choked with ferns fed by the constant spray of water from the cascading stream. When they pushed their way through the ferns they found a hollow space, perhaps forty feet across, which had obviously been cleared and levelled at some time, though the regrowth of small plants and mosses gave it an air of disuse.

Visible through the vegetation was indeed the lower end of a pipe, set in a heavy buttress of carefully laid stones. But the pipe itself was not metal or plastic, but formed out of lengths of a larger variety of the bamboo-like plant they had seen in the forest, with stems about a foot in diameter. Each section was bound tightly around with vines, over which had been poured some clear substance that had set like dense plastic. The same material had been used like a liquid cement to secure the stones on which the pipe was mounted. A natural resin, Turlough thought. Looking up the line of the pipe he could see it ran upwards at an angle of about forty-five degrees, cutting through the hillside in places and supported by more buttresses over hollows, until it vanished amongst the snow-covered peaks some three or four miles distant. Though there were obvious breaks and places where his view was obscured, as far as he could judge by eye the pipe was perfectly straight along its entire length.

A little way up the slope from the buttress, along a crumbling overgrown flight of steps that had been cut into the hill, was a curious mechanism. The pipe ran through the centres of two heavy stone slabs which were set perpendicular to its long axis with a space of about five feet between them. Filling this gap was a barrel-shaped object over a yard across, made of a bundle of carefully graded bamboos bound with thick vines and mounted on a heavy spindle set into the stonework on either side. Within the barrel were four cylindrical chambers, spaced so they could be rotated to align with the bore of the main barrel. The entire assembly was also heavily braced and sealed with more of the resin.

'Well, it's not a water pipe,' Turlough observed.

'No,' the Doctor agreed, examining the mechanism closely. 'I think it's a vacuum gun.'

'A gun?' Sinclair exclaimed. 'But it's monstrous.'

'I admit there is a resemblance to the chamber block of a revolver,' Haliwell said. 'But could it really serve in place of a breech mechanism for something so massive?'

'If for some reason your choice of materials was limited, this might be the most appropriate design,' the Doctor said. 'A conventional breech would require precision machining.'

'Come now, young man,' said the professor, who had also been inspecting the barrel. 'There are practical limits to the size of a gun. The displacement resistance of the air in such a length of barrel would alone limit the final velocity of a projectile.'

'Not if the far end of the barrel up there extends into the lunar vacuum, through the field that holds the air in the crater, and the remaining air in the barrel is evacuated,' the Doctor countered. He indicated a hole with a broken length of smaller-bore bamboo projecting from it in the side of the chamber block. 'If the stone facing slabs were greased and kept under compression they would form a reasonably airtight seal, but the block itself would still be free to rotate, allowing the charge and projectile to be loaded from the other chambers.'

'But I see no trigger mechanism,' Sinclair said.

'The charges might be triggered by a catalytic igniter,' the Doctor speculated. 'It wouldn't allow much time, which explains why the charge would have to be loaded after the barrel was evacuated.'

'But how did whoever built this draw the air out of the barrel?' Haliwell asked.

'Maybe with something like that,' Turlough said, pointing at a shadowy mass looming beneath the fern bushes.

A few slashes of the sailors' knives cleared the foliage and revealed a device of bamboo tubes and plungers linked to a water wheel by decaying drive belts. From it a channel ran some twenty yards up the hill to a small penstock that contained a pool lying in a hollow. The curious structure was now neglected and the stream had overflowed the pool and found its own course down the hillside. It was obviously some years since the improvised air pump had functioned.

Further cautious probing in the undergrowth revealed a discarded, blackened length of bamboo barrel that had evidently been blown apart from within. Professor Boyes-Dennison retreated into grumpy silence, since the new find seemed to confirm the Doctor's theory. Emily, however, still had some questions.

'This all must have taken a tremendous amount of effort to construct,' she said. 'But what was it for? If this is a gun then what was its target? It appears to be totally immobile. Was there an enemy of its builders that would only approach from the west?'

The Doctor smiled. 'That is a very good question,' he said. 'I just wish I had a good answer.'

They left the gun and continued on, angling away from the hills towards the British ships, making their way over ground none of them had traversed before. Turlough noticed Haliwell looking about with a growing frown as they progressed. Finally the captain asked: 'Where did you put your ship down, Doctor? If you landed as near to us as you say, I would have thought we would have seen it by now.'

'Oh, it's over there, somewhere,' the Doctor said, pointing vaguely to the scattered stands of trees. 'It's quite a bit smaller than your craft. You wouldn't have noticed it land.'

Before Haliwell could pursue the matter further, Turlough said quickly: 'What's that?'

Amongst the ferns lay the remains of a creature that in life would have been about the size of a double-decker bus. Now it was only scraps of scaly skin clinging to a frame of bleached bones. It seemed to have at least four pairs of legs and very large jaws. Turlough looked anxiously at the rolling heathland. He'd begun to feel they were safe up here, but if there were creatures of that size roaming around he wanted to know about it. However, all he saw and heard were the familiar darting insects and the occasional rustle of small animals in the longer grass.

In the next twenty minutes they passed the remains of two more large animals. Some of the bones had scratches on them that might have been teeth marks, but there was no way of telling if these were connected with what had killed them. They saw no fresh corpses.

A little later Haliwell gave an exclamation of relief. Appearing over the Moon's deceptively close horizon were the prows of the British spaceships.

A cheer went up from the ratings and unconsciously the whole party increased its pace. Turlough felt moved by an impulse to join the cheering. He wanted a reminder of civilisation as a buffer between him and the wilds of the crater.

In a minute a distant halloo from the camp told them they had been spotted in turn. Turlough saw figures moving about the base of the ships and waving. He had to resist the urge to wave back.

They were only two hundred yards away from the nearest ship when Sinclair halted abruptly, pointing to one side.

'My God... what's that?'

Gliding silently through the giant trees towards the British camp was a flying saucer.

Chapter Ten
Marooned

Even as they covered the last few yards to the ships in great leaps and bounds, Turlough could not think of a better description of the alien machine than the impression it had first conveyed. It really was shaped like a classic flying saucer, about twelve feet across and four deep through its centre, and silver in colour. Around the underside was a ring of half a dozen raised nodules, while set between these were what looked like small lenses.

The party came to a halt amongst the rest of the British crews. A dozen rifles were pointed at the saucer which now hovered silently about fifteen feet above the ground.

'Don't make any sudden moves,' the Doctor said, his voice suddenly taking on a commanding edge. 'It probably comes from the citadel, sent to look us over. If it can see we're peaceful there's no reason why there should be any trouble.'

'All right, lower your guns,' Haliwell ordered. 'But keep them handy.'

Turlough saw Emily say something quickly to her father then edge aside and make for one of the ships.

The Doctor stepped forward until he was almost underneath the saucer and raised his hands, palms outwards.

'I don't know if you can understand me, but we mean you no harm. If there's anybody inside we'd be glad to meet you.'

Haliwell stepped up beside the Doctor and said in a low tone: 'What do you mean, if there's anybody inside?'

'It's not very large, so it may be a remotely operated probe device, relaying our images to its controllers,' the Doctor said out of the corner of his mouth, not taking his eyes off the saucer.

'We've been here several hours. Why has it taken this long for them to show themselves?'

'I have no idea. Perhaps they wanted to observe from a distance before revealing their presence, or else they were waiting for you to make the first move.'

Haliwell looked up at the saucer and said loudly: 'I am Captain Richard Haliwell of Her Britannic Majesty's Navy. We have come in peace and good fellowship, and would be honoured if we could meet you in person.'

A pale pencil-thin beam of red light emerged from the edge of the saucer and began tracking methodically across the hull of the nearest ship. The sailors started and a few raised their rifles once again, causing the Doctor to wave his arms in a desperate appeal for calm.

'It's all right, I think it's just taking a closer look at your ships,' he said. 'They must be of an unfamiliar design.'

'Steady, men,' Haliwell commanded.

Emily emerged from the ship carrying her spare camera and tripod and began setting it up on the edge of the group watching the saucer. She stared in fascination at the rapidly moving beam as it flashed across to the second ship.

'Whatever is it?' she wondered aloud.

'Probably a laser topography-scanning beam,' Turlough said automatically.

Both the Boyes-Dennisons gave him the oddest look.

'And how would you know about such things, young man?' the professor asked suspiciously.

Before Turlough could think of an answer the beam finished with the ships and began to scan the group of onlookers.

'Just don't look directly at the beam and it won't hurt,' the Doctor said reassuringly.

Turlough blinked as the beam flickered across his face. An afterimage lingered for a few seconds, then faded. As long as there was no hidden infrared component in the beam he should be all right.

He saw Emily standing by her camera. The shutter release was in one hand while in the other she held an old-fashioned magnesium flash tray which she was raising over her head.

'No!' the Doctor said sharply. 'It might misinterpret the flash as a weapon.'

Hesitantly Emily lowered her hand. But the scanning beam was already flickering across her and the camera tripod. Suddenly the beam vanished and the saucer began drifting towards her.

'It's realised you're different from the rest of us,' the Doctor said, slowly edging towards her with Haliwell at his side. 'Don't make any sudden moves.'

'Emily,' Professor Boyes-Dennison said, holding out his hand. 'Leave your camera and come to me.'

For the first time Turlough saw real anxiety on Emily's face. She reached out for her father and took a hesitant step towards him.

One of the nodules on the underside of the saucer uncoiled, extending with a swish and crack into a whip-like metal tentacle that wrapped about Emily's waist and jerked her off her feet into the air. The Doctor and Halliwell leapt forward to pull her back even as two more tentacles lashed out. One caught Haliwell about the waist and chest, pinning an arm to his side. With a lightning reflex the Doctor managed to partially ward off the second and it could only fasten about his forearm. Even as the saucer began rising, lifting them off their feet, the Doctor twisted, wriggling his arm out of his jacket. The tentacle lost its grip and he dropped back to the ground.

Taking advantage of the low gravity, a couple of the sailors made prodigious leaps in an attempt to save the captives. One grasped Haliwell's leg, but his hand slipped and he dropped down again. The second managed to grasp the edge of the saucer itself. There was a crackle of electricity and blue sparks flickered about his hands. He shrieked with pain and fell to earth.

The saucer continued to rise, carrying the two remaining figures in its grasp.

'Emily!' the professor shouted, reaching up desperately towards the limp figure of his daughter. The saucer began to glide back the way it had come and he stumbled after it.

'Fire at the main body of the thing!' Sinclair shouted.

Shots rang out. Turlough saw bullets splash against the silvery hull only to ricochet away without leaving a trace. Then it was beyond their range, rapidly gaining height and speed, with the diminishing figure of the professor bounding futilely along beneath it calling to Emily, his coat-tails flapping. In a few seconds the saucer had passed over the tree tops at the end of the glade and headed out over the forest basin towards the central mountains.

Sailors ran to their comrade. He was trembling from the electrical shock from the saucer but seemed otherwise uninjured. Turlough helped the Doctor, who was holding his wrenched arm awkwardly, to his feet.

'Are you all right?' Turlough asked.

'Just bruised,' the Doctor said, looking very pale. 'Why did it act so aggressively when we offered no threat?'

Turlough shook his head. 'Keep on hoping for the best like that and you'll always be disappointed.'

'I trust I shall never become that cynical.'

Sinclair had pivoted the field telescope, which had been set up between the ships, to focus on the saucer. Now he began to call out orders.

'Green,' Sinclair said to the remaining commander, a slim, sharp-faced man, 'your helmsman Stanton is probably the best we have. Follow that thing in the *Draco*, but keep well clear. We don't want it to drop them. It's likely heading for the citadel on the central mountains but we must be sure.'

'Sir,' Green acknowledged, and dashed off.

'Bosun. Back to the *Cygnus* and tell Mr Forrester he now has command.'

'Aye sir!' The bosun saluted and made for his ship.

Turlough saw the professor still standing alone on the far side of the glade, away from the flurry of activity about the ships, staring at the spot where the saucer had passed over the trees. Turlough thought he'd never seen a person look so pathetically lost.

Then the old man seemed to fold in the middle. He toppled slowly to the mossy ground and lay still.

Even as a cry went up for the surgeon, the Doctor was bounding across the glade with Turlough at his heels.

The Doctor knelt by the crumpled figure and turned him over, feeling for a pulse in the neck. 'Nothing,' he said after a moment. He pulled back the professor's eyelids. The pupils were fixed and unresponsive. 'It looks like he's had a massive heart attack.' He sighed. 'I don't think there's anything we can do for him.'

'Can't you resuscitate him... or something?'

'Even if resuscitation worked briefly, the proper support facilities don't exist in this century. He wouldn't survive. I think this time we must let nature take its course.'

The *Lynx*'s surgeon arrived at their sides with a couple of sailors carrying a folded stretcher. Rapidly he made his own examination.

'He's gone,' he confirmed. 'No doubt due to his physical exertions earlier, then the shock of seeing his daughter carried off. Too much for a man of his age.'

Turlough felt sick, helpless and unaccountably angry. The suspicious, irascible, brilliant old man he'd known for a few hours was gone just like that. He'd seen violent death before, but why was this different? Perhaps because there'd been no great fuss, no heroics, only life departing. People shouldn't simply drop dead like that, just because they were old and tired... Then he realised he was reacting against his own inevitable mortality. It was the first time it had ever afflicted him in that way.

Sinclair glanced up from the telescope eyepiece for a moment as they returned. The Doctor shook his head. Behind them the professor's body was placed on the stretcher and covered with a blanket. Sinclair's face softened and Turlough heard him mutter under his breath: 'God grant him rest.'

Then he became the commanding officer with urgent responsibilities once more. 'According to Haliwell you seem to have a certain understanding of this place,' he said crisply. 'I must know if you have any idea who we're facing.'

'Obviously they are technically advanced,' the Doctor said. 'That craft, whether it was manned or remotely controlled, proves that. But until we know what purpose this crater serves, we can only speculate as to the motives of its inhabitants.'

Sinclair returned his attention to the telescope. 'Whatever these beings may be, we should have considered the possibility that they would also have flying machines. But these astral ships are so new that such concepts do not come naturally.'

With a clang the solar panels of the *Draco* swung inwards and locked against the hull. Its impellers started up with a hum and the ship lifted off the ground. Immediately, it dipped its nose and headed after the saucer. They watched it fade into the haze over the forest. Sinclair provided a commentary.

'They are overhauling the other craft rapidly. At least we seem to have the greater turn of knots. Now they're flying in parallel. Still holding the same course towards the mountain. I think…'

Even with his unaided eyes Turlough saw the blossoming explosion in the sky at the same moment as Sinclair let out a curse and jerked his head back from the telescope, blinking painfully. 'There was a brilliant flash from the top of the mountain, almost blinding.' He put his other eye to the lens. 'They're shooting at the *Draco*! It's taking evasive action…'

More explosions burst over the forest. A blue-white fireball seared high overhead trailing in its wake a thunderclap of sound that made them duck. Sinclair held his position.

'The *Draco*'s been hit! It's tumbling… they're trying to hold altitude… The prow is lifting…' There was an agonising pause. Sinclair drew back from the telescope, his lips pinched. 'It was too late. They've gone down in the forest.'

There was a groan of dismay from the men within earshot. Turlough sensed their barely contained anger. Over forty of their friends and comrades might have just died. Sinclair was holding himself steady with an obvious effort.

The Doctor asked gently: 'How far away would you say they crashed?'

Sinclair took a deep breath. 'At least halfway to the mountain. We can only hope they managed a controlled landing.'

'What about the saucer?' Turlough asked.

Sinclair looked again. 'Still on the same heading. Whatever that gun was, apparently we're within its range. But why isn't it firing at us now? Did they not see where the *Draco* lifted from?'

'At the moment they may be content to let you stay where you are as long as you don't threaten them,' the Doctor suggested. 'They're still curious about us.'

'You may be right,' Sinclair said. 'But I cannot permit them to indulge their curiosity through abduction, or firing upon our ships. That was an act of war!'

'We are the intruders here,' the Doctor pointed out.

'They could have made it plain they wished us to leave without resorting to such measures. Now they will learn they cannot treat British subjects that way. We shall go to their citadel and effect the safe return of Haliwell and Miss Boyes-Dennison by whatever means necessary. We must also mount a search for any survivors from the *Draco*. Since we cannot risk another launch while that gun is operational, we shall go on foot.'

'Through thirty or forty miles of forest,' Turlough said with feeling. 'That won't be a picnic.'

'If that is what is required, Mr Turlough,' Sinclair said tersely. 'The navy does not abandon either its captains, its guests or its crewmen. There is no other choice.'

'Perhaps there is,' the Doctor said. 'Our ship is smaller than yours and quite unobtrusive. We should be able to approach the mountain without being seen and we might even get the captain and Miss Boyes-Dennison back ourselves. At the very least we can make a reconnaissance so that you know what you're up against.'

'Of course, if you are prepared to take the risk then that would be capital, Doctor, though we shall proceed with our preparations just the same.' Sinclair hesitated. 'Should you be able to contact Miss Boyes-Dennison, do not tell her about her father until she is safely returned. That is my responsibility.'

'I understand.'

'Do you want some ratings to accompany you?'

'No, the fewer people the better until we know exactly what we're dealing with. Come on, Turlough.'

As they ran back to the TARDIS in ground-devouring slow-motion strides, Turlough asked: 'Do you think that saucer was sent deliberately to take prisoners?'

'Probably not. It simply took the opportunity we presented.'

'Why did it pick on Emily?'

'Perhaps because she was operating her camera, or she was physically different from the rest of us. Whatever the reason this is a terrible way for two intelligent species to meet. The British will only be too ready to shoot first next time.'

'If they've already met an alien species, doesn't this mean you have to let this timeline continue? I mean, that's getting pretty involved.'

The Doctor frowned. 'It's a significant factor. For the moment, though, I just want to prevent the situation getting any more violent.'

When they entered the TARDIS Kamelion was standing by the console, reminding Turlough of a faithful old retainer patiently awaiting his master's return.

'I trust you had an interesting time,' he inquired politely.

'That's one word for it,' said Turlough.

The Doctor closed the doors and began tapping buttons on the console, setting coordinates. 'We want to land on the central range within walking distance of the citadel but not too close,' he muttered half to himself. 'That should do. Here we go.'

The familiar low pulse of dematerialisation reverberated through the room and began to rise in volume. Suddenly the TARDIS gave a shudder and the time rotor froze. The sound pulse stuttered and faded away.

The Doctor frowned at the controls, checking the settings. Turlough scanned the displays on his side of the console. 'There's plenty of power and the coordinates are locked in,' he said. 'What's wrong?'

The Doctor was running through fault checks. Suddenly he said, 'Ah!' significantly.

'What?'

The Doctor stepped back from the console, thrusting his hands deep into his pockets in a gesture of frustration. 'The crater's energy field seems to have grown stronger since we landed, perhaps in response to the encounter we've just had. Now it's interfering with the dematerialisation process.'

'Can't you block it?'

'Not without using all the ship's power, and then there'd be none left to dematerialise. I'm afraid, until we can shut that field off we're marooned here – and so are the British.'

Chapter Eleven
The Citadel

Haliwell felt a cold hand close on his heart as he stared at the spot where the *Draco* had vanished. By reflex he clutched again at his empty holster. His pistol was somewhere back at the landing site where it had fallen in the confusion. Well, it probably wouldn't be any use anyway he thought bitterly, as the steaming forest rolled by a thousand feet below. Over the sound of the wind whipping past his head he heard Emily Boyes-Dennison say: 'Those poor men. They were trying to rescue us.'

He twisted his head around as far as his bonds would allow to stare at the woman suspended within her own cocoon of metal tentacles a few feet away.

'Miss Boyes-Dennison… are you all right?' he called over to her. 'I thought you had fainted.'

'I do not faint, Mr Haliwell, I was simply winded when I was lifted off the ground so violently. It has taken me a while to recover my breath.'

'I apologise for presuming you had fainted, Miss Boyes-Dennison,' Haliwell replied stiffly.

He saw her bite her lip. 'No, I must apologise. I spoke without thinking. We should not bicker over such trifles when good men have just died for our sakes.'

Haliwell inclined his head as well as he could. 'I accept your apology, Miss Boyes-Dennison. But do not give up on the *Draco* yet. There has been no sign of any smoke. If the ship had been completely destroyed the compressed oxygen cylinders would have exploded and burnt fiercely. There is a good possibility some of the men escaped. They may still be able to follow after us.'

To his surprise he saw her smile fleetingly.

'Thank you for trying to raise my spirits, Mr Haliwell. But I am fully aware of the realities of our situation. We are on our own without any hope of immediate rescue. That is true, is it not?'

There was no point in trying to deceive this perceptive woman.

'You're quite correct,' he admitted. 'There is little chance of any survivors reaching us from the *Draco*. And Sinclair would be a fool to launch another ship with the mountain defended by a weapon of considerable range. He can only proceed on foot and we know how hazardous an undertaking that would be. We merely touched on the fringe of the forest but there was every sign it grew denser further in. Assuming he met no insuperable obstacles I estimate three or four days for the journey.'

'So for at least that time we have just our own resources to rely upon. We can only trust that whatever beings are responsible for abducting us can be made to see we mean them no harm.'

'Their actions so far do not give me any great hopes in that direction,' Haliwell said bitterly. 'Firing upon the *Draco*…'

'I'm sure that was a misunderstanding,' she said quickly. 'The sophistication of this craft indicates they must be rational beings. As long as we can establish some form of mutually intelligible communication, we should be able to make our position clear.'

'Miss Boyes-Dennison, you asked me to speak the truth to you a minute ago. In all frankness, then, I suggest my experience of the realities of life is greater than yours. Our world is full of supposedly rational beings at war with each other who must have far more in common than we have with whatever manner of beings built this craft. Intelligence is no guarantee of civilised behaviour. Even the educated portions of the human race are no models of virtue, despite having the kind of ingenuity that carried us to the Moon.'

'I still have hopes of reaching an understanding. And besides, sir, you only speak for half the human race. Women as a rule do not start wars – Helen of Troy excepted…' She broke off with a grunt of pain.

'Are you hurt?' Haliwell asked anxiously.

'These tentacles are cutting into me. I fear I shall be badly bruised afterwards. And yourself?'

'Much the same. But I am trying not to move too much. Even if I could get free there is only the long drop to the forest, which I find unappealing. For the moment I think we can only bide our time until we land.'

'How long do you think that will be?'

'I would say we are making fifty or sixty knots. We should reach the mountains within twenty minutes.'

'At least they must set us down then. I will be very grateful to be free of these bonds.'

'You must face the possibility that they will only be exchanged for other bonds. But we may have a few moments of freedom. You must be ready if there is the slightest chance of escape.'

She looked at him oddly. 'Now circumstance has placed me in this position, I cannot run away from the first meeting with an entirely new species. The opportunity for new knowledge is so vast. I only wish my father could be there…' She faltered. 'Father will be so worried, he does depend on me so. No, for his sake I must go through with this. It will be worth the risk. You are free to escape if you can. Perhaps you can get word back to the camp.'

'Madam! My honour would never permit me to desert you under such circumstances.'

'Men's honour! I think some of the most foolish things are done in the name of men's honour. You set it so apart from everything else and nobody, least of all women, may encroach upon it. Will you not allow me to act as my principles dictate? Or is my choice to see this through foolish, while your decision to stay with me is heroic?'

Haliwell sighed. 'Miss Boyes-Dennison. If you are determined then I am, shall we say, *duty bound* to stay with you.'

She was silent for a moment, then said. 'Thank you, Captain Haliwell. I admit I would be grateful for the company.'

He realised she was more nervous than she cared to show. For a few minutes they said nothing, knowing they were in the hands of fate. The mountains grew steadily larger.

Then Emily Boyes-Dennison said: 'Despite our differences of opinion on many subjects, I think we can dispense with certain foolish formalities in our current circumstances. We are both adults, we have after all known each other for some months, and my surname does not slip lightly from the tongue. Please call me Emily.'

Haliwell took a deep breath. 'Then, Emily, you must call me Richard. But I must ask, when we return to the ships, that the formalities are maintained before the crew. It is how things are done, no doubt foolishly, but nevertheless so.'

'I understand perfectly, Richard.'

As they were carried helplessly onwards the central range grew before them, stretching perhaps ten miles to the right and left. The forest lapped its foothills, becoming a rapidly thinning band of scrub that clung precariously to clefts and ledges as the slopes became more precipitate. As they crossed the divide their transport began to climb, rising silently over the great crags of bare rock that guarded the sides of the central peak.

Suddenly, perpendicular planes replaced rough slabs. The top of the mountain had been shaped into an artificial plateau with sheer sides, two hundred feet high, carved from the living rock. They topped the outer ramparts and the citadel lay before them.

Haliwell had an impression of an acropolis of many terraces, from which impossibly slender minarets rose into the sky. Plazas and walled gardens were laid out between low buildings capped with fluted domes of white marble, shot through with threads of silver and gold. It was a scene of great beauty, yet at the same time quite sterile and lifeless, for of inhabitants there was no sign.

They dipped downwards, heading for a lower terrace that was filled with a curving line of shallow metallic domes, looking rather like inverted saucers, interspersed at irregular intervals with dark pits.

It was only as they skimmed across this curious formation that Emily exclaimed: 'It's a landing ground for more of these craft. There are dozens of them.'

Even as Haliwell realised the truth of her statement they had come to rest, poised over one of the vacant pits. The rim of the pit matched the undercurve of their transport exactly. The saucer craft sank downwards until it touched ground, settling into place like the cap of a well and fitting so perfectly that all light from outside was extinguished.

He heard Emily give an involuntary gasp of alarm as they hung suspended in complete blackness. The echo of her cry had scarcely died away when rectangular strips set in the sides of the pit began to glow with a pearly-white radiance, revealing a featureless shaft some twenty feet deep. The mechanical tentacles uncoiled, lowering them gently to the ground. As the two of them struggled free of the loosening grasp of their bonds the tentacles retracted into the craft once again.

They both stifled groans as they tried to move stiffened limbs. Emily sat down, rubbing some life back into her legs. Haliwell looked about him, flexing the fingers of the arm that had been clamped to his side.

'The arrangement of vessels and pits suggests they are used to receiving reluctant guests,' he said. 'This must be some transitional holding cell. Presumably we shall be taken to meet the masters of this place when they are ready to receive us.'

'Will we have to endure those tentacles again?' Emily said. 'I would much prefer to walk.'

Haliwell was circling the walls, examining them carefully.

'There's a seam here.' He traced its outline, which formed a circle as high as he could reach. 'I think it's a hatch or door, but very close fitting.'

Emily stood up and came over to his side. 'Yes, I believe you are right. I suppose there is no sign of a handle.'

Haliwell smiled grimly. 'Apparently it is not intended that we let ourselves out.'

'Then we must be patient. Meanwhile we should prepare ourselves for the encounter. My father has some theories –'

The door silently slid backwards like a plug from a hole and rolled aside. Silhouetted against the light from outside was a monstrous form.

Emily and Haliwell instinctively flinched away from the apparition, their reaction carrying them backwards ten feet in the light gravity. The thing entered the pit and they saw it properly for the first time.

It was an assembly of polished metal, taller than a man, supported by a low platform that rode on four large spherical wheels. A thick column rose from the centre of the platform, and arrayed about this were many jointed arms with various claws, hooks and other unidentifiable implements attached to their ends. Capping the column was something like a cowled helmet that swung about to face them. From its depths shone two unblinking red eyes.

The sight of familiar coiled metal tentacles amongst the array of devices it carried caused Haliwell to realise its purpose.

'It is just a mechanical servant,' he said quickly. 'No doubt controlled from a distance as the Doctor speculated the craft that brought us might be.'

'I believe you are right. It cannot be the ruling species here. Those gardens above us were created for beings with an appreciation of beauty, not machines.'

The machine extended a many-jointed arm in the direction of the portal through which it had entered, in an unmistakable gesture.

'Apparently it wants us to go that way,' Haliwell said.

'It must have been sent to escort us to its masters,' Emily said, her voice keen with excitement.

'It seems as though your wish is about come true,' Haliwell observed. 'As we have no choice, we may as well proceed.'

They edged past the machine and out into the corridor beyond, which was arched and lit by more glowing panels. The machine followed silently after them. The circular hatch, which had been resting to one side supported by a heavy arm, slid back across the opening and closed once again.

Haliwell and Emily walked along the corridor with their strange attendant at their heels. At intervals sliding doors that lay across their path opened for them as they approached and closed as soon as they were past. At a point where another passage crossed theirs, their guide swung around in front of them and held out a warning arm. Another machine identical to their own sped through the crossroads on some unknown errand without paying them any attention. Once it was past they were directed forward again.

'The passage has been level and we started from below the

lowest terrace,' Haliwell said in a low voice. 'We must be headed for some place deep underneath the main buildings.'

'Unless we are to ascend some stairway,' Emily suggested. 'Or perhaps a ramp, for I do not see how these machines could climb stairs.'

They came to a door larger than those they had so far passed. This one did not open automatically before them, but only after a significant pause. Beyond was a large chamber with a domed roof braced by heavy ribs and ringed with ramps and balconies on which were set banks of flickering lights and illuminated gauges, attended by more of the servant machines. Rising from floor to ceiling in the centre of the room was a massive pillar encrusted with pipes and cables. A broad glass band ran round the entire pillar, a little above its base, forming a circular tank that was illuminated from within by concealed lights. The tank seemed to be filled with green-tinted fluid that had some indistinct mass suspended within it.

Their escort indicated they should move towards the central pillar. They were ten feet from it when Emily gave a little gasp, even as Haliwell exclaimed: 'Good God!'

A living creature floated within the tank.

It was something between a sea anemone and a naked bloated brain, perhaps two feet across and reddish in colour. Tiny tendrils and sucker-headed arms ringed its body, swaying in a regular pulsating motion. A spray of fine wires and tubes emerged from the top of the creature's body and ran upwards into the heart of the pillar.

The mechanical hands of their escort pushed them onwards until they were almost touching the glass wall of the tank. With a ripple of its tendrils the creature glided forward until only inches separated it from them. Only then did they see that a dozen small eyes ringed its sides. These lidless orbs regarded them with cold interest for a full minute. Despite its grotesque appearance there was a fragility about the thing, Haliwell realised. It was hardly more than a mass of boneless jelly.

'I don't think it knows what to make of us,' he said softly.

'Perhaps it's myopic,' Emily replied, fighting the tremor in her voice.

A metallic voice suddenly issued from a grille set in the pillar above their heads, and a long phrase in some incomprehensible language boomed out at them. Then there was a pause, as though to allow for some response.

'It's trying to communicate with us,' Emily said excitedly. 'It cannot have vocal cords like ours, so it is using a mechanical speaker.' She looked at the thing in the tank and opened her arms in a gesture of incomprehension, shaking her head. 'I'm sorry, we don't understand you.'

The voice sounded again, but this time the words had a different pitch and rhythm, and included several glottal clicks.

'It's trying another language,' Emily said. She shook her head at the thing again. 'No, sorry, that's still not right.'

They proceeded though half a dozen equally incomprehensible languages with a similar lack of success. Some of the sounds coming from the speaker grille sounded so strange that Haliwell could not imagine what manner of being might employ them. Finally there was a long silence. The creature drifted back to the middle of its tank, rippling its tendrils in what might have been impatience.

'It's given up,' Emily said in dismay. 'But we must keep trying.'

'Apparently we have exhausted its store of languages,' Haliwell said. 'Either we must learn one of them, or it must learn English. Both procedures could take some time.'

'We might try mime,' Emily suggested. 'If we can somehow make it understand what we want...'

But it was evident the creature had decided on its own course of action.

A second servant rolled smoothly up to them. Before they could move the two machines had grasped their arms with heavy clamps. Even as they struggled futilely to break free more delicate mechanical limbs were unfolded. Each bore fine needles at the tips and Haliwell and Emily gasped in pain as these were driven into their immobilised arms. After a few seconds the needles were withdrawn and the clamps were released, leaving them bent over cradling their injured arms. The second machine took a glass ampoule red with blood from a cavity in its companion's needle-tipped arm, extracted an identical container from its own, and rolled away.

Their original guide now pointed back to the doorway through which they had entered. Still clutching his smarting arm, Haliwell said: 'It seems our audience is concluded.'

Biting her lip against her pain, Emily shook her head. 'But we must try to make it understand.'

The machine held out a clawed hand and electric sparks cracked and flashed menacingly between its tips.

'I do not think we have a choice,' said Haliwell.

They allowed themselves to be escorted out of the chamber and down the long corridor. Before they reached the pit they turned down a side passage and stopped in front of a heavy door. It opened after a few seconds and they stepped through. The door closed behind them, leaving their guide on the other side.

It was another room of white stone, lit by the glowing panels. There was no other visible exit.

Haliwell tried to keep his voice steady. 'I think it is intended that we should stay here for the time being.'

'It is a cell, Richard,' Emily said simply. 'I can see that.'

There were three alcoves opening off a common space, each furnished with raised pallets, formed out of the same material as the room itself, which were presumably intended to serve as beds. Opposite them was a recess in the wall through which a stream of water ran continuously. To one side was another alcove with a hole in the floor set in a shallow trough, whose function was obvious.

Haliwell felt a flush of embarrassment. They were intended to share these facilities with hardly any provision for privacy. The creature in the tank could not understand human proprieties. He strode back to the door and banged on it with his fist.

'This isn't good enough! We need proper rooms!'

There was no reply.

Emily was looking at him curiously and he realised he was simply making a fool of himself. She did not yet seem to appreciate the ramifications of their situation. Or perhaps she had her father's peculiar scientific detachment in greater measure than he had suspected.

'The machines were drawing blood and tissue from us,' she said thoughtfully as she rubbed her arm. 'Perhaps the creature means to analyse them to understand us further. We must seem as strange to it as it does to us.'

Haliwell felt anger rise within him and he gave vent to his true feelings for the first time.

'But what are we to it?' he said harshly. 'Does it recognise us as intelligent beings… or are we no better than animals that a medical student might dissect in his laboratory!'

Chapter Twelve
Aground

Every bone in Henry Stanton's body seemed to ache as he recovered his senses.

The ship, the ship!

He tried to jerk upright but the straps about the helmsman's chair held him back. Its gimballed mount meant he was still lying on his back, but the cabin didn't seem level. He forced his eyes to focus on the pendulum of the tilt gauge. Thirteen degrees off vertical. The *Draco* was still upright and the indicator showed the landing legs were extended. His head fell back on to its rest. He'd done it. Against all odds he'd set her down safely.

His father had been a coal miner. If only he'd lived to see him now; keeping his head and landing a stricken ship on the Moon!

When the fireball had struck and they'd lost half their lifting power there had been no time to follow the regular landing procedure, or wait for commands to do this or that. A falling astral ship wasn't like a ship at sea about to run aground, he now realised. Then you might have minutes to take action. He'd had seconds, even allowing for the slow way things fell on the Moon...

Somebody was shaking his shoulder.

He must have passed out again. He heard groans and curses from around him. The shaking again, and a voice:

'Stanton, can you hear me? Pull yourself together, man.'

It was Green's voice, with that buzzing waspish edge to it that he'd never liked.

'Aye, sir,' he managed to say at last. His tongue was thick and it was hard to shape the words. There was a pounding in his head. He must have given it a bang when they landed despite the padding on the chair, and his right eye felt bruised where it had struck the rim of the periscope. The last thing he'd seen through that had been the tops of giant trees flashing past.

He managed to focus on his surroundings. There was a thin haze of smoke hanging in the air of the bridge deck and he could smell hot metal and burnt rubber. A couple of men were lying in a corner being tended by the surgeon.

'Stanton, get down to the engine room,' Green said. 'They need all hands there.'

'Aye, sir,' Henry mumbled.

He unstrapped and staggered over to the companionway that ran through the centre of the ship and clattered down the steps. That was a fine way to talk to the man who had saved all their lives, he thought as he descended.

At the door of the engine room he had to give way. A grim procession of four contorted and blackened forms, hastily wrapped in blankets, were carried out past him and down towards the stern hatch.

'Who were they, mates?' he asked the bearers. Pale-faced, they reeled off the names. None of his close friends, but all men he knew well enough. He hoped the end had been quick for them.

The engine room was in a terrible state, its once gleaming machinery now twisted and smoke blackened. The fireball, or whatever it had been that struck them, had blasted a ten-foot-long section of hull plating clean away, leaving a gap through which he could see a slice of the towering forest that now surrounded them.

The explosion had also obviously damaged some of the batteries and one of the solar-reflector mounts. One of the civil electrical engineers was examining the mechanism of the impeller itself. To Stanton's relief it seemed to be largely intact. If we can get lifting power back we'll be all right, he told himself.

He was set to work hauling mangled debris clear. He felt curiously detached from his surroundings as he laboured, the elation over his miraculous landing seeming to negate worries over their current situation.

He knew now that he had a special talent for steering an astral ship, even though it was like nothing that had ever been done before. In fact, he could fly one better than anybody in the fleet.

He had the touch, the knack, call it what you will. He could balance the driving force from the impeller against the pull of gravity and the wind on the hull without even looking at the gauges. It just came naturally. Green hadn't got it. None of the other officers had it. And to think he might have lived his whole life and never known, had not Professor Boyes-Dennison come along. Henry didn't know how the device worked, nor could he plot a course across the heavens. But did that matter? Give him a piece of solid ground to aim for and he'd set you down safe, that was what counted.

The throbbing in his head was not helped by the rising heat as the heavy humid air penetrated from outside, but he wiped the sweat away and pressed on.

His thoughts seemed to become deeper. Maybe being on an astral ship was what he'd been born for. Weightlessness, for instance. After the first surprise it hadn't bothered him, while other men had been sick. Even Green had looked, ha yes, a little green about the gills for a time.

But then what did Green know? He'd heard that during training the captain had said it was improper for the crew to be seated at their posts, especially in the presence of an officer. He'd had to be convinced it was the only way to control astral ships during launch and landing, and that in orbit they'd only be floating about if they weren't strapped down. If only, Henry thought, he'd been assigned to the *Cygnus* or the *Lynx*. Haliwell and Sinclair were decent captains by all accounts. Maybe they'd appreciate what he could do.

After an hour the worst of the debris had been cleared. They could leave the repairs proper to the engine-room crew – already they were preparing temporary plates to cover the gap in the hull. Henry helped carry the last of the waste outside. There were a couple of guards by the gangway but they just nodded, mopping their brows in the sultry air.

As he looked about him he realised for the first time how lucky they had been to get down safely.

There was a narrow rift of blue sky five hundred feet above

them. All else was forest. He'd set the *Draco* down in a cleft between the trees that was barely wider than it was long. Indeed, in several places on the green walls there were blazes of pale wood where branches had been torn off by their descent and these now lay like an untidy garland about the ship.

Henry walked round the *Draco* inspecting the damage. A solar-mirror panel was completely gone, presumably now lying miles away, and one of the landing legs was buckled. Hardly surprising – there were deep furrows in the earth to show how they'd skidded as they touched ground. He'd have to be careful setting down on that leg again, especially when they landed back on Earth. The scar over the engine room was pretty bad, but it didn't look as though any of the main beams had been severed. They should be able to fix her all right.

He came upon Green, accompanied by a guard, talking earnestly to Sub-Lieutenant Cartwright. Cartwright was saying: 'If only the trees weren't so close we might send a signal rocket up, sir, but I'm afraid it would foul on those higher branches.'

Green looked round impatiently. 'Yes, Stanton?'

'Uh, nothing, sir. I was just taking a look at the ship, sir. Wondering how I got her down in one piece and thinking, if I've got to take her up again when she's sound, which way'll be best.'

'That's not your concern, Stanton. You'll steer the ship when and how I tell you. Now get back on board at once.'

Henry turned on his heel and slunk away. Damn his eyes! Not a word of congratulation for setting them down safely. Maybe Green didn't even realise what he'd done. Did he think the ship had flown itself down?

Two rifle shots cut through the still air.

Henry bounded round to the gangway with Green and Cartwright at his heels. The guards were standing with their rifles raised, peering intently into the green gloom beneath the giant trees.

'What is it?' Green demanded, his pistol in his hand.

'Something big, sir. An animal, maybe. We thought it was coming this way.'

'Did you hit it?'

'I don't know, sir.'

Green looked at the towering trees with a frown of displeasure. Henry followed his gaze. There was nothing to see now, but they could hear the whoops and cries of animals in the distance. Their sudden landing must have frightened away a lot of creatures, but how long before they returned?

'I'll have more men sent out,' Green said. 'Meanwhile stay alert. Stanton, I thought I told you to get inside!'

Christ what a place! thought Henry as he scurried up the gangway. And we're stuck here with a lemon-sucker like Green in charge.

Chapter Thirteen
The Exiles

'You're sure there aren't any weapons on the TARDIS?' Turlough asked once again.

The Doctor looked at him in mild disapproval. 'You should know me better by now. I never use or carry weapons except in the direst emergency.'

'This is an emergency,' Turlough protested. 'We might get killed out there.'

The Doctor handed him a walker's metal-shod staff to go with the larger camping packs he was assembling. 'You'll have to make do with that.'

Turlough swung the staff listlessly through a parody of moves he'd seen in a martial arts film. 'Oh, I'll really be able to beat off a giant spider with this,' he said.

'You don't have to come if you don't want to.'

Perhaps it was shame at the idea of being thought a coward, or perhaps it was that he had more of a conscience than he thought, but Turlough found himself saying almost indignantly: 'Of course I'm coming. I'm just saying I'd like something better than a stick to defend myself with. At least let's take the diary. If we've got to go to this citadel to shut down the energy-field generator, or whatever it is, then we'll have some idea of what we're up against.'

'I thought you understood that was too dangerous,' the Doctor said. 'We dare not risk learning about our own future.'

Turlough tried a different angle. 'What about Haliwell and Emily? The diary might tell us where they're being kept.'

The Doctor smiled brightly. 'We'll just have to rely on our own ingenuity to find them.'

'Even if it costs lives?'

'Even then, I'm afraid. Sorry, Turlough. The diary stays here.'

Turlough realised there was no persuading him, and shrugged

helplessly. The Doctor opened the TARDIS's tool box and began transferring several items from it to his pack.

'You think you'll be doing quick repairs along the way?' Turlough asked.

'I have no idea what might need doing. These are just a few general tools that might come in handy.'

He closed the tool box and shouldered his pack. 'I think that's everything.' He turned to Kamelion, who had been watching their preparations. 'Sorry to leave you alone again, Kamelion. We might be gone a few days this time. Keep checking the field intensity. If it drops suddenly then we've probably succeeded.'

'And if it doesn't then we're probably dead,' Turlough added darkly.

'You're developing a morbid streak,' the Doctor chided.

'No, just being realistic.'

'I shall maintain a proper state of vigilance,' Kamelion assured them.

The Doctor strode briskly out followed by Turlough, who walked hunched under his pack as though he was already trying to shield himself from whatever lay ahead.

Kamelion closed the doors after them, and watched their images dwindle on the monitor until they were out of sight. He turned about to go to his own quarters, then paused. He surveyed the control room carefully, then compared the image with his recollection of its appearance a few minutes earlier. Since his memory was mechanically perfect he had no doubt that an item which should have been present was now, inexplicably, missing.

The British rescue party was assembling on the ground between the remaining two ships when the Doctor and Turlough reached the camp. Turlough counted over twenty men, armed variously with rifles, hatchets and cutlasses, and carrying bundles of provisions, coiled ropes and other gear. One man had the folded tripod and mirrors of a heliograph-sender on his shoulder.

The Doctor reported the failure of their reconnaissance mission to Sinclair, explaining that the crater's energy field had interfered with the 'propulsion unit' of their own ship.

'Then it seems we have no choice but to proceed on foot and trust to God,' Sinclair said simply.

Looking around idly, Turlough was shocked to see a grave mound and a simple wooden cross set under the trees to one side of the landing area. Sinclair noticed his expression.

'We have no provision to transport the remains back to Earth, Mr Turlough,' he explained. 'Since we may now be here some days at least, I thought it best to act swiftly in these matters, as is the way in the colonies. I hope we may conduct a proper service with Miss Boyes-Dennison in attendance in due course.' He looked about him at the rolling highlands. 'For all that, this is not an unfitting place for him to rest. It was his genius that opened up this new world to us.' He frowned. 'And now it's our duty to see his daughter safely returned.'

Five minutes later the rescue party set off.

As they marched along Turlough realised they were now retracing the footsteps of Haliwell's party on its first expedition. In due course they passed the small volcanic cone as described in the diary. Turlough found it both reassuring and slightly disconcerting to know what they would come to next. Of course, things might have changed since Haliwell passed through. No, that had only been a few hours ago. Or had it? Turlough checked his watch. He and the Doctor had been on the Moon for almost twelve hours, so Haliwell couldn't have gone this way more than eight or ten hours before that at most. The unchanging light from the creeping Sun was distorting his sense of time. Thinking of the journey ahead he wondered how long could he could keep going. When they weren't being chased by giant spiders, ordinary physical activity was much less tiring thanks to the lower gravity. But presumably he'd still get tired mentally – and from what he'd seen so far, not being alert inside the crater could be fatal.

They reached the edge of the highlands in less than an hour and started down the winding cliff path. The marks left by Haliwell's party were still clearly visible, guiding their steps down the slopes and ledges of the shelving cliffside. At the foot of the escarpment lay the great forest basin. Turlough scowled down at it, feeling a sense of despair that increased with every step they took. What was he doing entering the place for the second time in less than a day? He must be mad.

Then a voice rang out though the thin air. A female voice calling out in some unknown language, but still conveying an unmistakable message of fear and alarm.

The whole party halted, turning about to try to locate the source of the cries.

'Up there!' The Doctor pointed.

A little way along the cliff from them, where the jagged rocks formed a sheer wall, a slim figure was hanging suspended in the air, supported only by the thinnest of vines that ran over the lip of a narrow ledge high above her head.

The girl cried out again, obviously imploring them to save her. There was something so plaintive in her tone that it pierced Turlough's self-imposed mental shroud like a hot needle, reminding him that there were other people in the universe in more desperate circumstances than his own.

Galvanised into action, he bounded forward ahead of the sailors and leapt from a ledge to grasp a cleft on the sheer rock wall. He hauled himself upwards and in seconds he had reached a narrow ledge above the girl. Immediately he saw that the upper length of the vine she was clinging to was hardly thicker than a piece of string. It emerged from a tangle of stalks and leaves that filled a crevice and ran tautly over the edge, looking as though it could snap at any moment.

Turlough threw himself flat and reached down over the edge with both arms. Below him he saw her frightened face looking upwards imploringly. He had an impression of skin the colour of burnished copper and a flowing mass of dark hair.

'It's all right,' he called out, knowing she could not understand his words but hoping his tone would reassure her. 'I'll pull you up. Hold still.'

Carefully coiling the vine about his fists, he began drawing it upwards, hand over hand. He could never have lifted anybody so easily on Earth, but here it was as though he had the strength of a muscle-bound action-movie hero.

The girl was calling out to him, whether in thanks or encouragement he could not tell, but it gave him a thrill of pleasure to hear her and caused him to redouble his efforts. Then a slim wrist came within reach and he grasped it, felt slender fingers close about his own arm and pulled.

Suddenly he was lying on the ledge with a very feminine body in his arms. A waft of wild scent filled his nostrils and brought a flush to his cheeks. She clung to him, trembling with both fear and relief, pouring out words in the same fluid but incomprehensible language. He tried to give her a reassuring pat on the back and found it was impossible to do so without encountering warm bare flesh, as she seemed to be wearing no more than strips and patches of some homespun fabric tied loosely about her. As she pressed her head to his shoulder he saw delicately pointed elfin ears protruding through the waves of her hair, which was so lustrously dark it seemed to shimmer with a faint green iridescence.

With an effort he disentangled himself from her grasp and held her at arm's length.

'Look,' he said with a smile, 'I'm sure you're being very grateful, but I don't understand you.'

Her brow furrowed at his words. Her eyes were as dark as her hair, but her lips were lighter than the copper of her skin, seeming almost golden by contrast.

She made an interrogative sound and he shook his head and shrugged.

From a little way across the cliffside he heard the Doctor call out: 'Turlough, are you all right?'

'Fine,' he called back. 'Just having a small communication problem.'

The girl smiled as though in sudden comprehension. She reached out, pressed the fingertips of both hands firmly to his temples and shut her eyes as though concentrating deeply.

'Hey!' He pulled her hands away. Her eyes opened and she smiled.

'I did not think you might not speak our language,' she said in clear, if slightly halting, English. 'Now I must thank you again for saving my life.' She caught his hand, pulled it to her and bent her head, brushing his fingers with her lips.

Turlough flushed again and gently pulled his hand clear. 'Uh, any time. Look, what did you do just then?'

'I drew the knowledge of your language from your mind, of course. Forgive me, but it was the only way.' She frowned delicately. 'You do not have the knowledge of telepathy?'

'No, at least not with most people…' He became uncomfortably aware of the rest of the party looking on curiously as he and the girl perched side by side on the narrow ledge. 'Can we get down from here? I think my companions are getting restless.'

'Of course… but may I first know the name of my saviour?'

'My name's Turlough.'

'And I am Lytalia.'

'That's… a nice name.'

They worked their way back to the broader ledges and Turlough presented Lytalia to the rest of the party. Sinclair was gallant and courteous, while the Doctor was his usual amiable self. The rest of the sailors eyed the girl's lightly clothed and shapely body with evident and barely concealed appreciation, which caused Turlough to feel both resentful and proud. Lytalia did not seem to notice anything amiss in their manner and merely smiled warmly at everybody without exception.

'I take it you don't live here alone?' the Doctor asked, once the introductions were done.

'No,' Lytalia said. 'My kindred, the few of us that are left, have a small settlement. It lies not far that way.' She pointed north along the line of the cliffs.

'And what is the name of your people?' Sinclair asked.

'We are Phiadorans.' Lytalia hung her head. 'Now perhaps the last of our line, I do not know. It was so long since they brought us here.'

'Who brought you here?' the Doctor asked, his eyes flashing intently. 'This is no ordinary colony, is it?'

'You had best ask our princess,' Lytalia said. 'Please let me take you to her. I know you will be most welcome.'

'Thank you for your invitation, but I'm afraid we have other business,' Sinclair said gravely. 'A flying machine from the central mountains has kidnapped two of our people. We are going to get them back.'

Lytalia's eyes widened in dismay. She turned to Turlough. 'You are going through the forest to the warden's citadel?'

'We don't seem to have much choice,' Turlough said. 'We're stuck here for good otherwise.'

'Tell us more about this "warden",' the Doctor said. 'What is he a warden of, exactly?'

But Lytalia was shaking her head grimly. 'It is a very dangerous journey you propose,' she said. 'You cannot know the perils that await you.'

'We've got a pretty good idea,' Turlough said heavily.

She flashed him a sad smile. 'Then you are very brave and I'm sure your deaths will be noble ones.'

There was an uncomfortable murmur from the sailors who were within earshot.

'Of course,' Lytalia added, 'if you told your story to our princess, she may be able to offer you aid and advice. We are also prisoners here. Perhaps co-operation will be to our mutual benefit.'

'That sounds good,' Turlough said quickly. 'Let's talk to the people with local knowledge. Find out what we're really up against so we can work out a proper plan of campaign. They must know the best route to take at least…'

Even as he babbled on he wondered if he was talking common sense or simply looking for reasons to postpone their descent into the forest. Then he saw Lytalia looking up at him with eyes full of warm approval and decided he didn't care either way.

When he had finished Sinclair frowned uncertainly. 'I follow your line of reasoning, Mr Turlough. However, we are constrained by time. We must reach the central mountains, undertake our rescue and return before lunar nightfall.'

'I think on balance we should accept Lytalia's suggestion,' the Doctor said. 'It might save us time in the long run and perhaps avoid unnecessary violence. This "warden" may be amenable to reason, but we can't tell until we understand his motives for behaving as he has.'

Sinclair nodded. 'Yes, perhaps you're right. Very well, Miss Lytalia. Please take us to your princess.'

Lytalia led the way back up the cliff, climbing in agile hops and steps. Turlough, moving quickly ahead of the others, made certain he stayed by her side. He saw the Doctor smile knowingly at his actions and could only shrug and grin back in return. They reached the top and set off at a brisk pace.

'This will not take long,' Lytalia explained as they went. 'We live not far from the place you set your craft down.'

'I'm surprised you didn't see us land,' said Sinclair.

'We did, but we were not certain who you might be, or whether your intentions were peaceable. I was one of the scouts sent to secretly watch over you. That was what I was doing when I missed my footing and you found me. I am so glad you proved to be a civilised people.'

'You seem to have overcome your suspicion of us very quickly,' Sinclair said.

Lytalia smiled. 'It was touching my brave rescuer's mind. Though I only took what was necessary to learn your language, I could sense the nobility of his character.'

Red-headed fair-skinned people should not be made to blush this often, Turlough thought, hastily avoiding the eyes of his companions.

'And who did you think we might have been otherwise?' the Doctor asked Lytalia.

'You'll understand once you have spoken to our princess.'

In twenty minutes they reached a line of boulder-strewn low hills that ran across the plateau. Lytalia halted them, went ahead and called out in her own language. In a moment another Phiadoran woman stepped cautiously out of cover. She was similarly dressed to Lytalia, but was holding a spear. She and Lytalia exchanged a few quick words, then the other woman nodded. She set off at a rapid jog ahead of them and soon vanished from sight.

Lytalia motioned them to continue. 'She will warn the others of your arrival so you will not be attacked,' she explained.

They entered a fold in the hills which became a narrow gully winding upwards. It was closed at the top by a heavy wickerwork gate set in what looked like the clear resin they had seen sealing the gun-tube back in the mountains. Two more women armed with both spears and axes stood guard by the gate. They smiled and beckoned the party through.

Beyond was a shallow bowl-shaped hollow sunk into the very hilltop and ringed by a stockade of posts interwoven with vines and branches. Within this enclosure was a handful of simple conical-roofed wattle huts around a larger central building. A few women were gathering, obviously alerted to the newcomers' arrival.

The Doctor's eyes narrowed and he turned to Lytalia.

'I don't see any children, or men, for that matter. Where are they? Out hunting?'

'You will understand soon,' Lytalia said.

They entered the door of the central building. Within was one large chamber, lit by slots in its sloping walls. Hanging banners formed of dyed and woven strips of plant fibre were drawn back in graceful curves, providing an awning for the wicker throne that rested on a raised dais in the centre of the chamber. Turlough thought Lytalia was beautiful, but the woman seated gracefully on the throne was even more striking; as perfectly proportioned and healthy as all the Phiadoran women they had so far seen.

Lytalia stepped up to the dais, bowed quickly, then touched her fingertips to the temples of the princess. For a moment the princess closed her eyes and drew in her breath, then she nodded and Lytalia withdrew. Liquid dark eyes passed over them, and Turlough felt the dignity and aura of command that lay behind them. Then she spoke.

'I, Nareena, last princess of the royal line of Phiador, greet you. Please accept what humble hospitality we can still offer.'

Sinclair gave a practised bow, the Doctor a measured nod, and the rest varying degrees of awkward bobs.

'Your Royal Highness,' Sinclair said easily, 'in the name of Her Britannic Majesty the Queen Empress Victoria, I thank you for your kind welcome. May all future dealings between our two peoples be as cordial as this.'

Lytalia stepped forward once again and introduced them. When they were done the princess said: 'There shall be rest and refreshment for you.'

Women brought in mats and laid them down for the British party to sit upon. These were followed by platters of fruit and pitchers of water. Lytalia herself laid a platter at Turlough's side and he found himself smiling his thanks foolishly at her. Fortunately he still had the sense to wait until the Doctor had sniffed the offerings cautiously and given his approval before biting into a translucent blue fruit the size of an apple. It had an elusive sharp flavour he could not place, but was pleasantly refreshing.

When they had all slaked their hunger and thirst, the princess sat forward in her chair and said: 'We had observed your arrival, but did not recognise the style of your ships. I am curious to know where you are from.'

'We are from Earth, Your Highness,' said Sinclair.

'I do not know of this place.'

'It is the larger planet that this world orbits,' the Doctor said, 'but it is not visible from this hemisphere.'

'That world!' the princess exclaimed. 'You have developed spacecraft so soon? We despaired of people from there ever reaching us in our lifetimes. I thought it was a primitive place.'

'Oh, it's coming along in leaps and bounds,' the Doctor admitted. 'Not always wisely or well, but its people are driven by a great curiosity about the universe around them.'

'And that curiosity has led you here, only to share our fate,' the princess said.

'That remains to be seen,' said the Doctor. 'But it would help if we knew what was going on here.'

'I will tell you our story,' said Nareena, 'then you will understand the cause of our despair.'

Chapter Fourteen
Alliance

'I shall not attempt to relate to you the long history of my world,' Nareena said. 'Its intricacies bear only in passing on our present circumstances. All you need know is that my line ruled Phiador and its dependent systems for ten generations. I do not claim we were perfect rulers, but I think we served as well as any could, guiding our realm to greater prosperity and general contentment.

'But there are always a few dissenting voices even during times of prosperity. One such group formed about a lesser branch of the royal line who had an ancient and tenuous claim to the throne that had long since been set aside. We believed they were best ignored, but we were wrong. In collusion with certain factions of the military, and by rousing the common people with false hopes and fears, they engineered a successful coup. My father was deposed and he and my brothers, who were next in line to the throne, were executed for supposed treason to the state. That left only myself and my cousins as survivors of our line.

'We would have died also, except that it was not done on our world, at least not then, to execute women. Yet equally the usurpers could not let us go free for fear we should become the focus of a counter-revolution. We had to be exiled in such a way that there was no possibility of return. And so we and our ladies-in-waiting were sent here, a place of terror we had never dreamed existed.'

She spread her arms wide to encompass the crater beyond the chamber.

'This is a hunting park, stocked with diverse predatory organisms from many worlds, for those wealthy enough to privately indulge their passion for danger and slaughter. We would not have allowed such a thing on Phiador, which was no doubt why the park was set up so far from our system. Nobody would think of searching the dead satellite of an undeveloped world for such an installation. Those worlds are left undisturbed until they are sufficiently civilised to meet with others on equal terms.'

'I didn't think this place felt right,' the Doctor said. 'We have already encountered some creatures with far too much persistence to be natural.'

'There is nothing natural here,' the princess said. 'The flora and fauna were chosen to provide a challenge to the skills of the most daring hunters. Many died in the quest for trophies, but others still came. And so it was here that we were exiled. In truth we were sent here to die, for it is the rule that any creature in the park is fair game. We learned it was not the first time intelligent beings have been disposed of in such a manner.'

'That is inhuman! You were treated monstrously!' said Sinclair with feeling.

'Perhaps, but it allowed the usurpers to claim that our blood was not on their hands, while knowing that our death was imminent. They supposed we would last only a few days at the most.'

'But you have survived for longer than that,' the Doctor said.

'Yes. It was partly luck that we were able to reach these highlands, though many of my companions died on the way. This is the safest area of the park, where it is possible to survive at a primitive level of existence, as you can see. Few large beasts come up here and we can defend ourselves from those that do. But that would not have saved us from the hunters, who would have soon tracked us down. Except that shortly after we arrived, their ships stopped coming.'

'Do you know why?' the Doctor asked.

'No. Perhaps the new ruling house on Phiador was overthrown by a counter-revolution, or there was some natural disaster. Whatever it was must have spread across a score of world systems to stop all communication. For a while we hoped to be rescued, but gradually the hope faded. Now I would almost welcome one last ship of hunters if they could tell us what has occurred. Does Phiador still exist? What of my people? I wish I knew.'

'Your Highness,' Sinclair said, 'if the hunters no longer come, who is it that lives in the citadel on the central peaks? Somebody must have sent the craft that took away our companions.'

'That would have been the warden's doing. It is the creature employed to maintain the park and tend to the wants of guests. The flying discs are just one of the many types of mechanical servant it has under its control. The warden must have been puzzled by your landing here and not at the citadel. But after so many years it hesitated before it acted. Perhaps it is becoming senile. It, like us, has no means of leaving this place.'

'Which leads me to a question I hope is not indelicate, Your Highness,' the Doctor said. 'Just how long have you been here?'

'We have observed the cycle of the local constellations. By that reckoning it is thirty-two years.'

'But that is impossible, Your Highness,' Sinclair exclaimed. 'You cannot yourself be more than twenty-five or thirty at the most.'

The princess looked surprised. 'Why, the youngest of us is twice that age. I do not understand. Do you age differently on Earth?'

Sinclair sighed ruefully. 'We do, Your Highness. You are older than any of us here.'

Turlough said nothing, casting an uncertain glance at Lytalia who was kneeling quietly to one side. She was old enough to be his grandmother – if he had a grandmother living anywhere. The Doctor was smiling unconcernedly. With hundreds of years under his belt he could afford to, Turlough thought.

'I thought you must have been here for some time,' the Doctor said aloud. 'Long enough to build that vacuum gun in the mountains.'

'You have found that device?' the princess exclaimed. 'No, that was here when we came. It must have been built by some earlier castaways. I suspect it was intended to fire flares to attract the attention of any science ships that passed by. Such vessels had been known to secretly observe the development of primitive worlds. Obviously the warden would have some means of disguising the crater itself, but there was a chance a flare might have been seen.'

'A very remote chance,' the Doctor said.

'This place drives one to take any chance, even the most remote and hopeless,' the princess replied simply.

'But why would the warden allow the building of such a gun?'

'The warden is a stupid creature in many ways. It will not act unless its safety is directly threatened or there is a chance some of its captives are building devices that might interfere with the function of the generators that maintain this place. It would detect the emissions from such things instantly and destroy them. It is through such fields of energy that we are held here, helpless to make any move against the warden.'

'How is that so?' Sinclair asked.

'The citadel, like the impalpable dome over the crater itself, is protected by screens of lethal energy attuned to the patterns of our body cells. If this was not so we would have risked everything and attacked the citadel years ago.' She leaned forward, copper cheeks flushing with excitement. 'But you are a different species whose pattern is not on record yet. You can go where we cannot. You could overthrow the warden, smash his machines and destroy this hateful place. Otherwise you will share our fate.'

'What do you mean?' the Doctor asked.

'Even though hunters may never come here again, the warden will follow its orders: to keep this place secret and also well stocked with game. By keeping you here both objectives are satisfied. It will never allow you to leave!'

There was a murmur of alarm from the British party.

'But there is a chance,' Nareena continued. 'We know the dangers of the forest. We can guide you to the base of the central mountains and tell you all we know of the warden and the citadel so that you are well prepared. Rescue your companions and destroy the warden's power. All we ask is that you take us with you back to your world. There are less than thirty of us left now. You must be able to find room for that number on your ships.'

Sinclair was silent for a moment, then nodded slowly. 'I promise when we leave your people shall accompany us, Your Highness. I would have it no other way in any case. Meanwhile, let us discuss how we shall assault the citadel.'

The Phiadoran women raised their arms into the air and gave forth a shrill ululation of delight.

An hour later Turlough walked out of the throne hut and took in a deep breath of air. Within, the princess, Sinclair and the Doctor were still talking. He looked around the compound and saw other sailors sprawled in the shade in groups of two or three, with Phiadoran women moving between them with more food and drink. Thanks to the relaying of Lytalia's telepathic touch it seemed that all the Phiadorans now spoke English. The words and laughter being exchanged between them and their Earthly guests suggested that any barriers between species were rapidly coming down. Of course, it didn't hurt that the Phiadorans in their brief costumes were not far removed from South Sea maidens in appearance, he thought wryly. Those elfin ears were really quite attractive when you got used to them. I wonder if there are any other differences...

'Are you all right, my saviour?'

Lytalia was standing beside him.

'Fine,' he said hastily, hoping she couldn't read minds at a distance. 'Just getting some fresh air. Might take a nap, you know. Looks like we're going to have a busy few days ahead of us, so I'd better conserve my strength.' To his horror he found himself giving her a confident and utterly false devil-may-care smile.

Fortunately he read only sincere delight in her face.

'I knew you could help us,' she said. 'I am so proud it was I who made the first contact. I'll leave you to rest, but if there is anything you want, just call for me.'

He watched her go and shook his head. Things were getting beyond him. He knew what he was feeling, yet couldn't quite believe it was happening. He'd only known her a few hours, for goodness' sake!

He found a patch of soft moss between two huts, threw his coat and pack down and stretched himself out. Just as he was getting comfortable a familiar silhouette eclipsed the sky.

'I'm trying to rest, Doctor,' Turlough said wearily. 'Go away.'

'I noticed you left the conference. I was just seeing if you were all right.'

Turlough squinted up at him. The Doctor's face was puckered in thought.

'You're not simply worried about getting into the citadel, are you?' Turlough said. 'You're thinking of the bigger picture, as always.'

The Doctor squatted down beside him. 'Turlough, it is the nature of my people to take the wider view. This time more than ever.'

'You mean the Phiadorans complicate things.'

'Exactly. What effect will bringing them to Earth have? Will their advanced knowledge bring confusion? They are obviously long-lived… will that cause resentment? Could they interbreed with humans? It doesn't make my decision any easier.'

Turlough rolled on to his elbow and gazed into the Doctor's troubled eyes. 'Look, hasn't it actually been made for you now? Sinclair's said he'll take the Phiadorans with him, and he's not the sort to go back on his word. Even if this expedition didn't return to Earth, other ships would be sent after them. It can't fail to open up a new timeline. Let it happen.'

The Doctor smiled slightly. 'I take it you approve of the Phiadorans. At least, one Phiadoran in particular…'

Turlough rolled away from him and closed his eyes. 'I'm going to get my head down. I think we're going to be pretty busy soon enough.'

He heard the Doctor give a light chuckle and walk softly away.

Turlough was tired, but he had something else to do before he slept. Making sure nobody was watching he opened his pack and pulled out Haliwell's diary.

He knew it was dangerous, but he had to take the risk. He would only read the passages that were relevant and nothing that hadn't yet taken place. Anything he could find out about the citadel could be useful. Just for once he might even impress the Doctor without him ever realising what he'd done.

He flipped over the pages describing Haliwell's account of their first meeting in the forest and the escape from the spiders, until he found a paragraph beginning: '*We were carried aloft in the clutches of the metal tentacles...*'

Turlough settled down and read on.

Chapter Fifteen
Tested

'What are you writing, Richard?'

Haliwell looked up from his diary with a start. Emily Boyes-Dennison was looking round the wall that divided his alcove from hers.

'I'm sorry. Did I disturb you?'

'Not at all. I know I should rest, but this unvarying light makes it hard to sleep. May I sit with you?'

'Of course.'

She sat down beside him on the edge of the raised sleeping pallet.

'Now you've closed up your book and are looking distinctly uncomfortable,' she observed. 'Were you writing something personal?'

'Not exactly. It's my diary. Despite our circumstances I'm trying to keep it up-to-date.'

'Ah, I thought I'd seen you working on it before now. It seems very important to you.'

'It is. I'm trying to set down more than a simple record of events. It is my belief that this remarkable journey of ours will have a profound effect on our appreciation of the universe around us. When travel by astral ships becomes generally available it cannot help but influence the greater population. I am attempting to note signs of the changes...' He faltered. 'I have not told anybody else about this. Does the idea seem odd to you?'

She clapped her hands together in delight and amusement. 'Not at all. You are applying method and reason to a most interesting field of study. You shall write a paper on the subject, let me see, yes: "Some observations on the effects of astral flight upon the perceptive scope of the human mind." We shall make a scientist out of you yet!'

He joined in her laughter. 'I'm not sure what my naval

colleagues would think of that,' he said at last. 'They already have me down as a bit of an "x-chaser".'

'I beg your pardon?'

Haliwell sighed. 'An "x-chaser", so it is popularly assumed, knows everything about algebra but is a hopeless practical seaman. It means I have shown an interest in too many subjects beyond those strictly necessary to my advancement. I regret that the navy is distrustful of intellectuals. Not that I have any pedigree in that line. My family are as solid and unimaginative as you could wish. But we are of the class that regards the naval quarterdeck as its exclusive preserve. My father and his before him were serving officers.'

'Yet you were given command of the first astral fleet. Perhaps that shows the navy is awake to the need for more capable officers in this new age.'

Haliwell smiled. 'If so it will be the first time they have made such an advance. They have hardly accepted the notion that steam is here to stay.'

'Well, they must have wanted somebody with a little more initiative than usual.'

Haliwell gestured at their cell. 'And see where my initiative has landed me.'

'You cannot blame yourself for our situation.'

'But it is ultimately my responsibility. I will have to account for everything that has happened to us… the loss of the *Draco*… Simon Granby.'

'You could not have prevented his death.'

'I could have taken a larger party, better armed.'

'There is no evidence that whatever took him would have been deterred by greater numbers. Was a single shot fired by your men? No. It happened almost before my eyes, yet had I had a gun in my hand I could not have done anything to save poor Mr Granby. Whatever took him was simply too fast for us.'

'Thank you. I will try to take some comfort from your words. I meant to ask, have you thought more about exactly what you saw? I know it was only a fleeting glimpse, but I would like to know.'

Emily's brow furrowed. 'I have thought about it, of course. If I could liken it to anything I would say it was as though a body of hot tar had grown limbs and been given the gift of independent movement. It had that same glistening fluid quality about it, combined with the speed of quicksilver. I know that sounds queer, but then I am still not sure if it was one animal or several acting together.'

'Who is to say what is normal on this world,' Haliwell observed.

They sat in silence for a moment, then Emily said: 'Do I appear in your diary?'

'Well, yes you do.'

'And does your record include our disagreements back on the ship?'

'It does, in passing. But be assured, assuming I am granted official permission, I intend to make none of my account public until you and your father have given your approval.'

Emily smiled. 'That's quite all right. As long as you have represented father and myself fairly. We were engaged in honest open debate and I will stand by everything I said.'

He looked at her with a touch of wonder. 'You know, Emily, if you will permit me to say so, I think you are the most singular woman I have ever met.'

'Because I speak my mind, or because I have something in my mind that is worth saying?'

Haliwell stiffened. 'I seem to have inadvertently given offence once again. I'm sorry.'

Emily was biting her lip. 'No, it is I who should be sorry. I did not think. My response was purely instinctive. You see, I have heard similar words from men in the past which have proven to be insincere.'

'Well, I mean exactly what I said. You are quite unique in my experience.' He hesitated, scratching his chin. 'Of course, my experience of the female kind is quite limited due to my time at sea. I may be quite wrong. Yes, on due consideration I withdraw my remark. You are no doubt quite commonplace.'

Emily caught in her breath to exclaim, then burst into laughter as realisation dawned. 'Captain Haliwell, I believe you are teasing me!'

'Very possibly,' he said, 'but only this once. Please believe that in all else that I say –'

Without warning the door of their cell swung open.

They sprang to their feet.

In the aperture stood another of the mechanical attendants. Whether it was the same one that had escorted them earlier they could not tell. It gestured to them to leave the room. Having no other choice, they complied.

'Are we bound for another audience with that monstrosity in the tank?' Haliwell wondered as they walked along the corridor. But in moments they had taken a turning in a new direction, away from the central chamber.

'Or perhaps dissection?' Emily said faintly.

Haliwell clenched his teeth, wishing he had never made the suggestion when they first found themselves in the cell. 'It was a foolish remark. I'm sure that will not be the case.'

'No, it is a possibility we must face, terrible though the idea is.'

He saw she was very pale. He wondered if he should take hold of her hand in reassurance but before he could decide they arrived at their destination, indicated by an open door. They were directed inside and the door closed flush with the wall, leaving them alone again.

The room was no more than twenty feet square with three plain walls. The fourth wall, opposite them, was anything but plain, being covered with a close array of stubby metallic rods that projected into the room. They looked at each other in puzzlement.

'What is supposed to happen here?' Haliwell asked.

Emily walked over to the wall of rods. 'And this curious arrangement. What is its function –'

As her fingers brushed the tip of a rod there came the flicker of a spark and a small crack of air. Emily jerked her hand away convulsively with a gasp of pain. 'They are electrified!'

Haliwell had sprung to her side. 'Are you all right?'

'Yes, the current is not high enough to be lethal.' She blew on the tips of her fingers. 'But it is very painful. Stay clear of them.'

'I shall.' He led her a few steps away from the wall. 'Now if that is all they have to show us then there is no point in remaining in here any longer.' He lifted his head, sure they were being observed by some means. 'Do you hear me?' he shouted.

Emily caught her breath in alarm. Haliwell spun about. The electrified wall was slowly approaching them.

They leapt backwards, but still the wall continued forward. They turned round to run, only to find that the opposite wall was receding.

'What madness is this!' Haliwell said.

'No madness… it's not the walls that are moving, it's us!' Emily said. 'The floor must be a continuous belt running the entire width of the room. It is carrying us towards the electrified wall.'

'And it's moving faster,' Haliwell said, beginning to lengthen his stride.

'You were partially correct, Richard,' Emily said, running at his side. 'I fear we are no more than laboratory specimens.'

'What do you mean?'

'We are being examined, tested. This is the simplest way to ascertain our speed and endurance.'

'They can't treat us like this! You are a lady!'

'I don't think such terms mean much to them. We must try to look on the bright side – it is better than dissection.'

He was amazed she could find the strength for levity. He tried to sound equally offhand. 'And I thought we had done enough running for one day… from those spiders. Does this test have a time limit, do you think, or must we keep running until we're exhausted?'

'I think you know the answer to that question.'

He did. The floor continued to roll ever faster under their feet.

'Richard,' Emily panted, 'take off your coat. It is heavy enough perhaps to jam the floor where it vanishes under the edge of the wall.'

Still running he shrugged off his tail coat and threw it down. It was carried backwards to the base of the wall where it was twisted into a long bundle like wrung washing. The floor continued to move.

'The clearance must be too fine,' Haliwell panted. 'Still, it was a good idea.'

In minutes their chests were heaving and they were lathered in sweat. Emily began to falter and stumble. Haliwell tried to support her but lost his balance. They fell together and were carried backwards into the wall. Twisting and tumbling they were thrown against the lowest row of electrodes. The air crackled and sparked as they received shock after shock.

After what seemed an eternity the power was cut off and the rolling floor slowed to a halt.

Pale and trembling, they dragged themselves away from the wall to sprawl exhausted on the floor, their limbs still twitching spasmodically from the unnatural stimulation they had received. It took Haliwell a full minute to recover enough control of his muscles to ask feebly: 'Emily... are you all right?'

'Just... I think. That was... horrible.'

'We are in the hands of a sadist. This is callous... inhuman!' Haliwell gasped.

'Of course it is... inhuman,' Emily said faintly. 'It is perpetrated by an inhuman intelligence... whose motives we do not yet understand.'

The door of the room swung open and they saw the mechanical attendant waiting for them.

'At least this test seems to be over,' Emily said. 'As long as they allow us some rest before the next trial.'

'You think there will be more?'

'I regret so.'

With what seemed a tremendous effort even in the low lunar gravity, Haliwell climbed to his feet and helped Emily up. As he supported her along the corridor to their cell, he asked:

'Would understanding the reasons behind all this really make it any easier for you to bear?'

'Yes it would, Richard,' Emily said, her voice sounding weak but carrying undoubted conviction. 'For with understanding comes reason, and with reason there is always hope.'

Chapter Sixteen
Mutiny

The last words of the funeral service hung in the heavy air. Captain Green closed the Bible with a snap. For a moment the surviving company of the *Draco* looked down in silence at the row of seven freshly turned mounds of earth. Then the bosun called out 'On caps!' and the ceremony was over. The dead were left to their rest.

They'd lost their first officer, one engineer, three engine-room assistants, a civilian electrical engineer and one ship maintainer in the attack, most of them caught in the blast of the fireball. There were also a couple of men with broken arms and their navigator was still unconscious with a cracked skull. Almost a quarter of their company dead or injured, Henry Stanton thought morosely. Still, if it hadn't been for his skill it could have been even worse.

Green addressed the men, his sharp clipped tones carrying through the glade.

'Though our ship is disabled and we have suffered losses, we still have a mission to complete. We were ordered to follow the craft that took Captain Haliwell and Miss Boyes-Dennison to its destination, and that I intend to do. We are already over halfway to the central mountains, and therefore well ahead of any party they might despatch from base. We shall not forfeit that advantage. The engineers and a skeleton crew shall remain with the ship to complete the repairs under Mr Cartwright's command. The rest of you will form the expeditionary party which I shall lead. Bosun, the list.'

The bosun read out a list of names. Green was taking the bosun, all the remaining fit general dutymen, the cook's and surgeon's assistants, both signallers and Henry himself and Tom Broady. That was both the helmsmen! What if anything happened to them? Who would fly the ship out of the forest then? Henry wanted to speak up but knew it would serve no purpose. Green would just think he was trying to stay with the ship, where it was safe.

'Those named will draw rations for five days,' Green continued. 'Armaments will be rifles, cutlasses and axes. We leave in an hour.'

Henry tramped back inside the ship and joined the line for rations. There were discontented grumblings from the others. When the men from the *Cygnus* had brought Davis back from the first survey word had got round about what they had seen in the forest.

'I never signed on for this,' Tom Broady said. 'They told us the Moon was a dead world. Just set the ships down easy like, then stay snug on board while the scientific types put on their diving suits and take their samples. That was the idea, not traipsing through the jungle to attack some castle. That's work for the marines, that is.'

There was a general murmur of approval.

'You said it right, Tom,' Henry agreed. 'But Green doesn't care, so long as the job gets done. Not that I don't want Captain Haliwell and the lady brought back safely, but this isn't the way to do it. We should all set to and put the ship to rights first. Then I could... I could fly her right up to that castle keeping her so close to the tree tops that they'd never see us!'

'You never could!' somebody said.

'I could,' Henry insisted. The certainty of his newly realised skill burned brightly within him. He knew he could do things with an astral ship that nobody had ever thought of before.

'Pipe down, Stanton,' the bosun said, coming into earshot. 'We've got our orders. We're doing this Mr Green's way.'

'Yes, Bosun,' Henry said. One day the bosun wouldn't talk to him like that, he thought to himself, because they'd realise astral helmsmen were something special. And then he wouldn't be just another rating.

The expeditionary party assembled outside the *Draco* at the appointed time. Green consulted his compass, then led them off into the trees at a brisk pace.

Henry shivered as the great branches closed over their heads, cutting off the Sun. He wasn't cold. He'd just realised that the great forest was truly alive. Every animal cry, shiver of foliage and crack of twigs proclaimed it. Unknown things flitted through the canopy high above them, while out of the corner of his eye he kept seeing the sparkle of dancing insects – yet when he turned his head they had vanished. And always in the distance he seemed to hear the ominous crash of some large beast that his imagination magnified to monstrous proportions. And here they were, interlopers in its midst. He clutched his rifle more tightly.

Yet for almost an hour they met with no trouble, and though their progress was not rapid it was steady. At regular intervals they blazed gashes into the trees so that they could retrace their steps when the time came. The men began to relax. A few started to whistle.

Then it happened.

They had passed under many trees that were thickly smothered by orchid-like blooms, bushy parasites and creepers that formed an aerial jungle of their own. So they gave hardly a second glance to the one arching over the way ahead of them, and the head of their little column passed under it unconcerned. Henry was far enough back to see the whole thing unfold.

With dream-like slowness half a dozen fuzzy bloated leaf balls detached themselves from the branches and dropped silently on to the men following at Green's heels. Yet so undramatic was the action that it took Henry a second to realise it might mean danger.

'Heads up, mates!' he shouted.

The column broke up as the men sprang instinctively aside and most of the leaf balls, spreading and swelling as they fell, struck only bare ground. But two men reacted just a fraction too late. The things fell over their heads and shoulders, completely enveloping them, and seemed to contract about their waists, trapping their arms by their sides.

The men shrieked in pain and terror, plunging blindly about in an attempt to free themselves. They fell to the ground and rolled from side to side, kicking and twisting in a frenzy of wild desperation. The other sailors had to throw themselves across their legs to hold them down as they used their knives to cut away the creatures that were choking the life from their comrades. Blood splattered across the ground as they slashed and tore at the rubbery outer hide of the shapeless things. With their bare hands they tore away strips of alien flesh and cast them disgustedly aside, until the bloodstained forms of their companions were freed.

But by then it was too late. The pair were unconscious and dying, bleeding from dozens of wounds too deep to stanch and beyond any aid they could give them. The things that had attacked them were no more than stomach sacs concealing internal rings of long curved needle-like teeth. They clearly killed by smothering and bleeding, gorged on the remains, then returned to their arboreal perches to await fresh victims.

In miserable, hopeless silence the men watched the life ebb away from their companions.

When it was over Green said quietly: 'Burial detail, Bosun. Make it quick.'

'Aye, sir.'

Another funeral, Henry thought wretchedly. How many more will there be?

When they were done and hasty respects had been paid, Green took a fresh sighting with his compass and they marched on again. But now they walked in silence and nobody whistled. They moved with hesitant steps, turning their heads at every sound and scrutinising every branch before they passed under it. Several men cut down bamboos as they went, sharpened the ends to fine points and walked with these pointing protectively up at the endless green canopy above them.

A little later, something half seen flitted past on the other side of a screen of trailing vines not ten yards from the column.

At the bosun's cry of warning it was subjected to such a hail of gunfire that it was stopped in its tracks. Green had to shout his command to cease fire three times before the frightened sailors obeyed. Cautious examination revealed the bullet-riddled remains of a lithe golden-coated six-legged beast crumpled in the bushes. Whether it had intended to attack them or was simply passing by they would never know. They continued on, Green striding determinedly ahead.

Tom broke the oppressive silence. 'He's no coward, you have to say that for him,' he said softly to Henry.

'Who?'

'Green.'

'That's because he's like cold mutton all the way through,' Henry said bitterly. 'He's never felt fear, he's never felt anything. That's not brave. And he don't understand people who do have any decent feelings. He'll lead us all to our graves, you mark me.'

The column halted. Ahead of them a twenty-foot-wide swathe had been cut out of the forest. The ground had been pressed down with tremendous force, compressing vegetation and earth alike. There were no individual tracks of any kind, but the centre of the track was depressed more than the sides, forming a smooth concavity. Sap was still oozing out of some of the pulped plant stems, suggesting that whatever had made the trail had not long passed by.

'It's like somebody rolled a huge cannonball through here,' a sailor muttered.

'No, that's not it,' said Tom. 'More like it was made by a giant snake.'

'Cut that talk!' Henry snapped. He hated snakes.

'This path runs close to our course,' Green announced. 'Since it appears to be recently made, most other beasts should have been frightened off. We shall make good time in greater safety.'

'But what if we run into whatever made it, sir?' somebody asked.

'If it is a beast, it must be of such dimensions that we shall see it in ample time. Follow me and stay alert.'

They trailed uncertainly after him. But the going was easier and the flattened wall of undergrowth on either side did give a sense of security. Nothing was likely to spring out on them and they could see ahead and behind as far as the gentle undulating curves in the path. Low branches overhead had simply been torn aside by the path-maker. Henry found himself curious to learn what the beast was, and at the same time fearful of encountering something of such obviously massive strength and bulk.

They had made three or four miles along the track in good time when the droning began.

They stopped, uncertain which direction it was coming from. It rose and fell in an irregular rhythm, but there was unmistakable power behind it that seemed to set up a resonance in their very bones. Suddenly the droning got louder. There was a flash of movement and light from the path ahead of them.

'Down!' the bosun bellowed.

A dozen glittering silver iridescent bodies flashed over their heads with the speed of an express train, even as the droning became a burring roar that threatened to burst their eardrums. Then it was diminishing as the glittering things receded down the path in a dancing, weaving cloud.

Three sailors were writhing on the ground, clutching at punctures in their coats where they had been stabbed, trying to stem the blood seeping into the cloth. One of them was Tom Broady. The others ran forward and hauled the injured men to their feet, but before they could carry them into cover someone shouted: 'They're coming back!'

The buzzing things swept back along the path again. This time the men managed to fire a few rounds, though without any apparent effect. Then they were enveloped in the midst of the whirring cloud and pounded by a droning so intense it set their teeth on edge. The things were insectile with bulbous bodies, as big as dogs, carried on wings a fathom long. Trailing behind each one was a long jointed tail tipped with a curving stinger that tapered to a needlepoint. As the creatures passed over the men they stabbed downwards with their stingers. Green emptied his revolver at them, but they were difficult targets. The men lashed out with their cutlasses and rifle butts, and stabbed with their improvised spears. A wing crumpled and a hard-cased body cracked, spilling its internal fluids. One of the insects fell to the ground buzzing impotently, but the rest of the swarm continued to attack with undiminished vigour. Another man reeled back clutching his bloodied cheek where a stinger had caught him.

'Into the trees!' Green shouted. Gathering up their wounded, they made a desperate rush for the woods, bursting through the shimmering deadly wall and plunging into the undergrowth. Here the hanging vines and thicker bushes gave them shelter and slowed the attack of the insects. Now the creatures presented easier targets and at last the rifles began to have some effect as, one by one, iridescent bodies dropped to the ground shattered and broken. Finally the remainder of the swarm gave up their pursuit and sped away down the path. The terrible droning receded into the distance and at last there was silence.

The *Draco* crew sank to the ground, momentarily overwhelmed by the conflicting emotions of shock and relief. Even Green looked dazed, numbly taking his cap off to mop his brow. Somebody laughed: 'Well, we showed 'em!' Others joined in. At least they'd survived this encounter without loss. They had won a small victory against the forest.

But then they turned their eyes to the men who'd been stung and their laughter died in their throats.

Silently, the venom they had been injected with had claimed them even as their comrades had driven the creatures responsible away. Henry looked into Tom Broady's fixed, contorted features then turned aside, feeling utterly sickened.

Green stood over the dead men for a moment, then said tonelessly: 'Burial detail, Bosun.'

'Aye, sir.'

Somebody pressed a shovel into Henry's hand and he looked at it blankly. It was one of the tools they had brought along to dig samples from the soil of what should have been a dead moon. Like Tom had said, this wasn't what they'd signed on for.

When the depressing task was done and the barest formalities complied with, Henry saw Green taking a fresh sighting with his compass. He couldn't mean to continue on?

'Sir, where are we going?' he asked aloud.

Green hardly spared him a glance. 'Forward, Stanton.'

'But we're not a third the way there and there's six of us gone already.'

'Regrettable losses. But we have our orders.'

'Not to get ourselves killed, sir.'

There was a faint murmur of agreement from the other men. It emboldened Henry. 'With respect, sir,' he continued, 'we've got to get back to the ship right now. We can't chance it, for everybody's sake. See, with Tom gone, I'm the only one who can fly the ship out safely.'

Green rounded on him, a thin smile of contempt on his lips.

'So that's it, is it, Stanton? Frightened for your own skin. Another word of dissent and you'll be put on a charge.'

'I'm not a coward, sir, but it's true. I'm the only one who can do it –'

'You have a strange idea of your worth, Stanton. I say we are proceeding ahead. You will obey that order without question, or face a charge of mutiny. Do you understand?'

'But sir –'

'Bosun, put this man under arrest!'

The bosun stepped forward unhappily and held out his hand for Henry's rifle.

Just then the whole forest floor shook gently under their feet. For a moment Green and Henry shared the same look of surprise.

'Earthquake!' one of the men muttered.

The reverberation came again, but more intensely.

'Be ready to move!' Green said, turning round in an attempt to locate its source. But it seemed to come from all about them.

A great thud shook the ground, and now they could hear the sound as well as feel it, along with a steady crashing of branches that grew louder by the second. High above them a flock of brilliantly coloured bird forms took flight. Somewhere in the distance an animal squealed in pain, only to be abruptly silenced.

The fourth impact dislodged a shower of dead leaves and twigs from the trees and sent the crew staggering drunkenly as they tried to keep their balance. A sonorous bellow, as though from the largest steam-driven foghorn ever built, ripped through the forest and the men clapped their hands over their ears to keep out the terrible noise.

As the echoes died away, leaving their ears ringing, a horde of animals of many sizes ran and hopped and bounded through the hollow between the trees in which the crew stood, taking no notice of them in the panic of their flight. As one, the men turned to face the direction from which the creatures had come. A crewman held out a trembling finger. 'There... Oh my God!'

They could only see the underside of the behemoth's body, but it must have been far larger than the greatest whale that ever swam the seas of Earth and was supported by legs that rivalled the giant trees themselves in girth. And from its sides depended grey tentacles, like the trunks of elephants but ten times longer and thicker. And as these tentacles coiled and twisted down from above and snaked between the trees towards them, the men saw that each had a single guiding eye mounted just behind its furled tip.

And then the tentacle tips opened to reveal a ring of cutting teeth.

All discipline and purpose were forgotten as the spell that had held the crew was broken. Their single desire was to escape this monster from their darkest nightmares. The men turned and ran, scattering to the four winds. And Green ran with them, too horrified himself to attempt to keep order. At their heels came the remorseless earthshaking thuds of the creature's twenty-yard strides as it ploughed through the forest in pursuit of its prey.

For a timeless interval Henry ran blindly on, leaping in great bounds through the forest, heedless of the trailing vines that snagged him or of the bushes he crashed into as he landed. He didn't consider his comrades or what direction he was taking. There was room for no other thought in his terror-filled mind but flight.

And then the ground ahead of him dipped and fell away. He crashed down into a small brushwood-choked gully, tumbling over and over until he splashed to a halt, sitting in the rocky stream that ran down its centre.

He was still shaking his head dizzily when he heard a voice: 'Who's there? Stanton? For God's sake help me!'

Not ten feet from him was Green. His face was deathly pale and he was lying twisted up against a rock, one leg turned under his body at an impossible angle.

'Stanton! I can hear it coming. Help me!'

Henry struggled on to his hands and knees and clawed his way towards Green. The booming footsteps were coming closer once again. The water in the stream began to shiver in response. The green twilight of the forest was eclipsed by a huge shadow. A leg, vast and wrinkled, with a footpad the size of a paddle wheel, crossed the stream and came down with a jarring thud on the far bank, setting a small avalanche of stones tumbling into the stream. A body the size of an airship filled the sky.

Instinctively Henry curled up into a ball and tried to control his ragged breathing. If only they were still and quiet it wouldn't know they were there. It was so big and they were so small, just like mice amongst the rocks and bushes. Please God let it pass by. Please God…

But Green wouldn't stay quiet. Perhaps he was in too much pain to understand. Perhaps to the very end he had to give orders.

'Stanton, help me get away!'

'Quiet, you fool!' Henry hissed.

'Stanton –'

Henry reached out and closed Green's mouth. 'You'll get us both killed!'

Another monstrous foot swung into view, then hesitated twenty feet above their heads; how many tons waiting to crush them? Green was struggling in Henry's grasp. His mouth wouldn't stay still.

'Shut up just for for once,' Henry sobbed. 'Shut up, shut up, shut up!'

The foot descended.

Chapter Seventeen
Through the Forest

Turlough found the beginning of his second expedition into the crater forest considerably less traumatic than the first. Apart from being part of a much larger and better prepared party, there was the reassuring presence of their Phiadoran escort.

What the British thought about being protected by a group of lightly dressed alien women carrying spears and bows he did not ask, but he decided that he personally wasn't going to become chauvinistic about it. He'd never worried about women doing so-called men's work and this was certainly no time to allow misplaced male pride to rear its head in objection. Besides, the Phiadorans looked like competent guides, despite their primitive weapons. After surviving thirty years in the crater they must have learned to take care of themselves.

However, it was easy to forget all that when presented with the undeniably attractive spectacle of shapely limbs and lithe bodies on show from every angle as they descended the snaking cliff pathway. From the looks of it the sailors also approved, offering helping hands that the women clearly did not need, but which they accepted gracefully. The men were, of course, behaving as one might expect, but Turlough wondered about the Phiadorans' reciprocal friendliness. To them, long-lived exiles from what had obviously been a sophisticated society, the Victorian sailors must seem very primitive and immature. Of course, the Phiadorans had been without male company for thirty years so they might not be so selective.

He looked at Lytalia, climbing down at his side, and she flashed a bright encouraging smile back. Was that the real reason she was being so warm to him? Maybe he should tell her where and when he was really from, so she would understand he was different from the rest. No, don't spoil it, he told himself. Enjoy having someone think you're special whatever the reason.

He looked again at the expedition winding its way down the cliff. Chatter and laughter floated up to him. The other men seemed to have the same idea. It had more the air of a picnic party and one would hardly believe they were about to enter a potentially lethal forest. Sinclair, who Turlough suspected of being a bit of a puritan at heart, might have objected to the casual mood as being undisciplined, except that Princess Nareena herself was keeping him close company. Perhaps her presence was mellowing him, for on at least two occasions Turlough saw him smile broadly, and once risk a light laugh.

Only the Doctor seemed to have escaped a special Phiadoran escort of his own. All his attention was directed to the forest below them and the hazy mass of the distant central mountain range. As they descended, the base of the mountains vanished, lost behind the sharp curve of the Moon's horizon, until only the highest peaks remained blazing golden in the lowering afternoon Sun. It was still over three Earthly days until local sunset, and Turlough fervently hoped they would have completed their mission by then. Despite their new companions he did not want to be out in the forest after dark.

They reached the base of the cliffs and the outskirts of the forest. The cacophony of strange cries filtering through the trees muted the party mood, and the men became grim-faced again.

Nareena split the Phiadorans into two groups. One would stay with the British party and make sure they didn't fall victim to any of the passive dangers of the forest, such as the mantrap plant they had already encountered. The second would scout the way ahead for the safest path and give warning of mobile dangers.

Lytalia was chosen for this latter group.

'You be careful,' Turlough said to her, and was surprised to find how much he meant it.

'Do not worry,' she assured him. 'I know the dangers of this place and the habits and weaknesses of its game better than any hunter who ever came here for sport.'

'Maybe I should come with you...'

'No,' she said firmly. 'Your task comes later when we reach the citadel. There we shall not be able to help. Until then allow us to guide and protect you. Be patient. We shall take turns scouting after a few hours and then we can travel together.'

He watched her and the other scouts melt away into the woods, then the rest of the party set off in their tracks.

Fifteen minutes later Turlough's worst fears seemed to be realised when a series of terrible snarling cries broke out somewhere ahead of them. The sailors held their rifles at the ready and Turlough instinctively started forward, but Nareena stayed them.

'There is no cause for concern,' she said. 'My people have dealt with it.'

Even as she spoke the snarls became squeals of pain, and then faded into silence. A few minutes later they passed the bloody corpse of a twenty-five-foot-long lizard-like creature with eight legs and a massive jaw full of dagger teeth. It was dotted with wounds from arrows and spears.

'Apparently the Phiadorans' confidence in their abilities was not overstated,' the Doctor said mildly, peering at the remains with interest. 'They remind me a little of Leela in that respect, though admittedly they have more refined table manners than she did.'

'Who's Leela?'

'A former companion of mine. You would have found her stimulating company.'

'Tegan was quite stimulating enough, thank you.'

'Compared with Leela at her most determined, Tegan was quite self-effacing.'

Turlough gave him a disbelieving glance. The Doctor nodded soberly. Turlough whistled.

As they proceeded their guides pointed out the hazards along the way. There were plants to avoid touching because of their acid sap, bare patches of ground that concealed the subterranean burrows of a species of carnivorous 'mole', the splayed roots of a shrub that could coil up and trap a man's legs. A pool of clear water under a certain tree was not water at all, but the resin they had seen used to seal the gun. Trapped by the substance's powerful adhesion, the unfortunate victim would soon find the tree's branches closing about him to begin the digestive process.

After a few hours the scouting group changed places with the escorts and Turlough had the pleasure of Lytalia's company once again. The Doctor smiled benignly at them and gave them space.

The main party was threatened only once, when a huge bird clad in what looked like silver scales plunged down upon it, talons spread wide to snare any likely target. Here massed rifle fire proved adequate for defence and the creature was dead before it struck the ground. The Doctor examined it intently, and was only dragged away to keep up with the rest with great reluctance.

'I know it is unavoidable,' he said, 'but I wish there was a better way to protect ourselves than crude force.'

'It is force that rules here,' Lytalia said. 'You kill, or you are killed. There is no middle ground.'

Turlough could think of no response to such a statement.

'By the way,' the Doctor said. 'Some of our party encountered an unusual creature the first time they entered the forest. I wonder if you know it.' He described the fleeting impression of the thing that had taken Sub-Lieutenant Granby.

Lytalia's face clouded. 'It must have been a Vrall,' she said. 'There are only a handful in the park. Pray to your God that you do not meet one, for even we could not protect you then. They are the most cunning and deadly of all the creatures here. A dozen hunters have died trying to take a Vrall carcass home with them as a trophy.'

Eighteen hours' march took them over halfway to their objective. Turlough doubted if they could have managed even half of that in the same time without their guides, and certainly not without suffering heavy casualties.

They camped under the spreading boughs of a massive tree with foliage so thick that it reduced their surroundings to a premature twilight. A ring of fires lightened the gloom and the homely smell of wood smoke displaced some of the less pleasant odours from a nearby swamp. They ate a cold meal from their rations and then rolled up in their blankets to try to snatch a few hours' sleep. Lytalia was standing guard again and the Doctor was lying with his hands crossed over his chest in that disconcerting deep trance state that would, in twenty minutes, serve him as well as eight hours' normal sleep. Turlough surreptitiously drew out Haliwell's diary and read on by the light of a pencil torch.

We were allowed to rest for several hours in our cell after our ordeal in the running chamber. A sort of bland food was provided which we had no choice but to consume as we had to maintain our strength. We then slept, rather uneasily.

Emily's suspicion that we had only started on a series of tests was confirmed when we were roused and taken to another chamber. Here was the same ominous panel of metal contacts, but this time set at an angle under a wall studded with many projections and pitted with holes and slots. It was evident that our ability to climb was now to be ascertained. Having no option, we set to as well as we were able, finding that the climbing wall was mounted on a continuous belt, whose motion gradually accelerated. This time it was I who missed my footing first and fell. But the power was not turned off until Emily also dropped. I believe she did so on purpose to reduce my suffering.

The pain of those electric shocks is quite terrible, and it is only the knowledge that they will leave no lasting damage that makes it possible to face them. Nevertheless they are the most brutal of devices that can be applied to innocent beings. If I ever get the chance I will gladly smash the tank in which that monstrosity controlling these experiments resides, even if my own life is forfeit as a consequence.

However, I can only bear these misfortunes with as much courage and fortitude as my companion. She is, as I freely confessed to her earlier, the most remarkable of women…

Turlough paused. He was beginning to feel like a voyeur and it was troubling his conscience, something that up until now had never bothered him much. His approach to life had been

'Turlough first' for as long as he could remember, and other people's feelings simply hadn't counted. Reading the diary was confusing. Its form and language made the events seem distant and unreal, yet he knew they had just happened to people he had met in the flesh.

Still, he rationalised, for their own good he should know what happened to them. The more he learned of the geography and routine of the citadel the better. And of course, his sudden show of 'perception' when the time came would impress the Doctor... and Lytalia when he told the story later. He read on.

After another rest period we were taken to a new chamber. This contained a long narrow water-filled pool. Apparently our ability to swim was to be assessed. There was no electrical wall to drive us on this time, as such a device would have been confused by the conductivity of the water itself, but our mechanical guard made it quite clear we had to enter the water and swim lengths until allowed to stop. Here some embarrassment ensued. Emily began removing her outer clothing, stating that she was not going to risk drowning for the sake of social convention and that her underclothing still provided adequate covering. She urged me to do the same. Her logic was impeccable as always and I could only follow suit, averting my gaze from her person as far as possible. We swam for an hour monotonously to and fro until cramp and exhaustion threatened to overcome us. Only then were we allowed to exit the pool and collect our discarded clothing.

We had to return to our cell in our wet undergarments, which we then had the problem of drying without proper means. Knowing that Emily was only a few feet from me in a state of undress was, if anything, more discomforting than our sharing the pool. Emily, however, kept up a brisk and lively conversation through the intervening wall, pointing out that at least this test had been less painful than the last two.

Was she covering her own embarrassment or sparing my own, or even trying to keep my spirits up? I wonder if, in moments such as these, women are the more pragmatic and tougher-minded sex. Perhaps Emily is simply unique. I do know that I could not have wished for a more stalwart companion…

Turlough switched off his torch, put the diary away and pulled his blanket over his head. He felt like a real intruder now, prying into something that didn't concern him. If it had really been a hundred years since it was written, with the participants long dead, mere names and just part of history, it would not have felt so intimate. But travelling with the Doctor sometimes had the unexpected consequence of bringing history to life, with all its attendant hopes and fears and tragedies. Perhaps if he knew how the diary had come into the Doctor's possession he would have felt better. It wasn't the sort of thing he imagined Haliwell would have given up willingly, certainly not in its unedited form, which suggested… No, he didn't want those two people to die!

He turned over restlessly. By an ironic twist the very thing he had joked about only days before was coming true. Haliwell was falling for Emily Boyes-Dennison in a reserved, hesitant, English sort of way, only the process had been accelerated because they'd been thrown together in unusual circumstances. And now he, Turlough, was reading about the romance as it unfolded, but by a means never intended for public consumption in this form. How would he feel if his private thoughts about… well, Lytalia for instance, were read by somebody else?

Was his guilt the sign of a balanced conscience? The diary had become part of the attempt to know himself better, which he had initiated by asking Kamelion to replicate him. It was another means of holding a mirror up to his soul… and he wasn't yet sure he liked what he saw.

Turlough must have fallen asleep then, for the next thing he knew was that a warm body was pressed against his back and a slim arm had reached around him to lie against his chest. The scent in his nostrils was unmistakable: Lytalia.

How could she do this? They would be seen. Or would nobody

notice in the flickering firelight? Perhaps everybody else was asleep. If he didn't move they wouldn't realise she was there. Perhaps a gentle embrace was as intimate as it would get – though he half wished for much more. Minutes passed and Lytalia didn't move. She was asleep! Was that a compliment or an insult? He wished he knew the proper etiquette in such situations. He wished he knew so many things…

When he awoke again Lytalia was gone and the camp was being roused. He half wondered if he had imagined the encounter. He would have to ask her, very tactfully, later for she was already out with the scouts again. Like the Doctor, the Phiadorans didn't seem to need much sleep.

They set off once again. The forest was definitely getting darker as the shadows lengthened and the sunlight retreated from the deeper hollows. The cool of a long evening was settling in.

Sinclair had asked the Phiadoran scouts to keep a watch for any sign of the downed *Draco* since it had crashed in this general area. But they reported no trace of it. Of course, in this forest they could have passed within a hundred yards of the ship and not noticed. Once again Turlough resolved not to get himself lost.

They forded a small river using lines. It wasn't deep or particularly fast flowing and they could easily have waded – except for the flat fish some six feet across that inhabited it. They were exactly the colour of its sandy bed and Turlough would never have noticed them had Lytalia not pointed them out. He didn't ask if they were dangerous because he knew the answer.

'Doctor,' he said as they took a short break for rest and rations. 'Have you any idea yet how we're going to get into this citadel? It's got pretty high walls… so I imagine. I mean they'd have to be, to keep out the game animals. This warden thing could just sit tight and ignore us.'

The Doctor didn't appear to have noticed his slip. 'You may be right. A frontal assault is probably out of the question. We simply don't have the equipment. Unless some other means presents itself, it may be necessary to induce the warden to come out after us.'

'Why do I think that's going to be a dangerous job?' Turlough said.

'Everything here seems to be tinged with danger,' the Doctor said grimly. 'This could have been a place of great beauty, but instead nature has been perverted to serve the desires of hunters. To kill for the sake of killing, to take pleasure in slaughter merely for self-aggrandisement. That is the most terrible crime in the universe –'

There was a flash of light and an ear-splitting bang. A pressure wave knocked them off their feet. The British crew fell flat, rifles ready, looking for the source of the cannon shot that seemed to have exploded in their midst. Turlough twisted round to see the smoking remains of one of the smaller trees, the leaves stripped from its branches by the force of the blast, slowly topple over and crash into the undergrowth. Through the ringing in his ears he heard a man calling out: 'Charlie, where are you? Charlie... Oh God, he's gone!'

The rest of them climbed warily to their feet. Sinclair, pistol in hand, was looking intently about him. 'Stay alert! Watch for a muzzle flash.'

The man calling for Charlie was holding something in his trembling hand. Turlough blinked for a moment, then realised with a spasm of nausea that it was a boot with the bloody stump of a leg still within it.

The princess was examining the shattered remains of the fallen trunk. She moved quickly to another tree, peering at something low down, then called out: 'This was no attack. Have your men stay back from these trees, Captain, and I will show you the cause.'

Sinclair, the Doctor and Turlough joined her. She pointed to a growth of yellowish fungi near the base of the trunk.

'Your man must have struck one of those. They are not common in this part of the forest. We did not think we would encounter any or we would have warned you. I am sorry for your loss.'

'You mean those things explode?' Sinclair said incredulously.

The Doctor was already crouching to examine the fungi. Turlough caught his breath as he appeared to squeeze the growth then stood up with a drop of yellow fluid on his fingertip. He flicked his wrist and sent the droplet flying on to a rock projecting out of the undergrowth. There was a sharp bang and a puff of smoke.

'Good God!' said Sinclair.

'I wondered where the propulsive charge for the vacuum gun came from,' the Doctor said. 'This fungus seems to exude a natural form of nitroglycerine. I'm sorry we came across it under such tragic circumstances, but we might have a use for it if we can make some reliable fuses.'

'We've got fuses and guncotton with us… the supply we carried for mineral sampling,' Sinclair said.

'Good,' the Doctor said.

The princess was shaking her head. 'The citadel walls are massive. It would take many powerful explosions to open a way through. The warden would intervene long before then.'

The Doctor smiled slightly. 'I don't intend anything quite as crude as that. Now we must find some more fungi. As long as it's kept cool and isn't allowed to sweat, I think it should be relatively safe.'

They carefully gathered fungi while the remains of the dead sailor were buried. Carrying the explosive slung on a pole wrapped in water-soaked blankets, they continued on.

Gradually the ground started to rise and Turlough realised they were nearing their objective. The trees thinned and he saw glimpses of the peaks of the central range rising beyond them. Through telescopes they could see the sheer white walls of the citadel. In conference with the princess they planned the final stage of their route.

The foothills were not as steep as the edge of the highland shelf and in the low gravity they ascended rapidly, refreshed by the cooler drier air. Fingers of forest snaked upwards through the mountain valleys and they kept to these for concealment.

Finally, over thirty hours after they set out, Sinclair called a halt. The base of the citadel was perhaps five hundred feet beyond the line of trees and scrub in which they were sheltering. But between them was only a steep expanse of bare rock leading up to sheer ramparts. Sinclair surveyed the scene again, then turned to the Doctor.

'I hope you really have some plan in mind, for I cannot see how we shall ever gain entry to that place. Unless there is some gate we can't see that can be forced.'

'There is no gate,' said Nareena. 'The only access is by flying craft.'

'Rather as I suspected,' the Doctor said. 'Now, we have the materials and labour force to hand. It shouldn't take too long to prepare. This is what we're going to do.'

And they listened intently as the Doctor laid his plan before them.

Inside half an hour the copse was a hive of activity. Vines were being plaited into ropes, trees and bamboos were cut and trimmed and stones gathered. Turlough slipped away behind a tree with the diary. There wasn't much time left and he wanted to make a last check so that he would be prepared for the assault. If he was going to play the hero then he wanted to do it right.

In his haste he flipped further ahead than he intended and his own name seemed to leap up at him from the page. Before he could stop himself he had read the paragraph in which it appeared.

He snapped the diary shut, cursing his carelessness, but it was too late.

He'd seen his part in what was to come. Now he had to make things work out exactly right – or else people would die.

Chapter Eighteen
The Survivor

The lookout stationed at the *Draco*'s upper porthole saw the ragged figure break out from under the trees and head for the ship, moving in leaps and bounds that only Earthly muscles were capable of on the Moon. With a pistol in one hand and a cutlass in the other, the man fell upon the ring of creatures that surrounded the ship.

He'd emptied his revolver into the nameless things before they could react to this unexpected onslaught, and then began to hack and slash those that still stood before him. Talon and tentacle alike fell before those great double-handed swings driven by that wild excess of energy that comes to those utterly determined to prevail.

The astonished lookout found his voice and shouted down the speaking tube: 'Open the hatch – it's Stanton!'

The *Draco*'s lower hatch cranked open. Two men crouched in the airlock began firing into the horde that surrounded them. Under cover of their fire Stanton made a final leap, scrambled up the ramp and tumbled into the ship.

The hatch clanged shut and the guards stared down in amazement at the figure of their shipmate as he lay gasping for breath on the deck. It hardly seemed possible that it could be the same man who had set out for the central mountains barely two days earlier. His hair was matted and his clothes hung in tatters about him, ingrained with dirt and stained with the fresh blood and sap of the things he had killed.

'What happened to you, mate?' one asked, as they tried to help him to his feet. 'Where the others?'

Stanton shrugged off their hands and hauled himself upright so that they saw his face for the first time. It was Henry Stanton's, more haggard but unmistakable, yet it was also changed. It had the mask-like quality that lingers after every shade of terror has been played across a face so many times that the muscles have been numbed. But in stark contrast to this blankness were his eyes. There was a fire within them that had never been there before.

'The others…' he said, but his voice was no more than a dry rasp and his words broke into a hacking cough.

He hauled his way up the ladder to the hold, and the bay where the rum cask was kept in its locked frame. With the butt of his rifle he smashed the lock, turned on the tap and sucked the spirit straight from the spigot. Only when he had had his fill did he turn to the two men who had followed him.

'They're dead,' he said.

'Green, the bosun, all of them?'

'You heard! And unless you want to end up like 'em, you'll tell Cartwright to ready the ship. There are things out there that can eat us whole. But I can fly us out.'

'It ain't as easy as that, Henry. Like for a start, Cartwright's dead… and the lieutenant, and the surgeon and navigator. Maitland's in charge.'

'An engineer?'

'He's all that's left.'

Henry shook his head and for a moment a terrible smile played about his lips. 'My, but the ship's gone to hell while Henry's been away.'

He stared into their confused faces and they flinched away from his burning eyes. 'What happened?'

'Well… we'd just finished the platework on the hull when things of every shape and size just poured out of the trees at us. Like they'd been waiting, gathering in the shadows. A few got into the ship… God, what a slaughter it was… their slime's everywhere. We had to butcher them before they stopped moving. We saw 'em off in the end but the rest settled down to wait, like they knew we weren't going anywhere.'

'We are going somewhere,' Henry roared. 'We're going straight up!'

'But they can't get the engine fixed properly. We ain't got the power to lift!'

Henry became aware of curious faces appearing round the hatch frame. He pushed past them and headed up the ladder.

He halted just inside the engine-room hatch. The breach in the hull had been repaired but the impeller drive mechanism lay half dismantled, with tubes and coils scattered across the deck. Maitland and a civilian electrical engineer were huddled over the confusion, with the surviving engine-room ratings looking on anxiously over their shoulders. Maitland lifted a haggard face as Henry entered.

'Stanton? Where are the others?'

'Dead!' Henry snapped, raising his voice. 'Did everybody hear that, so you don't have to keep asking the same damn fool question? They're all dead, I'm alive. Got it?'

They were staring at him uncertainly. One of his shipmates put out a gentle hand. 'Maybe you'd better have a rest, Henry. You must be all in.'

Henry shook off the hand. 'I don't need to rest! Now, who else have we got left, apart from what's here?'

'Well, the cook, a couple of maintainers on lookout and the special navigator.'

'Enough to run the ship,' Henry muttered, 'if we can get her off the ground.' He turned to Maitland.

'What's stopping us lifting?'

'Stanton, get to your quarters –'

'Just tell me!'

Maitland was too weary to argue and could only shake his head. The civilian electrician answered for him. 'We're only getting power through half the coils. The ship rocked a bit when we tried them, but not enough to lift. The other coils are dead, but we don't know why.'

'Then put more power through what you have got.'

'We can't. Any more and they'll burn out.'

'But what lift we have got is nearly enough, right?'

The engineer looked doubtful. 'Maybe. We don't know for sure.'

'Right,' Henry said. 'We need to lighten the ship. We throw out everything that we don't need. The exploration gear for a start.'

'Stanton, I'm in command,' Maitland said. 'I'll say whether we lighten the ship or –'

He stopped because Henry had unslung his rifle and levelled it at him. The silence in the engine room became absolute.

'We lighten the ship, do you hear me?' Henry said slowly.

Maitland found his voice again. 'Don't be a bloody fool. Put it down or else –'

'You'll have me arrested for mutiny? Queer thing but Captain Green wanted to do the same thing out there in the forest… but he died. And the bosun would have done it, but then he died. Maybe it was chance, maybe it was providence. Want to try your luck?' He looked about him at the frozen figures in the engine room. 'Anybody else want to face me?'

As they met his eyes several men had to turn aside because there was little humanity left in them, only the absolute and indomitable will to survive at whatever cost. Yet even as the sight chilled their blood it offered hope. It denied the possibility of failure and, whether it was a product of mania or higher reason, they needed to believe in such certainties at that moment.

When no one spoke up, Henry looked back at Maitland.

'See, I'm finished with people telling me what to do. I can fly this ship better than anyone, so I reckon I'm due some proper respect at last.'

Maitland could only shake his head in despair. 'I haven't the strength left to fight you, Stanton. But it doesn't matter who gives the orders. If we can't fix this we're all dead anyway.'

Henry's face creased into a contemptuous scowl. 'You're engineers, it's your job to know how these things work. You fix it, I'll fly it. That's the deal.'

Maitland gave a mocking laugh, quite without any humour. 'You can wave that gun about all you like, Stanton, because it won't change the facts.' He gestured at the array of components strewn about him. 'Only Boyes-Dennison really knows how these things work. If the fault's too deep, then it's beyond us.'

Henry leaned forward slowly, the very incarnation of cold menace.

'Then you'd better learn, Maitland, 'cos otherwise our only chance'll be to lighten the ship further... and you'll go out with all the other dead weight!'

Chapter Nineteen
To the Limits

Haliwell and Emily could only stare in amazement at the items racked on the long wall. Their guard gestured again, then stood waiting with mechanical patience.

'I think it means we should choose something,' Emily said.

'But why, in God's name?' Haliwell said.

The wall held the largest single array of armaments he had ever seen. Though there were no guns or explosive devices, there were numerous muscle-powered projectile weapons together with every other implement imaginable for clubbing, cutting, ripping or stabbing.

'We are prisoners,' he continued. 'Why would they arm us?'

'I fear it is another test,' said Emily. 'They have ascertained our general physical capabilities. Now they wish to see what skills we have in combat.'

'Against what?'

'No doubt we shall find out as soon as we make our selection.'

'And they expect you to fight as well? It's outrageous!'

'We have already agreed, Richard, that they do not make any distinction between us on the grounds of our sex. Now, I do not wish to go into battle, I find nothing glorious in warfare, but we certainly have the right to defend ourselves. If this follows the pattern of the previous tests, we will be given no choice in the matter. I shall find something I can use and I think you must do the same.'

Haliwell shrugged helplessly and walked along the line of weapons until he came to the swords. There was everything from blades as long as he was tall, that he could hardly have lifted, down to needle-slender foils. He found something not unlike a cutlass and checked its balance. He took up a defensive stance and ran through the positions from prime to octave, finishing with a quick lunge. He recovered and nodded.

'It will do. I am a fair swordsman, so I think I should stay with something familiar.'

'You look very formidable,' Emily said. She had found a light bow and quiver of arrows. 'I have done some archery and even hit gold a few times.'

'But you've never fired at a living target?'

'No. But I think I can make myself, if it is a matter of life and death.' She moved along the wall and selected a long-bladed knife. 'You should have something in reserve as well.'

'Will it let us take more than one weapon each?'

'There is only one way to find out. I do not think this is going to be an encounter with many rules. You notice we are not being offered any armour. We should take all that we can carry without encumbrance.'

Haliwell chose a small axe. As he swung it to gauge its weight he eyed their escort thoughtfully. Emily saw him and said quickly: 'No, Richard. I'm sure they are not foolish enough to give us anything that might be effective against our guard.'

'If I can just distract him long enough, you might be able to…'

'To do what? Where shall I run? There are many guards and closed doors which only they seem to be able to open. It would be a brave gesture, but a futile one. If we are to escape we must find a better moment than this.'

He sighed. 'As you say.' He thrust the axe through his belt and looked at their guard. 'All right, we're ready.'

They were led down another corridor to a door larger than those they had so far encountered. Haliwell tightened his grip on the sword while Emily nocked an arrow and held her bow ready. He saw the set of her face and her tight lips, and knew she was fighting to control her fear. At that moment he would have given anything to spare her whatever ordeal was to come.

The door swung open, revealing an empty chamber beyond with a similar door at the far end.

'This looks rather like our double-airlock hatches, but much larger,' Haliwell said. 'Perhaps the atmosphere on the other side is poisonous… or is it a vacuum?'

'Then there would be no point in arming us,' Emily pointed out. 'More likely it serves as a trap for animals to prevent them escaping.'

'You are right, of course.' He stepped forward. The door behind them closed. After a moment the door in front swung open. 'Let me go first.'

Beyond was a vast round pit covered by a glass dome that caught the rays of the lowering Sun and gave them their first sight of natural light for over two days. The floor of the pit was layered with earth, supporting a variety of small lunar trees and shrubs interspersed with outcrops of rock and a few pools of water, giving the effect of a wild garden. Haliwell looked about intently, probing every shadow for danger. But the scene looked perfectly peaceful. Without any wind there was not even the rustle of a leaf.

Emily was following at his heels and the door closed behind them. 'It seems deserted,' she whispered.

'For the moment,' he agreed. 'I think we should explore while we have a chance.'

They edged along, keeping the wall at their backs. Soon they came to another door similar to the one they had passed through.

'There may be half a dozen of these around the sides,' Haliwell said. 'I don't suppose they will have carelessly left one open for us to escape through.'

'It will be like gladiators in the Roman Coliseum,' Emily said bitterly, 'facing whatever beasts they send out of their cages to fight us.'

'At least they were properly armed and trained men.'

'There were also *gladiatrix* – female gladiators. They fought as savagely as any of the men and died as brutally.'

'I did not know that. I cannot in honesty say I approve.'

'Neither do I…' They heard the soft thud of a door closing on the other side of the pit. 'But perhaps we would be grateful for their company right now.'

Straining their ears they heard the pad of feet and a snuffling sound.

'If we could climb one of those larger rocks we would still be protected and could see further,' Emily suggested.

'That's an idea… but too late!'

Something like a lion with six legs burst out of the undergrowth and gathered itself to spring upon them. Emily's bow twanged and the arrow buried itself in the creature's right shoulder. As it stumbled Haliwell leapt forward and swung his cutlass. The blade cut halfway through the creature's neck. Frothing with blood, the thing twisted and spat, rolling on to its back and raking the air with its talons. As Haliwell and Emily shrank back against the wall its death throes gradually subsided and it lay still.

Haliwell looked at Emily's pale face. 'That was a fine shot.'

'It was lucky,' she said.

'Perhaps. I do not think they will let us go with one easy kill, so let us find a perch before our next adversary appears.'

They had just reached the top of a sizable boulder some twelve feet above the ground when another door opened. Crouching at the ready, they heard an indistinct rustling without any clear pattern to it. Then out of the bushes rolled what appeared to be a ball of moss some five feet across. A couple of dozen six-inch spikes protruded from its body, and the thing apparently moved by selectively withdrawing and extending them.

It circled their refuge, then began butting up against the base of the boulder as though in a futile attempt to climb after them.

Despite their circumstances Haliwell chuckled. 'We seem to have outsmarted this one. How long must we wait until it gives up, do you think?'

'I don't know. I'm not even sure whether it is plant or animal. Can you see any sign of eyes?'

Haliwell leaned forward to get a better view. 'Not that I can see. Perhaps it – ahhh!'

There was a bang like compressed air being released. One of the creature's spikes had shot upwards, trailing a glistening sinew behind it, and passed through the shoulder of Haliwell's jacket, burying itself in the folds of material. The sinew contracted and started to pull him downwards. He fell to his knees scrabbling at the rock to keep his place. Emily fired an arrow into the ball of moss, and then another, without any apparent effect. Haliwell managed to bring his sword around and slashed at the sinew, but the blade only slid along the slippery elastic cord. Another contraction pulled him flat, slithering towards the edge of the boulder top. Emily dropped her bow, pulled out her knife and sliced across the sinew where it lay tight over the rock. It took three cuts before the sinew parted, snapping like rubber, and was rapidly drawn back into the creature's body.

Haliwell rolled on to his back, panting. He carefully took hold of the tip of the spike protruding from the shoulder of his jacket and pulled it and the trailing length of sinew through the hole, then tossed them aside in disgust.

Emily leaned over him anxiously. 'Are you wounded?'

'Just grazed, I think. My own fault. Never underestimate anything in this place. It may not have eyes, but it knows exactly where we are by some means. And now it has us trapped up here.'

'Perhaps not. The shafts of my arrows are still protruding some way out from its body. Bearing in mind its means of locomotion, I think I can at least immobilise it.'

The thing was feathered with a dozen arrows before it was stopped. The projecting shafts left it rocking back and forth, its spikes extending and retracting futilely as it tried to push itself along. Haliwell climbed down the other side of the boulder, found the largest rock he could lift, and threw it at the creature. The side of the thing crumpled inwards and the spikes stopped moving. Greenish fluid began to seep out from under the still body, staining the sand.

Emily dropped to the ground and, overcoming her revulsion with a visible effort, began removing the embedded shafts.

'Richard, we must recover as many of my arrows as we can. We may yet need them.'

They had retrieved eight arrows when they heard another door open. Immediately there came a peculiar whirring flutter, then another and another.

'Birds?' Haliwell said.

Black shapes flitted about the sides of the dome, half seen

through the trees. They made a circuit of the walls, then gathered into a knot of spiralling bodies and plunged down. Emily managed to loose one arrow before the shapes were upon them, and they could only cower at the base of the rock as the things swirled around them in a black cloud. Haliwell counted seven forms ringed by claws and supported by wings, ten feet across, that did not flap but somehow whirred round continuously like a ship's propeller.

Emily shot down two of them, at the cost of many misses, before she ran out of arrows. She snatched the small axe from Haliwell's belt and joined him in cutting and slashing at the rest. One by one the things fell, fighting with single-minded ferocity to the end. When the last was downed they stood, panting with their exertions, their sleeves ripped and bloody, amid a ring of twitching claws and torn and broken wing membranes.

'One man without cover would not have survived against them,' Haliwell gasped.

'All these creatures attack on sight, before we even threaten them, and they fight to the end,' Emily said, wiping her brow with a bloody hand.

'You're hurt!' Haliwell exclaimed anxiously.

'No more than you. Just scratches, fortunately. As you said, if we had not had the rock for cover they might have overcome us. It is not natural.'

'Like the spider beasts. The Doctor said such behaviour was abnormal.'

'I begin to understand why. Such savagery may be inbred.' Emily hesitated. 'Are we being groomed to join them?'

Again they heard the sound of a door opening.

'Will they give us no time to rest!' Haliwell said, as Emily began to scrabble about for any arrows she could find.

Something heavy shuffled into the pit. There was a soft slithering rasp, a pause, then another slither. There came a distinct hiss, then the shuffling resumed. Undergrowth swished and cracked as a large body pushed it aside.

They looked at each other in dismay. There was something

unspeakably disturbing about that curious combination of sounds.

There was more shuffling, growing steadily louder. Then a flattened head reared over the bushes. On its crown rose two horns, while set between them was a single slotted eye.

As they sprang away a second identical head rose up beside the first and fixed them with its unblinking gaze.

'I thought I could only hear one beast,' Haliwell said.

A third head appeared followed by the sinuous, twining necks of all the heads which merged into a single flattened, legless body that stretched and contracted, shuffling its bulk forward.

'A hydra!' said Emily, as they took another leap back from the approaching beast. The thing hissed, its three heads bobbing up and down as it wriggled and squirmed its thirty feet of length towards them.

'As good a name as any,' Haliwell said lightly even as his mind raced. 'And somehow we must kill it or it will kill us.'

'But how? It is massive.'

'We run until we can think of something. See if we can make it circle the walls. I do not think it is very fast. Come on!'

They set off along the relatively clear strip of ground that edged the pit wall. The hydra shuffled after them, hissing angrily. By maintaining a moderate pace they found they could quite easily stay ahead of it.

'But we cannot run for ever,' Emily said. 'It will be like the spiders. We will have to make our stand eventually.'

'Yes, but at a point of our own choosing. Where is it vulnerable to the weapons we have?'

Emily twisted her head over her shoulder to look at the nightmare beast behind them. 'Its skin looks to be heavily scaled. Even your sword might not penetrate it.'

'Its eyes, then. If we can blind it.'

'I do not think I am a good enough shot. Those heads bob and weave about too much – and I only have five arrows left.'

'Then we must get it to a place where the heads are restricted. If it is foolish enough to follow us in circles, it may be easily trapped. The rock we climbed. Come on!'

They cut away into the miniature forest and the hydra followed. As they reached the rock they split up, running left and right about either side of it, and vanished from sight. The hydra reached the rock and hesitated, uncertain which way to go, its heads instinctively separating around the obstacle, stretching out in an attempt to catch sight of its prey again. Fang-toothed jaws gaped wide. For a moment the heads were almost stilled.

An arrow pierced the ball of the hydra's right eye as the tip of a sword simultaneously burst its left one. The creature reared up in agony and confusion, hissing like a trio of steam valves, its two blinded heads whipping back and forth. Crouched in the lee of the rock, Haliwell and Emily could only huddle tighter into their shelter. The side of one of the hydra's heads, larger than that of a shire horse, beat against the rock and slammed into Emily. In the low gravity the blow sent her tumbling out into the open ground. The hydra's remaining eye fixed upon her. Instinctively the central head arched over and down on its tormentor.

Haliwell leapt upwards with all his strength, meeting the descending head with his sword. The blade passed through the eye socket and deep into the cranium beyond, only to be wrenched from Haliwell's grasp even as he collided with the great jaw and was knocked aside. The flattened snout smashed into the ground just a yard from where Emily lay winded and gasping for breath.

The head lifted again and the great beast rolled completely on to its side, hissing and spitting, flattening saplings and lashing the ground with its tail. Haliwell, his nose bleeding, crawled out of the bushes into which he'd fallen, caught hold of Emily and pulled her away from the monster's death throes.

Only when they reached the pit wall did he put her down.

'That was very brave of you, Richard,' she said huskily. 'And foolhardy, of course. But I should expect that by now.'

He managed a smile. 'That's the navy way. Sorry… tradition, you know.'

He withdrew his arm from her back where he had supported her and caught his breath. His palm was covered in blood.

'Emily, you're bleeding.'

'I think it was the hydra's horn. Its head struck my back and side. Is it bad?'

Very carefully he turned her over. The back of her jacket and the shirt beneath had been ripped clean through and were soaked with blood. Whatever had done it had cut deep.

'Not too good, I'm afraid,' he said. 'You'll need some bandaging.'

'By which I take it you really mean stitching?'

He could not deceive this woman. 'Yes.'

'You may have to improvise…'

A door not ten feet from them began to swing open.

'No!' Haliwell shouted. 'Not again!'

But it was their mechanical guard that rolled into view. It pointed back through the door.

Emily laughed, though it obviously hurt her. 'It seems we have overcome our quota of adversaries. We live to fight another day.'

Haliwell helped her up.

'Shall I carry you? It is easy here.'

'Thank you, but I can walk. My spine at least is not damaged.'

With his support she hobbled out into the corridor.

'Maybe they'll help,' Haliwell said. 'We have to try.'

'What do you mean?'

He waved his hands to attract the machine's attention and turned Emily round so it could see her injury.

'We must have medical aid,' he said, miming cleaning the wound and drawing the edges together. 'Do you understand me? You must help treat her, or else your tests will be finished.'

The machine hesitated, seeming to study Emily's back for a moment, then indicated they should move on again.

'Did it understand?' Emily asked faintly. Her face was now deathly pale.

'I don't know.'

They were put back in their cell.

Haliwell lay Emily face down on her sleeping pallet, then pulled off his jacket and ripped the sleeves from his shirt. He moistened the material in the drinking fountain, then sat down beside Emily.

'I can at least clean the wound,' he said gently. 'Then I will bandage it as best I can. But I'm afraid I must remove some of your clothing.'

'Of course you must,' Emily said. 'This is no place for foolish modesty. You should know me better by now.'

She eased herself up so that her jacket and shirt could be pulled off. He realised he still had the knife in his belt, and used it to cut away her chemise.

The gash ran from just under her right shoulder blade diagonally downwards across her spine and finished at the bottom of the left side of her rib cage. He cleaned it as best he could, though the blood continued to flow, then tore up more of his shirt to make a bandage. The injury was so long and deep there was no doubt it should be stitched, but he had no needle. Somehow he had to close the sides of the wound with bandaging alone and hope it would be enough to stop the bleeding. Then pray it would not turn gangrenous.

There was a click from the cavity in the wall where their food was delivered by some form of dumbwaiter. He glanced over his shoulder automatically, only to see that the usual containers weren't in the receptacle.

'What is it?' Emily asked.

Haliwell crossed the room and picked up the items that had been delivered. One was a small tub of translucent pinkish-tinted ointment, the other a reel of clear ribbon about two inches wide.

He brought them back to Emily, who examined them as well as she could. The ointment had a faint chemical tang to it that she could not place. The ribbon was clear as glass, yet pliant. When Haliwell tried to lift the end from the reel with his nail he found that it peeled back with some resistance.

'It has some adhesive on its inner side that is still slightly wet,' he said. 'I think this is what I asked for. But I must be sure first.'

He place a tiny drop of the ointment on one of the minor cuts on his own arm. Immediately he felt the relief of sensation and after a minute it seemed to him that the wound was closing slightly.

'Use it, Richard,' Emily said. 'We both know there is no other choice.'

He carefully applied the ointment, working it deep into the gash. Emily gave a sigh of relief as the pain eased. In a few minutes the bleeding had stopped and the sides of the wound, as if by magic, were pulling together. When there was just a thin pale line left he cut a length of the tape and laid it in place, smoothing it down so that it held the skin firmly.

'That is so much better,' Emily said. 'But I am tired. I don't think I have the strength to wash, though I must be filthy.'

'You rest,' he said gently, covering her. 'Doctor's orders.'

She was asleep in moments.

Wearily Haliwell cleaned himself up and used a little of the ointment on his own wounds, then sat watching her. He knew they had been granted a reprieve, nothing more. It seemed as though the remarkable medication of their captors would save her from this injury, but he could not believe she would be completely healed for days at least. Would they wait that long… or expect them to face their next test in just a few hours' time with Emily still incapacitated? This last encounter had almost proved too much for them. What would the next one bring?

He pulled out his diary and brought his entries up to date. His darkest forebodings filled the last lines.

What torture will come next? Will there be an end to these tests, or are we to be pressed to our limits… and beyond? If we are to escape, or by some miracle be rescued, please God let it be soon.

161

Chapter Twenty
Attack

The throwing arm of the catapult slammed into its stops, sending the projectile hurtling upwards. In the low gravity and thin air it cut an incredibly long arc through the sky. Just as it passed over the top of the citadel walls it exploded.

'Another two seconds on the fuse, please,' the Doctor called out, observing the flight of the bomb through his telescope.

The adjustment was made as the catapult was cranked back into firing position. In a minute a second package of terrestrial guncotton enhanced by lunar explosive fungi flew upwards. This time it exploded somewhere on the far side of the walls.

'Good,' said the Doctor. 'Now swing it round by five degrees to the right.'

The sailors levered the catapult mount around to open up a new line of fire and another projectile was prepared.

'Your friend the Doctor is most inventive,' Lytalia said to Turlough as they and the main group watched the attack from their shelter further back in the trees.

'He's OK on planning this sort of theoretical stuff,' Turlough said quickly, 'but he relies on me for the practical things. I mean when we get into the citadel I'll have to spend half my time watching him to see he doesn't wander off, or something. You know these cerebral types. Yes, I'll be pretty well running things then.'

'But you have the plans we gave you as a guide.'

'Yes, but as you admit, you were taken through the place pretty quickly all those years ago and didn't see everything. For instance, I'd suspect there's a lot more hidden underground. Captain Haliwell and Miss Boyes-Dennison are probably being held down there... I guess. Still I'll probably be able to work it out as we go.'

For a moment he forgot his concerns about what was to come, nor cared that he was being deceitful and boasting wildly. He just wanted to see that look of admiration and approval on her face again.

'I know you'll be very brave,' she said. 'We'll never be able to thank you for what you are doing for us.' Turlough basked in the warmth of her smile. 'But your Doctor does have a fine mind,' she added.

'Mind isn't everything,' Turlough said shortly.

Lytalia frowned. 'Yet he doesn't seem to care for our companionship. He seems apart from the rest of you. I hope we have not offended him in some way.'

'No, I'm sure you haven't. Everybody else likes you. It's just that the Doctor doesn't go in for close female company that much. It's because he's a... well, it's complicated. You see neither of us are quite what we seem – '

Two saucers rose up over the citadel walls.

'Everybody move back through the trees as planned, please,' the Doctor called out.

They retreated quickly. The silver saucers dropped down outside the walls and swooped towards the belt of trees. A handful of sailors fired a few rounds at them then turned and ran. The saucers dived under the overarching forest canopy and down the aisle between the trees. Ahead of them a number of figures were running in apparent panic. Jointed tentacles uncoiled from beneath the saucers and electric sparks crackled across their hulls as they prepared to repulse those who disturbed the sanctity of the citadel.

'Now!' Sinclair shouted from his perch in the high branches.

A dozen knives sliced through supporting ropes and the camouflaged nets dropped out of the tree tops. The saucers flew right into them and spun about as they became entangled. Heavy vines securing the nets jerked tight as they took up the strain, preventing the saucers from pulling away. The lower ends of the vines were tied around felled tree trunks. Soldiers and Phiadoran women burst out of cover, ran to the trunks and began rolling them forward, coiling the vines about them and inexorably pulling the saucers down to earth.

Electrified tentacles twisted their way through the nets and reached out towards the attackers, only to be caught by thrown nooses and pegged down where they could do no harm. Still crackling impotently, the two craft struck the ground, rocking and straining at their bonds.

'Cover the sensor ports!' the Doctor shouted.

Phiadorans ran nimbly forward and threw handful after handful of mud at the glass eyes ringing the saucers until the ports were completely obscured.

The Doctor and Turlough sprang on to the nearest saucer, lengths of plaited dry grass wrapped about their feet and knees to insulate them from the current that still coursed through the hull. The Doctor searched frantically until he found an access panel. Turlough handed him a tool from their pack and the panel popped open, revealing a tangle of cables and instrument boxes. The Doctor examined them for a few seconds then called for a new tool which Turlough slapped into his hand. He reached inside the cavity and there were three rapid clicks. The electric crackling of the hull died away, the writhing tentacles went limp and the frantic rocking of the craft ceased.

The Doctor and Turlough leapt down from the saucer and bounded across to the other one where they repeated the process. As it fell still and silent a cheer went up from the sailors. The Doctor waved them urgently into silence.

'Well done, but this is only the first part of the job. Clear away these nets and lines as quickly as possible to make way for the harnesses, please.'

By the time Sinclair came up to them, still brushing mould from his trousers where he had shinned rapidly down a tree, the Doctor and Turlough had exposed a large cavity in the very top of the saucer and were working intently on the mechanism within.

'Can you do it, do you think?' Sinclair asked anxiously, eyeing the immobilised craft with some trepidation.

'Easily, given time and the right equipment,' said the Doctor. 'Unfortunately my equipment is limited and we only have as much time as it takes the warden to decide to send down more of these craft. Hopefully it'll think we've simply destroyed these. That might cause it pause for a bit while it thinks up a different way of chasing us off.'

Sinclair eyed the tools they were handling and glimpsed the mechanism within the cavity. A curious frown creased his brow.

'These machines cannot be constructed on the same principles as our own ships. How can you work on them so surely?'

'Oh, there's a certain logic about how machines must be put together,' the Doctor said lightly. 'You just apply first principles, you know.'

Princess Nareena and several of her women ran up carrying long coils of plaited ropes.

'Do you wish these put in place now, Doctor?'

'Yes, please. I think we're ready here. Have you got the command sequence straight, Turlough?'

'I think so,' Turlough said doubtfully. He saw Lytalia running towards them carrying more ropes. 'Of course I have,' he added in ringing, confident tones. 'You get on with fixing the other saucer. I'll manage this one. No problem.'

As the Doctor began working on the second saucer the Phiadorans tied a latticework of ropes about the curving upper hulls of both craft. As soon as the rigging was complete, a picked group of ten sailors armed with rifles and improvised grenades began climbing on board, hooking their arms firmly through the netting lines.

Lytalia crouched by Turlough as he squatted in the cavity in the top of the first saucer studying the improvised controls.

'I wish I could go with you,' she said, 'but the protective field runs along the walls.'

'Don't worry about it,' he assured her. 'In an hour that field will be gone and you can go anywhere you want.'

'Ready!' the Doctor called out from the other saucer, and Turlough's complement of sailors, led by Sinclair, climbed aboard. Lytalia gave him a quick kiss. 'Good luck,' she said, then dropped to the ground.

Feeling like a mahout astride some strange mechanical beast, Turlough tentatively pressed a contact. The saucer stirred and lifted silently into the air. A few yards away the Doctor's saucer did the same. The remaining sailors on the ground cheered and the

Phiadorans waved their spears, a few blowing kisses; they were learning Earthly gestures rapidly.

The saucers turned and glided through the trees, then rose upwards. In a few seconds they skimmed over the walls of the citadel and were lost from sight.

'I thought I heard thunder a few minutes ago,' Haliwell said to Emily as they were escorted along the corridor to the pit.

'You're just trying to distract me, but thank you for trying.'

'But I really did hear thunder,' he insisted. 'It seems they have storms on the Moon as we do.'

'That may be, Richard. But I doubt it will change their plans for us.'

His expression became grimmer. 'How is your back?'

'Little changed from when you last asked. I am not in any pain, except when I try to move my arms, especially my left one. Bending is also difficult.'

'That is hardly surprising. I could not help but notice considerable bruising on your back and side when I checked your dressings. But at least your wound is healing wonderfully. I think there will be hardly any scar.'

'We both know that may only be of academic interest, Richard. If we face combat again, I will not be able to use my bow. I could just about hold a knife, and though it will not be pleasant I can run a little way. That is all. I will not be able to fight.'

'Then you must let me handle the physical side while you plan our strategy. You are the most intellectual member of this crew in any case.'

She laughed, then winced. 'You are incorrigible, Richard.'

'I fear I must look such a long word up in the dictionary before I can reply to such a charge. I'm only a simple sailor, you know, ma'am.'

They reached the outer door of the chamber leading to the pit. Their weapons from the previous test were lying waiting, Emily's quiver restocked. The sight of them dispelled the last of their banter.

'Carry your bow anyway,' Haliwell suggested. 'Let us not show them you are unfit.'

Emily slung her quiver with an effort and took up her knife even as Haliwell rearmed himself. The door opened and they stepped through. In a few seconds they stood in the pit again.

'Everything seems as it was before,' Haliwell said softly, his eyes flickering about ready for any sign of danger.

'They have at least cleared the carcasses away,' said Emily. 'Shall we make for that useful rock of ours or wait here?'

'If you are better fitted for running then let us stay in the open. Be prepared to move either way. We shall try to assess whatever is sent against us from a distance before we are forced to confront it.'

'But what will it be? They have not repeated themselves yet.'

They heard a door on the far side of the pit close.

'We shall know soon enough,' Haliwell murmured.

They strained their ears for some clue as to what creature had entered the pit. But there was nothing. The tiny forest before them was perfectly still. A minute passed.

'Why does it not attack us?' Haliwell whispered. 'None of the other beasts waited so long.'

He heard Emily draw in her breath. 'They were driven by an instinct to kill or overwhelming hunger. This one seems different. This is stalking us... Richard – what if this is a true hunter? A thinking being!'

Haliwell caught Emily around the waist and leapt to one side with all the strength he had. At the same moment there was a bang of compressed air and a dart flashed out of the undergrowth and struck the wall where they had been crouching. Haliwell snatched a glance over his shoulder as they bounded clear and glimpsed the outline of a figure as it moved in the bushes. It was carrying a rod-like shape cradled in its arms.

'Keep moving!' he said, and they leapt again along the curving wall. Another dart smacked into the wall at their heels. Then a stand of trees was between them and their pursuer. They came to a halt on the opposite side of the pit from where they had been attacked.

'It is a hunter,' Emily gasped.

'Yes. A man… or what looks like a man.'

'One of the real masters of this place, perhaps?'

'Perhaps. I could not make out any details. He seemed to merge in with the undergrowth. It was only when he moved that I saw him.'

'He is wearing a form of camouflage dress then?'

'It must be.'

'And he has a gun.'

'We have a bow.'

'You must use it, for I cannot. Have you used one before?'

'Like yourself, I have done some archery for sport,' Haliwell said. 'We also have our Earthly strength, which must make us more agile than any targets he is used to facing here. If he is well camouflaged he will want to stay in cover. If we taunt him enough he will have to give chase and then I can get a shot at him.'

'Then I will draw him out. I am no good for anything else.' She handed over her bow and quiver. 'Let me have your axe, Richard. I must try to look threatening.'

'Emily –'

She snatched the axe from his belt with a grimace of pain. 'There is no time to argue. You know there is no other way. Stay ten yards behind me. We can divide his attention and perhaps confuse him if nothing else.'

And she leapt away around the side of the pit again, yelling at the top of her voice as she went: 'Come on! Here I am! Catch me if you can!'

Haliwell pushed his sword through his belt, nocked an arrow to the bowstring and leapt after her, fighting to quell the sick despair in his heart. It was a desperate scheme, but it was all they could do.

Emily bounded towards the centre of the pit where the trees were thickest, hacked weakly at a shrub then leapt back to the wall again. Haliwell fixed his eyes on the undergrowth, straining for any sign of movement that Emily's actions might provoke. At the very least the hunter must keep shifting his position to watch the two of them…

He saw the tiny flicker of movement as the gun was raised, and drew back and fired his arrow almost before he realised what he had done.

The gun went off even as the arrow passed into the thicket where the hunter was crouching. There was a flurry of confused motion and a crash of branches. Haliwell sprang high in the air and managed to nock and fire a second arrow into the thicket before he landed. He struck the ground with his knees bent, cast aside the bow and leapt forward, drawing his sword. He plunged into the heart of the thicket, saw an indistinct figure before him and swung at it with all his strength.

Seconds later Emily bounded up to the thicket with the axe held ready. Everything within was deathly silent. 'Richard?' she called fearfully.

'It's all right,' he called back. 'But it's not quite what we thought.'

She pushed her way through the brush and twigs to find him crouching over a still figure sprawled on its back. It was wearing a peculiar helmet and visor that completely covered its head and face, and a one-piece coverall of some material that exactly mimicked the mottled patterns of leaf and earth on which it rested. A long slash in the chest of the garment showed where Haliwell's blade had struck. But there was no blood around the wound, only a bundle of fine wires sliced in half by the sword.

Haliwell pulled up the helmet visor. Two glass lenses stared up at them from an otherwise featureless metal face.

'A machine!' Emily exclaimed. 'An automaton.'

'But a machine made to look and act as a hunter would,' Haliwell said. 'Apparently we are not worthy of facing a living hunter yet.'

'What do you mean?'

'We are being assessed as prey for hunters. That is what this place must be for!'

On the other side of the pit another door opened.

I have to make this work out just right, Turlough thought as he sent his saucer skimming over the ramparts of the citadel, hoping the warden's plasma cannon, wherever it was mounted, couldn't be brought to bear on targets this close. Now they had to find their objective before the warden realised what was going on and sent more saucers up against them.

The acropolis of the citadel opened out before them in all its marble perfection, bringing forth a gasp of approval from one of the sailors clinging to the netting. It was very beautiful, Turlough acknowledged, just as Haliwell had described it in the diary – until you knew it was a place where hunters rested between their expeditions down into the forest for game. How many had brought back Phiadorans as trophies? He suppressed his anger and strained his eyes for the thing he had to find.

'Let's try over there!' he shouted across to the Doctor, pointing to a shallow dome of glass rising on a lower terrace not far from the saucers' landing ground.

'Why?' the Doctor shouted back.

Turlough had his line of reasoning ready. 'Everything above ground is obviously for show and for the clients to enjoy. But that looks like the top of some sunken greenhouse. I bet they can control the local weather, so why would they need an underground garden unless it was for hunting practice?'

'It's worth a look,' the Doctor agreed.

The saucers banked towards the dome and dipped downwards. Turlough suddenly felt a cold sweat break out down his spine. What if he was too early… or too late? Why had he ever brought the diary along!

They circled low over the glass dome, peering through its honeycomb facets. A sailor shouted: 'I see them, sir!'

'Open that roof now!' Sinclair said.

A fuse fizzed into life and a demolition charge was tossed over the side of the saucer.

There was a flash and bang and a shower of glassy fragments glittered like a rainbow as they lazily fell back to earth. With the smoke still billowing about the gaping hole that had been torn in the dome, the Doctor dropped his saucer down and through it with Turlough following in his wake.

On the edge of the miniature forest below them was a tall

camouflage-suited figure, apparently undisturbed by the destruction of the roof. Guns were held in a firing posture in both its pairs of arms. In its sights were Haliwell and Emily, who were crouched against the pit wall evidently in the last stages of exhaustion.

Gritting his teeth Turlough drove his saucer forward and down. There was a bump, a metallic crunch, and then they were on the ground.

'Smartly done!' Turlough heard Sinclair exclaim.

But in his mind were the words that had held him hostage to fate for the past few hours, and which now, to his heartfelt relief, dropped into their proper place and became just another part of history.

…I thought we were done for when the glass roof was blown in by a powerful explosion. To our amazement, two of the saucer craft, with ratings clinging to their sides and piloted by the Doctor and his assistant, dropped into the pit. With great presence of mind, Mr Turlough drove his craft straight at our many-armed attacker an instant before it could fire upon us and crushed the machine man into the ground…

Chapter Twenty-One
Under Fire

A door swung open and a service robot rolled into the pit, its many arms raised threateningly and sparks crackling between its heavy-duty claws.

The British crewmen scrambled off the saucers and started to pour fire into it. Bullets sparked and ricocheted off its metallic bodywork.

'Aim for its sensors!' the Doctor shouted over the din. 'The eye lenses on its head section!'

A lens shattered and a bullet tore a panel from the side of the head, spilling wires and coils. The machine spun about wildly, arms thrashing, then toppled over on to its side and lay still.

'Stand guard on that door!' Sinclair ordered. 'Ready a grenade if another one of those things shows itself.'

'That was a most timely arrival,' Haliwell said breathlessly, as he and Emily Boyes-Dennison got slowly to their feet. Their stained and torn clothes looked like something a tramp had discarded and their faces were grey and drawn from the strain they had been under. Sinclair must have been shocked by their appearance, but nevertheless shook Haliwell's hand firmly and bowed to Emily with as much formality as if they were meeting at some society function. Then, in a practical gesture appropriate to his ancestry, Sinclair passed over a hip flask from which they both drank gratefully, coughing a little, and some colour returned to their cheeks.

Emily said, 'Thank you, Captain Sinclair,' very quietly, and Turlough realised she was fighting back tears of relief.

The Doctor stepped in. 'Sorry to hurry you, but we must make our next move before more reinforcements arrive. Have you seen the main control centre and can you guide us there? Otherwise we've got to find a way in from above.'

'I think I know the place you mean, Doctor,' Haliwell said. 'But why do you have to go there?'

'There's a being called the warden who runs this place – never mind how we know – who we must persuade to release certain fields of energy that cover this crater. Otherwise we're trapped here for good.'

'I think we may have met this warden,' Emily said, 'but I do not know how it can be persuaded, for we have no common language.'

'That won't be a problem,' the Doctor assured her.

'Unfortunately there are several substantial doors along the way which only the machines seem to be able to open, though I never saw how,' Haliwell said.

'We can blast our way through them if necessary,' Sinclair assured him.

'Or we could use the remote key the robots must use,' Turlough said, walking over to the disabled machine and tapping it. 'What do you think, Doctor... sonic, radio or infrared?'

As the British looked on in bemusement he and the Doctor pulled tools from their packs and tore into the machine. In a minute the Doctor had extracted a small circuit-card and a lens trailing a spray of wire.

'Infrared it is,' he said. 'If we attach it to a power cell from the multidriver it should do the trick.'

He carried the improvised device over to the guarded entrance to the pit and pointed the lens at the inner door of the pair. It swung smoothly open revealing another robot waiting in the corridor beyond. The Doctor dived to one side as the sailors blazed away at the machine, shooting out its sensors and leaving it immobilised, a smoking hulk.

He got to his feet, brushed off his knees, then beckoned to Haliwell. 'Please lead the way.'

'First section will accompany us,' Sinclair said. 'Second section to remain here and guard the saucers. Miss Boyes-Dennison, you will stay with them.'

'But I want to...'

'Please,' Haliwell said to her. 'Just this once, for my peace of mind.'

To Turlough's surprise she nodded meekly.

They headed off along the stark white corridors. Robots appeared at each intersection, charging at them with claws snapping, only to be disabled or blasted by grenades. They also lurked behind almost every door the Doctor opened, and suffered the same fate.

'Fortunately they're not really fighting machines,' the Doctor observed as they stepped over the latest pile of smoking metal. 'They're more like general-purpose service robots. The warden also seems to have little grasp of tactics and is employing them very unimaginatively.'

'They obviously don't have revolutions here very often,' Turlough said. 'Let's hope the warden's a slow learner.'

They reached a corridor closed by an unusually large door.

'That opens on to the central chamber,' Haliwell said.

The door did not respond to the Doctor's key. Sinclair had a couple of grenades with long fuses laid against them and the party retreated behind the last corner while the explosives did their job. Before the echoes of the blast had died away everyone had dashed through the haze of smoke into the huge chamber beyond.

A ring of a dozen robots was waiting for them, edging forward and back restlessly, flexing their claws as though they were barely kept in check. A couple held oddly shaped hand weapons. Turlough flinched backwards, but the robots did not fire.

'Don't shoot!' the Doctor yelled, waving his hands urgently at both sides. 'I think the warden wants to talk.'

The sailors hesitated, faced with superior odds for the first time. Turlough tensed. Was the warden learning tactics at last?

'Hold your fire but stay alert, men,' Sinclair said.

The sailors stood their ground, trying to face down their expressionless mechanical opponents.

'It lives in the central pillar,' Haliwell said quietly. 'Be prepared, it's not a pretty sight.'

'We probably don't look any better to it,' the Doctor replied.

Peering between the robots' bodies Turlough could see the creature in the tank shivering in agitation. The Doctor took a few

175

steps forward and Turlough followed at his side, trying to live up to his new confident image. A couple of the robots edged apart a little so that they could see what they were talking to more clearly, and be seen in return.

'I'd like to settle this peacefully,' the Doctor said loudly and clearly.

A rapid chattering came from the speakers over the tank. The sounds translated in Turlough's mind as: 'Return to the forest and you will not be harmed.'

'That was one of the languages it tried on us,' Haliwell said. 'Unless it's learnt English since then we won't get very far.'

But to their evident astonishment the Doctor replied in the same tongue.

'You are imprisoning us here unjustly,' he told the warden. 'Release the energy field that interferes with the function of our ships and traps the Phiadorans and we will do no more damage.'

'Phiadorans?' the warden said uncertainly.

'The princess said it was getting senile,' Turlough whispered.

'It does not matter,' said the Doctor. 'Cut all emissions except the molecular dampening that contains the atmosphere, and we will leave you in peace.'

'Not allowed,' said the warden, twitching uneasily in its tank. 'The builders' rules say no unauthorised landings allowed to leave again. Only the hunters can leave. You are not hunters. You must stay. You have tested well. You will provide good sport for the hunters.'

'But the builders went a long time ago and the hunters haven't come here for many years, have they?' the Doctor said. 'They may all be dead. Any understanding you had with them is meaningless now. You can make up your own rules.'

'Make up my own rules?' the warden said slowly. 'There are only the builders' rules. I follow their rules. That was the agreement... I think. So long ago...'

Turlough could not help asking: 'How long have you been here?'

A long silence, then: 'Too long...' There was a pause and for a moment Turlough thought the warden had forgotten they were there. Then it said: 'Now you must return to the forest. You must be ready when the hunters come. The hunters must have their sport. Only the best, the most skilled, come here. Yes. They hunt only the most dangerous prey. Always keep a few of the most dangerous for the most daring. That is the rule: kill or be killed. That is how it ends... how it always ends...'

The voice faded into incomprehensible mutterings. The Doctor shook his head sadly.

They turned away from the warden to find the British party looking at them with more than a trace of suspicion in their eyes.

'You were talking with it. How can you possibly know its language?' Haliwell asked.

'Later,' the Doctor said impatiently. 'What matters now is that the warden has been conditioned to follow orders... or else through routine or endless repetition it's become too set in its ways to change. It's as much a prisoner here as the rest of the animals. Another crime to lay at the door of those who built this place.'

'You'll forgive me if I do not feel much sympathy for its plight,' Haliwell said heavily. 'If you had been treated the way Miss Boyes-Dennison and myself have been, I think you would understand.'

'So what do we do if the thing is as intractable as you say?' Sinclair asked.

The Doctor's face set. 'I don't think it cares for itself any more. Only a sense of duty and routine is sustaining it. Death might be a merciful release. Perhaps it wants to die and that's why it's holding its robots off. But it can't simply surrender to us. We may have no choice but to fight.'

'Then we simply destroy it and its machines,' Sinclair said.

'Just a moment,' the Doctor said. 'There are a few things we have to know.' He turned back to the warden again. 'If you wanted to shut down the systems I mentioned earlier, what controls would you use?'

'I must not shut them down if there is a danger of escape. Not allowed.'

'I know, but if you did when there was no such danger. For maintenance purposes, perhaps?'

There was a long pause, then two panels on the second level to their right flashed.

'I see,' said the Doctor gently. 'Do your robots function autonomously, or are they controlled from a central unit?'

'All control is centralised.'

'From this room, perhaps?'

A panel flashed to the middle on the bottom row.

'And the plasma cannon?'

A pause, then the warden said: 'Part centralised, part automatic. Not controlled from a panel here.'

'All right. You know what we have to do now?'

'Kill or be killed,' said the warden. 'That is the only way.'

The Doctor turned away slowly, taking Turlough with him, and walked back to the others. In a flat voice he said: 'The second panel you saw light up. It controls these machines. Have your men destroy it. They'd better all fire together and do it quickly, because as soon as they begin the machines will attack.'

The two captains looked totally bewildered, but wisely did not argue. In precise phrases Sinclair gave the orders, cautioning the men not to move until he gave the command.

'Fire!'

The sailors swung about, aimed and fired a volley into the control panel even as the robots jerked forward. Claws clacked and snapped and the two that were carrying hand weapons fired, sending searing bolts of light into the wall over their heads. Another volley smashed into the panel. Turlough leapt backwards as a robot swung at him. There was a shower of sparks and the panel front blew out.

The robots' limbs dropped limply to their sides and they rolled to a halt. Turlough let out his breath with a sigh. The sailors cautiously prodded the now lifeless robots, then began to laugh. Haliwell mopped his brow with a filthy handkerchief.

'How did you know what controls to destroy?' he asked the Doctor.

'The warden told me.'

'Told you! You tricked it?' Sinclair exclaimed.

'Not really.' The Doctor appeared to stare at nothing for a moment, as though trying to fathom another mystery of the universe, then he shrugged. 'In its way, perhaps it was trying to help us.'

'And look at it now,' Turlough said.

The lights in the central pillar and within the warden's tank had gone out. The creature's tendrils had ceased beating and the colour seemed to have drained from its body. Slowly it sank to the bottom of the tank and lay still.

'Without its robots it had no purpose left,' the Doctor said sombrely. 'It must have known the hunters would never come back, but it couldn't let go until now.'

'Are we finished?' Turlough asked, suddenly feeling sick and very tired.

'Almost.' The Doctor crossed to the panels controlling the energy-field generators, studied them for a moment, then began pressing buttons. Display lights flickered and blinked out. 'I'm shutting down the defensive shields,' he explained. 'The Phiadorans will be able to leave and the interference to our own ships' systems should cease. I'll just be a minute.'

Sinclair and Haliwell began conversing in low tones. The sailors were pushing the deactivated robots to and fro and laughing. Turlough paced about, hands thrust into his pockets.

He'd played his part, showed he could be as smart as the Doctor and helped save Haliwell and Emily, even if it was with help from the diary. Plenty to impress Lytalia. And they were free to travel again. So why did he feel despondent?

A symbol on a control panel caught his eye and he stopped pacing. It looked like a stylised representation of one of the flying saucers trailing its mechanical tendrils. Below it was another image showing a figure riding on the saucer. This symbol seemed to be linked with a line of buttons that led to a long locker-type door set to one side of the main panel. He pulled the door open. Inside was a rack of joysticks mounted on plug-pin bases.

'Ah,' said the Doctor, joining him. 'Manual control sticks for the saucers. The hunters must have wanted to pilot themselves occasionally. These can't have been used in years.'

'Well, we can use them now,' Turlough said. 'Save trekking back through that forest, especially as the Sun'll be down soon.'

'No reason why they shouldn't work,' the Doctor agreed. 'We'll take a few and –'

An alarm came on with a shrill wail, rising and falling in an urgent rhythm. Control panels lit up all round the chamber, bathing them in a flickering display of coloured lights. The British party clasped their guns at the ready and looked round grimly for some new danger.

'What's happening?' Haliwell shouted.

The Doctor was running from panel to panel checking the displays. The expression on his face was not reassuring. Suddenly he spun round to face them.

'An automated countdown process has begun, probably initiated by the death of the warden. I really should have anticipated something of the sort. There are also indications that a hyperspace transmitter has been activated, presumably to alert the controllers of this place.'

'What is this transmitter?' Sinclair asked.

'A long-range signalling device.'

'But… the controllers are probably dead,' Turlough said.

'That does complicate matters,' the Doctor admitted. 'I'm not sure how long we have, but I suspect it might not be a good idea to be near to the citadel when the countdown ends, or the system concludes that nobody is coming to sort things out. Turlough, bring those control units. Now everybody; back the way we came!'

They pounded along the corridors to the pit, startling the sailors on guard who were already agitated by the alarm. Turlough glimpsed Emily's look of relief as she saw Haliwell appear, then they were clambering back on to the saucers.

Turlough pulled out their improvised control switches and plugged one of the joysticks into the appropriate recess. It wasn't shaped exactly for the human hand, but his fitted well enough. There was a trigger switch that had to be for power, the grip slid up and down for vertical control, twist to turn, and angle for horizontal flight. He depressed the trigger slightly and slid the grip upwards. The saucer lifted smoothly.

He waved to the Doctor. 'It works fine!'

The Doctor's saucer also lifted. Together they flew out through the shattered roof and headed for the saucers' landing ground. The Sun hung golden above the western horizon, sending the shadow of the distant crater wall creeping across the highlands. Already Turlough imagined a gathering coolness in the air, though it would be another six hours at least before actual sunset.

They landed beside the row of parked saucers and began fitting three of them with joysticks. A minor argument broke out behind them.

'Why should I not steer one?' Emily said to Haliwell. 'We need a fifth pilot and no one else is any better qualified. I have been watching the Doctor and it seems perfectly straightforward, even simpler than riding a horse. After all, when astral craft become commonplace, I fully expect to fly my own.'

Haliwell could think of no answer to that, and wisely gave in.

In a minute Haliwell, Sinclair and Emily were seated on the newly commandeered saucers and together the little fleet lifted off. As far as Turlough could see, Emily controlled her saucer just as well as the two captains.

They topped the walls and plunged down towards the forest. As they glided between the trees, the Phiadorans and the remaining sailors appeared from the shadows. A cheer went up as they saw they had the captives with them.

'Please prepare more harnesses,' the Doctor called out as they set down. 'We're going to fly back to the ships, and we're taking everybody at once.'

Lytalia sprang up the side of the saucer and embraced Turlough. 'Is the warden destroyed, are we really free now?' she asked anxiously.

'He is and you are,' Turlough said.

She hugged him tightly. 'I knew you could do it. I think you're wonderful.'

Turlough didn't argue. As they sat together on the top of the saucer, he saw Haliwell and Emily staring at the Phiadorans.

'As you said, they are most striking allies,' Haliwell said to Sinclair, contemplating the women's bronzed forms as they helped sling nets about the three new saucers. He turned to Emily. 'Would you care to meet a princess, Miss Boyes-Dennison?'

'Thank you, Captain Haliwell,' Emily said with, Turlough thought, a distinct trace of stiffness. He smiled as she was presented to Nareena.

The princess was polite, but seemed more preoccupied with the saucer Emily had flown.

'I owned craft like this before our dispossession,' she explained, stroking its hull. 'I would so wish to pilot my own people out of the forest for the last time.'

'I'm sure Miss Boyes-Dennison would be happy to give up her place,' Haliwell said eagerly. 'It is a more dignified way for one of royal blood to travel.'

'Of course,' Emily said tersely. 'Be my guest.'

The princess climbed on to the saucer and took up the pilot's position. The Doctor must have been watching the changeover because he climbed down from his saucer, saying: 'If Miss Boyes-Dennison would like more flying practice, she's welcome to take my place.'

'Thank you, Doctor,' Emily said graciously, and did so, leaving Haliwell looking oddly puzzled.

'You'd better ride with us,' Turlough told the Doctor.

The last of the passengers were just scrambling on to the nets when the sky blazed with light. The plasma cannon had fired. A second later there came the the crack and rumble of superheated displaced air.

'What's it firing at?' Sinclair demanded.

'It could be a random pattern, or simply anything that moves,' the Doctor said. 'It must be on automatic control now.'

Another bolt flashed overhead.

'If they're trying to hit us, then they're well off target,' said Haliwell.

'My God!' Sinclair exclaimed. 'What if they're firing at the ships? They're in line of sight and we know those fireballs have the range.'

'For want of a better target they might be programmed to eliminate any unauthorised presence in the crater,' the Doctor said.

'Everybody aboard!' Haliwell shouted, climbing on to his craft. 'Ready to lift.'

'We must stay below the level of the tree tops,' the princess said. 'I have done this before. Follow my lead.'

'We'll take up the rear and make sure everybody stays low,' the Doctor said, scrambling on to Turlough's saucer along with Lytalia and the last couple of sailors, and twining his arms through the netting.

The princess took off, guiding her machine with a sure hand. Sinclair, Emily and Haliwell followed. Turlough smiled reassuringly at Lytalia and headed after them.

The saucers wove their way upwards through the great trees until the branches thinned and they had room to pick up speed. The tree tops began to flash past as Turlough banked and turned, following the line of saucers ahead of them. It was like an arboreal slalom, he thought. The saucer felt hot and responsive to his touch and he realised he was having fun. Even the crack of the plasma bolts overhead added a wild sense of exhilaration. He was flying the local equivalent of an open sports car; impractical but exciting. That was probably why the hunters had used them. A different thrill in between their slaughter... or were the craft for running down their prey? For the moment he didn't care.

They covered five miles, then ten. Surely there wasn't much chance of them being spotted now.

The crown of a giant tree ahead of them exploded even as the sky over their heads blazed with white heat.

The bolt's shock wave hammered into them and Turlough fought to keep the saucer level. They sped through a cloud of choking wood smoke and flying chips of bark and he flung up his hand to protect his eyes. Then they were through into clear air.

The Doctor was holding his hand up against the glare of the setting Sun, trying to spot the other saucers, but in those seconds of confusion they seemed to have vanished. Another bolt flashed into the trees a few hundred yards to their right. Was it firing at the others or simply bracketing the general area with fire?

'Bear left!' the Doctor said. 'It may be predicting our line of flight –'

The world seemed to explode into searing light and sound.

Turlough saw trees spin about him, there was a crashing of branches, then only blackness.

Chapter Twenty-Two
The Falling Glass

Surely there has never been such a graveside scene as this, Haliwell thought sombrely.

He, Emily and a couple of crewmen holding lanterns stood under the impossibly tall and slender lunar trees, enveloped in the shadow that covered all the highlands. Above, the first stars shone in the purple-black sky. They were bundled up in heavy coats against the growing chill of night, though the last rays of the invisible Sun still touched the central peaks of the crater. Every half-minute or so a dazzling white pinpoint appeared on the peaks at the spot where the citadel stood, discharging a fireball over the forest to strike the ground not a quarter of a mile away from them.

Emily paid the shattering explosions no notice, simply staring down at her father's grave.

Sinclair had withheld the news of the professor's death from Emily until they had set down their little fleet of saucers close by the ships, so that there would be no distraction from their escape. It was an understandable decision, but did not make breaking the tragic news any easier. Once Emily had recovered from her initial shock she had steadfastly insisted on visiting the grave, and they could not refuse her despite the danger.

When the bombardment had started earlier, Forrester had prudently ordered the ships lifted just clear of the ground and moved a few hundred yards into the cover of a broad stand of trees, so that they were no longer in line of sight of the citadel. The fireballs had followed them, but at least they had some shelter for the moment. In between shots it was possible to cross back to the old landing site on foot. As soon as the Phiadorans and the rest of the crew were safely inside the ships, and Haliwell and Emily had replaced their tattered clothes, this was what they had done so that they could pay their last respects.

'At least he lived to see his life's ambition achieved,' Haliwell said quietly. 'One day we shall return and erect a proper stone to mark his resting place. The man who opened up the way to the planets will not be forgotten. I hope that is some small comfort.'

Emily nodded, sniffing into her handkerchief.

Haliwell gently took Emily's arm.

'You're getting cold. We must go now.'

'Any sign of them?' Haliwell asked Forrester, after he had seen Emily to her cabin and was back on the bridge of the *Cygnus* once again.

'No, sir.'

Come on, Doctor, Haliwell thought. You seem to be a resourceful man. If you're still alive, let us know somehow.

'We've divided up the, uh, Phiadoran ladies between us and the *Lynx*,' Forrester continued. 'It puts a strain on the accommodation, but the men don't seem to mind giving up the space for them. Well, they really are quite charming creatures.'

Haliwell could not help but smile at the expression on his lieutenant's face. 'I had noticed, Mr Forrester.'

Another bolt of fire from the citadel's cannon struck the rolling ground not a quarter of a mile away. Haliwell shook himself and returned his attention to the matter in hand – and perhaps the hardest decision he would ever have to make in his career.

Their earlier move had bought them some grace but sooner or later the cannon would range in on them again, and without the Sun to recharge the ships' batteries they could not keep moving them. The next time they would have to make for open space with all speed, because the cannon had already shown what it could do to a ship in flight. And while it remained active they dare not return to the crater.

Haliwell paced about, pausing to look out of a port. If there was a sign from the forest he was ready to use the saucers to make an attempt at rescue. But without some clue and with night falling any random search would be both futile and foolhardy.

A flash on the other side of the sheltering belt of trees signalled another fireball strike. This time he felt the ground tremor of the impact transmitted up through the body of the ship. They were running out of time.

'Secure the lower hatch in case we have to lift at short notice,' he told Forrester. 'Put the engine room on alert for maximum power output. Signal the *Lynx* to do the same.'

Forrester nodded grimly, fully aware of the implications of the orders.

A light step on the stairs and a slight stir amongst the bridge crew told him they had a visitor. He turned about and smiled politely at Princess Nareena, who was looking about her with intense interest. Despite his other more pressing concerns, Haliwell made a mental note to do something about the Phiadorans' immodestly brief costumes. They had seemed acceptable in the wilds of the crater, but were quite out of place, and disturbing, within the confines of the ship.

'I trust your quarters are adequate, Your Highness,' he said. 'I'm afraid we cannot offer better under the circumstances.'

'Think nothing of it, Captain. What is a little discomfort when you have been freed from prison? I merely came to learn when we would be taking off, since the fire from the citadel seems to be getting closer.'

Haliwell hesitated. 'I still have some hope there will be a sign from the Doctor. Apart from my men and his assistant, he does have Lytalia with him.'

She fixed him with her dark full eyes. 'You think I am being heartless? Perhaps my time here has taken its toll. One lesson I have learned is that sometimes you must sacrifice a few for the greater good. The survival of the group or race must take precedence over all else.'

Even as she spoke, the signaller handed Haliwell a message slip.

'Heliograph from Captain Sinclair in the *Lynx*, sir.'

The message read: *Check barometer. Glass falling rapidly. Are we in for a storm?*

Chapter Twenty-Three
Into the Night

'Turlough… Turlough…'

The voice kept on at him, but he just wanted to sleep. Then cold water was dashed into his face. He sat up gasping, consciousness returning with a rush.

In the gloom he could just make out the pale blur of the Doctor's anxious face as he crouched over him. Far above him the tree tops were aflame with the last rays of the Sun, but down here amongst their roots it was already almost pitch-dark. Over the Doctor's shoulder he saw the shattered remains of the saucer. Beside it were two crumpled figures lying very still.

'We were shot down and crashed,' the Doctor said slowly and clearly, in answer to his unspoken question. 'If it hadn't been for the low gravity and some fortuitously placed branches to cushion our fall we'd all be dead. As it is I'm afraid the sailors didn't make it.'

'Lytalia?' Turlough said. 'Is she…'

'I don't know. I think she was thrown clear as we came down through the trees. I couldn't leave you unconscious to search for her.'

'Well, I'm awake now, so let's go.'

Turlough tried to spring to his feet, but instead he almost fell over. Even in the low gravity he felt desperately weak and dizzy. It was only the Doctor's arm that kept him upright. His head throbbed and he ached all over, but nothing seemed to be broken. Nothing that would stop him finding Lytalia.

They drew out torches from their packs and backtracked along the line of their descent, calling out Lytalia's name. The forest loomed about them, full of uneasy rustles and cries. Perhaps the nocturnal creatures were beginning to stir, Turlough thought. How long would it be before he and the Doctor attracted the attention of something dangerous?

A crashing of undergrowth and terrible snarling broke out somewhere ahead of them. The sound rose to a climax as the snarls became squeals of pain. For a moment Turlough froze in his tracks, unsure if they should run from whatever the conflict was. Then another possibility struck him and he sprang forward.

'Lytalia!'

The brushwood stirred and Lytalia staggered into the dancing circles of their torch beams. She was scratched and shaken but still clutched her spear, the blade of which was dripping red. From the bush behind her came the bubbling moans of some dying animal.

Turlough clasped her shoulders and peered anxiously into her face. 'Are you all right?'

'Yes,' she panted. 'The better for seeing you. I was torn free as we came down, but fell into a high branch. It has taken me a while to climb down. Then the night crawler attacked me... but that is nothing. Where is the saucer?'

'Completely wrecked, I'm afraid,' said the Doctor. 'We're on foot from now on.' He checked his compass and frowned. The needle was jerking from side to side, and every so often it span wildly. There was a flicker like distant lightning from high above, then seconds later a long-drawn-out rumble. 'Considerable magnetic interference. Probably due to the cannon's energy pulses.'

'What's it firing at?' Turlough wondered.

'The British ships, I presume,' the Doctor said. 'If that keeps up they may be forced to leave.' He took another small device from his pocket and checked it. 'At least the TARDIS tracer is still functioning. We can home in on that.'

'The TARDIS?' Lytalia asked.'

'Our spacecraft,' Turlough said. 'Don't worry, that'll still be there even if the others have gone.' He looked about him. 'But I don't fancy walking twenty miles through this lot at night.'

'It will be dangerous,' Lytalia admitted.

'Perhaps we can make a signal,' Turlough said. 'What about a fire?'

The Doctor shook his head. 'It's already too dark to see the smoke, so the light would have to be visible over the tree tops. It would take quite a blaze to do that and this is a fairly damp forest.'

'Could we climb a tree and use our torches?' Turlough thought of negotiating hundreds of vertical feet in darkness avoiding whatever else might be living in the branches. 'Stupid idea. Sorry. We haven't anything in the tool box we could use?'

'The British aren't equipped to receive any electromagnetic signals we might generate,' the Doctor pointed out. 'I'm afraid we're going to have to walk and take our chances.'

Turlough shrugged in resignation, then winced and swallowed hard. 'My ears just popped.'

The Doctor was staring at him. 'So did mine.' He looked at Lytalia. 'Does the air pressure here fall significantly at night?'

'I have never noticed any change,' she said. 'Why?'

The Doctor pulled out a multimeter of his pack and examined it closely. As he did so Turlough realised the sounds of the forest around them had changed slightly. Instead of settling into some sort of rhythm they were growing louder and more disturbed.

'The beasts know something is wrong,' Lytalia said, taking a fresh grip on her spear.

The Doctor looked up from the meter. 'The air pressure is falling steadily,' he announced. 'The rate looks too constant for it to be a natural fluctuation.'

'You mean the pressure curtain over the crater has failed?' Turlough asked.

'It's possible the continuous firing of the plasma cannon has drained too much power,' the Doctor said. 'In which case there should be some automatic cut-out to prevent it going too far. Or else…'

'What?'

'If the automatic systems in the citadel have received no answer to the alert they sent out, they may be programmed to shut everything down to hide the evidence.' He looked at Lytalia. 'Perhaps to prevent your people, or exiles like you who might have been marooned here, from revealing who was responsible for building this place.'

'By killing every living thing in the crater?' Lytalia said.

'Yes.'

'How long will it take?' Turlough asked.

The Doctor frowned in thought. 'Some air will pool in the bottom of the crater and traces might remain through the lunar night, but it won't be breathable. And with the air thinning so quickly the temperature's going to fall dramatically. I'd say we can remain active for eight or ten hours more at most.'

They had perhaps twenty miles of forest to traverse, a cliff to climb, then another hour's walk to reach the TARDIS. Over level ground in good conditions that was perfectly achievable in the time. But Turlough knew how long the outward journey had taken them, and now they would be fighting increasing cold and thinning air. It was just not possible.

It was at that moment of despairing silence that they heard the peculiar sound murmuring through the trees, far deeper and more sustained than any of the animal cries.

'That was no beast I have ever heard,' Lytalia said.

'No, it was something mechanical,' the Doctor said. 'Come on!'

They plunged through the trees, ignoring the small creatures that flapped and hopped and scuttled past them as the panic spread. Turlough's ears popped again but he ignored the twinge of pain. They heard the sound a second time, but now it was distinctly louder.

The forest opened before them, revealing a narrow glade like a chasm between the giant trees, lit by the faint twilight from high above. The shadowy forms of larger beasts were scattering across it, grunting and hissing in confusion as they tried to escape the invisible doom that lay upon them. In their midst was the metal tower of the *Draco*, pale yellow light shining from its ports.

'It's about time we had a little luck,' Turlough said, feeling his heart lift.

As they watched, the humming drone came again and the ship rocked on its buckled supporting legs. They could almost believe the craft was straining to break free of the Moon's hold to return to its natural element. One leg, then two, lifted clear of the ground then the humming faded and it settled back again.

'They seem to be having some mechanical trouble,' the Doctor said. 'I think we might be able to hitch a lift if we offer to help with the repairs.'

They bounded across the mossy ground to the base of the ship. Turlough was about to make another leap towards the lower hatch when the Doctor held him back and shone his torch about them. The ground was littered with discarded items: twisted metal plates, acceleration chairs, gas bottles, wooden crates, a couple of modified diving suits, various personal effects – and a body dressed in naval uniform.

The man was already stiff and cold. The bloody hole and powder burns on his chest suggested he'd been shot at close range.

'There is another over here,' Lytalia said.

The second man looked as though he'd been shot in the back, which made him a no more pleasant sight.

'Are there any more, I wonder?' the Doctor said in a flat voice. 'Or have the forest creatures already taken them away?'

Turlough looked up at the ship. 'What's been going on in there?'

'We can only guess,' the Doctor said. 'But we have no choice. We have to get inside and they must be convinced to let us in. Say nothing about finding the bodies. They may think we missed them in the gloom.'

He found a twisted length of metal spar, reached up and began banging on the hatch. It was a minute before the light within came on and a face appeared at the thick glass portal. The Doctor waved at it.

'Let us in and we can help you!' he shouted. 'We've got tools. We can fix your engines.'

The face goggled at them and then vanished. A couple of minutes later a different face appeared, only to be pushed aside by a third. They heard the faint sounds of an argument from within, and then there was a clank of bolts and the hatch slowly dropped open. A figure holding a rifle was silhouetted in the electric light of the airlock.

'Who the hell are you?' he demanded.

'I'm the Doctor, this is Turlough and this is Miss Lytalia. We are what you might call private spacefarers. We nearly met when we came back to your base with Mr Sinclair's rescue party, but the appearance of that flying saucer interrupted the introductions. We saw you shot down, by the way. You were obviously very fortunate to survive.'

There were low words from someone out of their line of sight.

'The girl with you,' the man with the rifle said, 'what's wrong with her ears?'

'Actually she's not human, she's a Phiadoran, one of the local inhabitants. They've been very helpful to us. Mr Haliwell's offered to take them back to Earth.'

More soft words.

'Haliwell's safe?' their inquisitor asked.

'Yes,' the Doctor said loudly. 'Both he and Miss Boyes-Dennison should be back with the other ships by now. Unfortunately we got separated from the main party and ended up here. Still, it's lucky for you because I happen to be familiar with impeller drives. Would you like me to check yours over? It sounded a little rough. I suggest you decide quickly because it's going to get rather cold and airless out here very shortly. I hope your hull is still sound. Can we come in now?'

Another exchange with the unseen voice, then: 'All right. Come aboard.'

They stepped up the ramp and into the airlock compartment. Three men were waiting for them, holding their rifles close to their chests and looking anything but friendly. They saw the owner of the unseen voice for the first time. He was not a big man and like the other two was haggard and unshaven, and smelt slightly of alcohol. But he held himself more erect with a certain air of self-importance. His eyes, though puffy and darkly circled, were unnaturally bright. As the hatch was slowly cranked closed the Doctor beamed at him in his most innocently disarming manner.

'I'm Stanton,' the man said sharply. 'I'm in charge.'

'I thought this ship was commanded by Captain Green,' the Doctor said gently.

'He's dead,' Stanton said. 'The officers are all dead. The beasts got them, right? I'm in charge because I can fly her, see?'

'I see,' the Doctor said easily. 'Most unfortunate. Well, perhaps you'd better lead us to the engine room and we can get on with the repairs.'

Stanton was still looking at them with the deepest suspicion. Lytalia spoke up.

'Yes, let us help you. You have done so much for my people already by releasing us from our exile.' And she smiled warmly.

That seemed to unbend the men a little and they grinned back foolishly, eyeing her up and down with evident approval as though seeing her properly for the first time.

'Well, I'm sure you'll be welcome there,' Stanton allowed. 'We need somebody who knows about the engines. But maybe the lady would rather go up to the mess where it's warmer.'

'Where she can tell you what a fine hunter she is,' Turlough said quickly. 'See the fresh blood on her spear? Do you want to know how big the thing was that she just killed out there? No, right, let's all get to work.'

They climbed up the companion ladders through the cargo deck to the engine room. There were four men inside. Two held rifles and were leaning against stanchions. The other two, one wearing civilian dress, were bent over the partly disassembled impeller. As they entered the pair looked up with frightened eyes.

Stanton explained who they were in a few terse sentences, glanced lingeringly at Lytalia once again, then left the room.

While Turlough and Lytalia made a show of unpacking the tools the Doctor squatted down by the two workers.

'Now, what seems to be the problem?' he asked genially.

The civilian electrical specialist licked his lips, glanced fearfully at their guards, then said: 'Well... We seem to have the power, but we can't maintain output through the lifting coils...'

The man's voice trembled as he spoke. His manner alone told the story of what had happened aboard the *Draco*. They were the

195

last survivors of some mutiny in which Stanton had won the upper hand. They were only spared because they knew about the engines.

Turlough glanced at Lytalia and saw the same grim understanding in her face. They were safe only as long as they were useful to Stanton and his followers. If they couldn't fix the drive they'd all die anyway. And if they did repair it, he still wouldn't give tuppence for their chances.

Chapter Twenty-Four
The Dying Crater

Kamelion stepped cautiously through the outer door of the TARDIS. Frozen moss crunched under his metal feet. His circuits registered the drop in temperature and adjusted his pseudometabolic rate to compensate, ensuring his systems were functioning at optimum efficiency. The thinning air bothered him not at all.

The energy field that had disrupted his circuits when they landed on the Moon had gone, but in its place he had a new concern. Where were the Doctor and Turlough, and what was happening to the crater?

He turned to look at the mountains that rose over the highland plateau and formed the western rim of the crater. A seething sparkling cloud seemed to be hanging over them as air and water-vapour boiled away into space in the last rays of the Sun. Above him the stars were shining ever harder and colder. Already he doubted whether an unprotected human could have stood beside him and survived more than a few minutes.

A plasma bolt streaked from the citadel across the forest and struck some target a few miles to the north of his position. He deduced it was aimed at the landing site of the British expedition. That was the most likely place for the Doctor and Turlough to be sheltering. Should he cross to the British camp to find out?

But that would take time. If they were there then they were relatively safe and he could wait for them to return to the TARDIS by their own means. If they were elsewhere he had to find out as soon as possible. Perhaps, as there were so few human-like minds within the crater, he could divine their location.

He increased the sensitivity of his empathic circuits, searching for the familiar mental patterns of the Doctor and Turlough. The Doctor's powerful mind alone should be detectable at a considerable range, since it would stand out clearly against the lesser mental activity of the mass of animal life in the crater –

Kamelion reeled in shock as an appalling cacophony thundered through his circuits.

The crater was screaming its death at him!

A million creatures were fighting for air even as the life was being frozen out them. Their confused cries of mental anguish merged into one all-encompassing shout of pain and fear that submerged all else.

His empathic circuits overloaded and cut out. Kamelion staggered back into the TARDIS and shut its insulating doors against the wails of the dying.

Haliwell checked the latest barometer and temperature readings and shook his head sadly. The external pressure was now the equivalent of only eight inches of mercury and still falling, while the temperature was minus forty-three degrees Fahrenheit. He had already had to order the ship's heaters to be put on to prevent the chill penetrating the hull. Without a moderating atmosphere to contain it or sunlight to replenish it, the living heat of the crater was radiating away into the void of outer space. Under such conditions there could be no hope of survival for any of the macabre, incredible creatures in the crater – or for the Doctor and his companions.

Now Haliwell's duty was to ensure there were no more casualties.

'Send to *Lynx*,' he said to the signaller. 'Prepare to launch on my command. Rendezvous in lunar orbit for recharging.'

The *Cygnus* rocked and a flash of bright light shone in through the ports. The fireballs had methodically destroyed the screen of trees. In minutes the ships would be directly exposed to the citadel's gun.

'All hands to launch positions,' he ordered, settling back in his chair and fastening the straps. 'Prepare for maximum acceleration. Send to *Lynx*: Launch immediately after next shot from citadel.'

The last anxious seconds ticked away. Haliwell chewed his lip. As long as the citadel's cannon could not reload, or whatever it did, in the time it took them to get clear…

There was a blaze of light through the ports and the thump of a concussion wave, enough to shake them even through the thinning air.

'Now!' he said.

Power surged into the driving coils and Haliwell was pressed back into the padding of his chair.

A single plasma bolt seared into the sky after them, only to melt into a cloud of glowing mist as they sped away beyond its range.

The surviving ships of the Imperial British Space Fleet were on their way home.

Chapter Twenty-Five
Deadweight

The Doctor sat back on his heels and wiped his grimy hands on a piece of engine-room rag.

'I think that's the best we can do,' he said to the others.

For hours they had slaved over the impeller. Pieces that had been destroyed in the blast that had crippled the ship had been painstakingly refashioned with help from the TARDIS's tool box. Other damaged elements he had bypassed with an ingenious series of haywire circuits and improvised parts. Turlough felt weary and he had only helped the Doctor. The electrician and his assistant, Sumpter and Draycott, looked ready to collapse. Only Lytalia still seemed alert and fresh, snatching quick glances at their guards with a hunter's eye.

The Doctor attracted the men's attention.

'You'd better let Mr Stanton know we're ready to test the impeller. He might like to watch this.'

Stanton was with them in a minute. The Doctor was standing by the main power switches and rheostat panel.

'You'd better send one of your men down to the lower hatch to check we clear the ground.'

'Pat, get down there,' Stanton told one of the guards.

The Doctor threw the switches and turned the heavy dial. The impeller tubes glowed and a low humming began, rapidly rising in pitch until it reverberated through the hull and then passed their range of hearing. They felt the ship sway, then lift a few feet from the ground.

A voice from below shouted: 'We're clear – five feet and more!'

The Doctor cut the power and they settled back to Earth.

'You have about 85 per cent of maximum thrust,' he told Stanton. 'That's the best we can do. With the spare mass you've discarded already, and the reduced ship's complement, that should be plenty for lunar takeoff and enough to land back on Earth if you're careful.'

'Oh, I'll be careful,' Stanton said. 'So you're done then.'

'Not quite. You'd better work the bridge controls to check the power linkages to the impeller. They may still need adjusting. It wouldn't do to lose control halfway up, would it?'

'I never lose control of anything!' Stanton snapped back. 'I got us down here in one piece, didn't I? Who else could have done that? That lemon-sucker Green never knew how lucky he was to have a helmsman like me. He had it coming...'

Stanton faltered, as though frightened that he'd said too much.

'I'm sure you did your job most skilfully,' the Doctor said gently. 'Now you'd better check the bridge controls.'

Stanton blinked, then nodded and went out. Turlough watched him go, unsure how close the man was to a complete breakdown.

'Help me get these cover plates back on, everybody,' the Doctor said briskly. As they bolted the panels into place he lowered his voice so that their remaining guard would not hear him. 'Stanton will be back down here in a couple of minutes and then we'll know what he plans. Are you willing to fight if he intends to dispose of us?' he asked Sumpter and Draycott.

The men nodded. Sumpter whispered: 'He's mad. He shot Maitland and the others who tried to stand up to him. I think they're holding the special navigator up on the bridge. They still need him to –'

'Tell us later,' the Doctor interjected. 'For now we've got to get to the bridge ourselves to fly the ship. Turlough and Lytalia, that's your objective. The controls should be straightforward enough. Lock the crew out with the internal doors – they're pretty solid. We can do the same down here to make sure they don't cut off the power. We only have to hold out for a few minutes. Land close by the TARDIS and Kamelion can bring spacesuits across for us.'

'We'll need a diversion to get past the crew,' Turlough said.

'I have one planned,' the Doctor said. 'Listen...'

A minute later Stanton returned. He had his other two followers with him. All were armed. The Doctor, standing once again beside the main switch panel, beamed at them.

'Well, the linkages seemed to work perfectly so I think we can say the ship is functional once again,' he said. 'Now if you'd be so kind as to drop us off by our ship. It's not far from where you first landed. You've got enough battery reserve to make the diversion and still reach a recharging orbit. We can take Mr Sumpter and Mr Draycott with us if you'd like. They seem to want a change of scene.'

'We're not risking any side trips with that cannon out there, not after what it did to us last time,' Stanton said. 'When we leave we're going straight up at top speed.'

'Oh dear,' said the Doctor reasonably. 'Well, I suppose we can go back to Earth with you, then arrange for another ship to bring us back to collect our craft when it's safer.'

'And have them two tell what happened here?' Stanton sneered. 'Do you think we're stupid? We're not going back to the glen. I can fly us anywhere... somewhere they'll be very interested in this ship. Somewhere they'll appreciate what I can do. An astral pilot, that's me!'

Despite himself Draycott said: 'Traitor! You swore an oath to Queen and country –'

'What has the bleedin' country ever given me or mine?' Stanton spat back. 'Father died down the pits, sisters working for a pittance in the mills. What chance have we ever got of bettering ourselves? I have this special talent, but the brass'll never own up to it. Never let the likes of me on the quarterdeck. Well, damn their eyes, I say!' His own eyes blazed with all the resentment that had accumulated within him over the years and which had now found release. 'We're going where I say – and we're going without you!'

The rifles had lifted barely two inches when the Doctor clasped a heavy switch on the panel and threw it open. Every light in the ship went out.

'Shoot blind in here and you'll destroy the impeller for good!' the Doctor shouted in the darkness.

Turlough and Lytalia had lined themselves up with the engine-room hatchway and as the lights went out they threw themselves forward. A flailing arm caught Turlough's shoulder but he twisted free and plunged on. They scrambled through the hatchway and grabbed for the handrail of the companionway ladders, then bounded up them.

All they had to do was follow the ladders up to the top of the ship before anybody realised what they were doing. Turlough pulled his pocket torch out, ready to use it when they reached the bridge. They heard an electric crackle and shriek of pain from below them and he grinned. Under cover of their work the Doctor had loosened one of the secondary power cables and now, as planned, was using it to keep the mutineers at bay.

They were bounding up the next flight when Turlough realised he could see about him. It was as though the stairs and bulkheads had been splashed and streaked haphazardly with faintly luminous paint. What the cause was he had no idea.

They had reached the cabin deck when there came a cry from Lytalia, climbing just a few steps ahead of him, mingled with a man's shout of alarm and a sudden scuffle of feet. In the faint illumination Turlough made her out struggling with a larger figure. Her spear clattered down the metal steps together with a heavier object that could only be a rifle. There was another crewman up here! They had hoped they would all be on the lower decks. Turlough lunged forward, wrapped his arms around the man's body and hauled, pulling him away from Lytalia and at the same time ramming his knee into the small of his back.

'Keep going!' he gasped, and Lytalia scrambled on upwards.

His opponent kicked out, driving them both back into the handrail, which caught Turlough painfully in the ribs. The man broke free of his grasp and turned to strike him. Turlough kicked out desperately, his heel thudding into the crewman's stomach. With a cry of pain the man lost his balance and began to fall. His fingers closed around Turlough's ankle and jerked him off his feet. Together they bounced down the companionway in a strange slow-motion tumble. They hit the deck and Turlough's hand closed on the barrel of the fallen rifle. Before the other could get to his feet he swung it like a club. It struck the man on the side of the head with a sickening crack and he slumped back limply against the bulkhead.

Still clasping the rifle, Turlough scrambled to his feet, wheezing as he tried to recover the breath his fall had knocked out of him. Even as he hung on to the rail he heard half a dozen shots from the engine room, a man moaning in pain and a cry of triumph.

Then the lights came back on.

Turlough shrank back against the stairs. It was all going wrong!

'Get rid of them!' he heard Stanton shouting. 'Then find the other two.'

There was the shuffle and scrape of bodies being moved and boots descending the ladders to the lower deck. The airlock! They were going to throw them out of the airlock into the freezing and almost airless night.

Turlough never knew if it was blind panic at the thought of losing the Doctor or some twisted notion of living up to his fragile new image, but he found himself leaping down the stairs waving the rifle. He hit the deck above the engine room, saw a group of figures through the open stair treads and fired a wild shot.

Before he could force the unfamiliar bolt mechanism to lodge another cartridge in the chamber, a volley of shots from below ricocheted off the ironwork and sent him scurrying back the way he had come. He crouched trembling on an upper deck, cursing himself for being a fool and a coward.

He heard the clank of hatch bolts being sealed, the rattle of a lever, a bang and rush of air… and then silence. He covered his mouth to stifle a despairing moan of anguish, shaking his head in disbelief.

'Right,' he heard Stanton's faint voice. 'Get up there after them… and cut the impeller power before they try to lift off.'

With a huge effort Turlough tore his thoughts away from the Doctor. He must think of himself and Lytalia now. If they cut the power to the engines they would never get away. They would be hunted down to share the same fate as the Doctor. He had to get back to Lytalia and warn her. He started up the stairs. Perhaps if they could barricade themselves in and threaten to damage the controls…

There was a terrible shriek of pain and fear from above. For a moment his heart leapt. But it was a man's voice, not Lytalia's. Then came a series of bangs and thuds as though a struggle had broken out.

'Lytalia!' he yelled, and started forward again.

The engine hum reverberated through the ship and rose to a shrill peak. The *Draco* stirred, then lifted from the surface of the Moon – not gradually, but with the full force of the remaining engine output.

An overhanging branch shattered as the craft soared upwards, gouging the hull from stem to stern and knocking the ship a few degrees off the perpendicular. Then the *Draco* was clear of the forest canopy and driving into space before the plasma cannon in the citadel could be brought to bear upon it.

Inside the ship, instinct made Turlough drop flat a second before five gravities of acceleration did it for him, pinning him to the deck as his body weight rose to thirty times what he had become used to over the past few days. And there he lay absolutely helpless, fighting to fill his lungs with air against the pressure that seemed about to crush his chest at any moment. Groans and choked curses from below told him that Stanton's men had been similarly immobilised.

The batteries could not sustain the frantic acceleration for long. It was less than a minute before Turlough felt the pressure easing even as the lights began to flicker and cut out. Before it had reduced to one gravity he had levered himself to his feet and begun hauling himself up the stairs. He had to reach the bridge ahead of Stanton's men.

He scrambled up the last flight and threw himself into the bridge, now lit only by electricity-starved carbon arcs that sparked behind their frosted shades. He meant to slam and lock the hatch behind him, but the sight that met his eyes drove all thought of his pursuers from his mind.

In stark contrast to the immaculately polished wood, brass and copperwork of the bridge fittings, the body of the civilian astral navigator lay horribly contorted in his chair. Blood from the wound in his head where a hole had been punched through his skull was dripping slowly on to the deck. His rigid hands were still locked about the harness of ropes knotted at the back of his chair, no doubt the means by which Stanton kept him at his post, as though in his last seconds of life he was trying to tear them loose. Turlough's gaze was dragged reluctantly back to the ruin of the man's head. There was something horribly familiar about the wound –

He heard a low moan and spun round.

Lytalia was huddled in the space between two lockers.

The curve of her naked back was facing him, the light clothing torn from it. Scored across it from shoulder to hip were three parallel scratches oozing blood.

Turlough ran across and knelt by her, taking her shoulders gently. 'It's all right, it's me… what happened?'

She turned to him, still huddled and shivering. There were more triple scratches down her front as well. Her coppery skin was unnaturally pale and her eyes were wide with horror, the first time he had seen her show real fear since he had saved her on the cliff.

'I fell against the controls when it attacked… the sudden acceleration confused it… but it's still in the ship!'

The sound of an indrawn breath made Turlough spin round, his rifle pointing towards the hatchway. Stanton and his cronies were frozen in a strange tableau, poised halfway into the bridge, momentarily petrified by the sight of the dead navigator. Then the spell was broken and they turned their guns back on Turlough and Lytalia.

'You can shoot if you like, but I'll take at least one of you with me,' Turlough said. 'Now who's volunteering to go first?'

It was a line from some B-movie he'd seen, art supplementing a momentary deficiency of imagination. But in the grip of a cold fury, he realised that he meant the words quite literally. If he was going to die then it wouldn't be alone.

The mutineers hesitated, the conviction in Turlough's voice penetrating even Stanton's manic obsession. Lytalia broke the silence.

'It might be quicker and kinder if we did all kill ourselves,' she said. 'For we are all going to die anyway.'

That flat statement held their attention. Lytalia climbed slowly and stiffly to her feet as though suddenly weary almost beyond endurance, exposing fresh wounds for all to see. A couple of the rifles shifted to follow her. They could have gunned her down at any moment but curiosity, and the first stirring of fear, held them back. Turlough held his rifle steady in turn, locked into the strange standoff, waiting for the balance to tip one way or the other.

'Forest creatures were in this ship,' Lytalia said. 'I know because I saw the secretions of one of them glowing on the walls when the lights were turned off.'

Stanton's eyes darted about wildly as if suspecting some sort of trap but found none. 'So what?' he rasped. 'They got in, they were driven out or killed.'

Lytalia shook her head sadly, hopelessly. 'No. At least one remained. It hid somewhere dark. They like the dark. When the lights went out it made its first move.' She pointed to the body in the chair. 'It is satiated for the moment, which is perhaps why it spared me. But it'll be back. They always come back. It is the most cunning and ruthless predator in the forest, and will not stop until we are all dead. It is a Vrall!'

Chapter Twenty-Six
Cold

Amongst the piles of jettisoned items that marked the spot where the *Draco* had stood, something stirred. One of the three figures that had been tumbled out of the airlock minutes earlier rolled on to his hands and knees. Frost was already forming on his hair, the intense cold congealing the blood that had flowed from the bullet graze across his temple. He stood up with painful slowness and took one lurching step forward, then another, moving like some ancient clockwork toy. His lips were clamped shut against the air that would have frozen his lungs. He was sustained only by his Time Lord metabolism, bioengineered and enhanced over a thousand generations, and his determination not to die. Regeneration here would not be an option.

The Doctor's thoughts spun in confusion from the cold and the shock of his injury.

Another five steps and he would reach his goal, just visible in the starlight... Poor Sumpter and Draycott. Nothing he could do for them now. Their bid for freedom hadn't lasted long... Just four more steps... Betrayed by the inexplicable presence of some luminous substance splashed over every surface in the engine room and only visible when the lights had gone out... Three more steps... No need to breathe, he told himself... plenty of air left in his tissues... Two more steps... Stanton's men had been able to see to use their guns, instead of fumbling futilely for the emergency lanterns that he'd carefully moved during the repair work... One more step... Always expect the unexpected... but wasn't that a contradiction in terms?

He slumped over one of the piles of discarded items, cold-numbed hands fumbling for what he wanted. With the last of his strength he dropped the brass dome of the modified diving helmet over his head and twisted open the valve on its air cylinder. Air hissed into the helmet, sluggishly at first and icy cold, but warming quickly. An insulated cover with an electric coil buried in it was wrapped about the cylinder. An automatic heater, no doubt the idea of Professor Boyes-Dennison. Very clever.

The air was rushing out of the unsealed collar of the helmet of course, but he could gain some sustenance from it, taking in great mouthfuls and grunting to force it into his lungs. Gradually his head began to clear.

It took him ten minutes to put on the rest of the cumbersome suit and seal it properly. Within its insulated layers he began to feel the warmth returning to his limbs. The suit was a masterpiece of Victorian engineering and ingenuity, but probably would not have kept a human functioning for more than half an hour in a hard vacuum under intense heat or cold. The Doctor was hoping he could survive in it for rather longer than that. He had no choice.

He found a discarded lantern, a heavy self-contained carbon arc unit that must have been specially made for the voyage, and turned it on. By its harsh light he used a buckled hull plate and a length of cable to make a crude sledge. On this he piled spare oxygen cylinders and batteries and lashed them firmly into place.

He took one last look around the dismal remains, then glanced up at the stars.

He did not know what had happened to Turlough and Lytalia, but the fact that they hadn't been thrown out with him gave him some cause for hope. The abrupt manner of the *Draco*'s departure suggested Stanton was not in complete control. Had that been their doing? Could they reach the TARDIS and convince Stanton he had nothing to gain by preventing them from leaving the *Draco* unharmed? At least there they would be safe, for years if necessary. But if the sudden launch had been unplanned and unguided, then the ship might be heading anywhere in space. He would have to track it down as soon as possible.

He checked the TARDIS tracer to orientate himself, took up the reins of the sledge and set off through the frozen forest.

Chapter Twenty-Seven
Into the Unknown

'A truce,' Turlough said. 'We have to work together to fight this Vrall, or else we're all dead.'

He hated making the offer to the mutineers. The idea of forming an alliance with the men who, only minutes earlier, had killed the Doctor sickened and revolted him. But now they all faced a common enemy and there was no other choice if he, and Lytalia, wanted to survive. So he had to smother his feelings. Together they might all stand a chance, divided they were finished.

The standoff continued on the dimly lit bridge, he and Lytalia on one side, Stanton's men on the other, the setting made macabre by the presence of the dead navigator. One of his hands had drifted free of the ropes and was half-raised as though mutely indicating that he wanted to interrupt their conversation. The drive had cut out as the main batteries drained, leaving them in free fall, clinging to straps and handholds, but still holding their rifles at the ready. In the back of his mind Turlough considered the effect weightlessness would have if they started firing. The recoil of the weapons would knock them flying unless they were properly braced. Did the others realise that? It only needed one wild shot through a porthole and it would be the end for all of them.

Stanton spoke up. Turlough thought he had lost the impetus of anger and resentment that he apparently needed to kill in cold blood, and the other mutineers seemed to follow his lead.

'How do we know this Vrall thing is as dangerous as she says? Killing a man tied to his chair doesn't take much. Maybe we can handle it ourselves. Maybe we don't need you.'

'You need all the help you can get,' Turlough assured him. 'I've seen that sort of head injury down in the forest. Granby was like that when we found him. You must have heard he'd gone missing. That was why Sinclair took out a relief party. Well, the Vrall had taken Granby right in front of his group. They were all armed but it happened so fast nobody could stop it. Listen to Lytalia. The Vrall are the only things her people are really frightened of, and they've lived in the crater thirty years so they should know.'

Lytalia was huddled beside Turlough with his jacket draped over her shoulders and wrapped around her as if she was cold. Her manner was listless, as though she was resigned to her fate. She spoke up again.

'Did you see the Vrall that did this?' she asked simply. 'Probably you passed it as you ascended and did not even notice. They know how to conceal themselves and take their prey one by one. That is how it will hunt us.'

The mutineers stirred uneasily.

'This ship's not so big,' Stanton said. 'We'll go though it cabin by cabin. We'll find it.'

'You may not even see it,' Lytalia explained wearily. 'The Vrall are not like any creatures you have ever encountered before.'

Stanton's eyes narrowed. 'What d'you mean not see them?'

'They are not large creatures, perhaps half a man's weight, though they are shaped quite like you. Their skins are normally dark to blend with shadows, but they can alter the colour and texture at will to merge with most objects. Their bodies bend and flex like rubber when they wish them to, so they can flatten themselves to no more than a hand's thickness. They could be resting against a deck or bulkhead and you would not notice them unless you knew they were there, or detected them by touch or a chance shadow. They can also combine together to form a larger organism of greater strength.'

'So this thing'll be hard to spot. We'll look real close.'

'And then what? I doubt if your simple weapons will do more than irritate it. Vrall do not bleed, and any cuts or punctures quickly heal over. It will not die unless you can completely dismember it. But you will not get the chance to land more than a single blow because it will move too fast for you.'

'Are you saying we can't kill it?' Stanton said, angrily. 'Something must work.'

'A large enough explosion. An all-enveloping fire.'

'We'll destroy the ship if we try that!'

'Then we're dead,' Lytalia said simply.

Stanton's men were looking frightened. There was something very compelling about Lytalia's frank admission. Turlough felt a sense of despair creeping over him as well, but with an effort shook it off.

'No!' he said firmly. 'We're not going to give up without a fight.' He looked at Stanton. 'Well, do we do the Vrall's job for it or work at this together?'

Stanton said slowly: 'If we get out of this, you don't say a word about what happened here, ever. In return we set you and the girl down somewhere safe. Agreed?'

Retribution wouldn't bring the Doctor or the rest back. 'Agreed,' Turlough said.

'Your oath on it?'

'My oath on it.'

Stanton took out a jackknife and ran the tip of the blade across the palm of his right hand so that a line of blood appeared, then handed the weapon to Turlough. Turlough took a deep breath and matched the gesture, then clasped Stanton's hand so that the blood mingled. Gazing into the man's unnaturally bright eyes he wondered if the promise would hold. Oddly, he thought it might. None of Stanton's despised officers would have sealed the bargain with such a gesture.

'All right,' said Stanton, unclasping hands and turning to his followers. 'First thing, we've got to open the sun panels and recharge the batteries. That'll also give us more light and get the air machine going.' He looked at Lytalia. 'They keep away from light, right?'

'They prefer shadows,' she said. 'They are easier to hide in.'

'Then we have to find out where we're headed and figure some sort of course back to Earth.' He glanced at the dead navigator. 'That was meant to be his job.'

'I can probably work out our rough course and speed if I can use his charts and instruments,' Turlough said.

'I don't see him objecting,' said Stanton. 'Good with the figuring, are you?'

'Most of it's only basic trigonometry,' Turlough said. 'It'll take a while but I don't think there's any danger of us falling back to the Moon. I'm pretty sure we passed escape velocity.'

'Well, you just figure away,' Stanton said, 'and you put us on course for Earth. But once we're back amongst the clouds again, it'll be me who lands us, because I'm the helmsman and I really fly this ship and don't you forget it.'

'I won't,' Turlough promised.

'Right. You stay here with the girl and do your trigo-nometry. We'll get things started below, watching our backs as we go. Once we've got power and some weight under us, then we'll take care of this Vrall.'

'It has just fed,' Lytalia said. 'For a while it will be less ready to attack if undisturbed. But do not take too long.'

'We're not going to hang about, lady. You'd better secure the hatch after us. But be ready to open up real quick when we call. Remember, we can always shut the impeller down from below.'

'We've made a bargain,' Turlough said sharply. 'You keep your part and I'll keep mine.' He pointed to the dead navigator. 'And you can take that out of here with you.'

Stanton led his men through the hatchway, towing the corpse after them, and they pulled themselves down the stairwell towards the dim lower decks. The helmsman didn't lack courage, Turlough had to admit, as he closed the hatch.

Suddenly he felt the beginnings of a nervous reaction setting in. If it hadn't been for the free fall he'd have had to sit down. He looked at Lytalia and once again she seemed to divine his thoughts.

'You did what you had to do,' she said. 'You must continue on bravely, even while mourning for your friend.'

'There was nobody like the Doctor,' he admitted as he began to examine the lockers. 'I can't really believe he's... not coming back.' He found the charts and assorted navigation instruments. There was also a beautifully made chronometer mounted in a padded case.

'You started to tell me about him before the attack on the

citadel,' Lytalia said. 'He sounded… an unusual man.'

Turlough found himself chuckling dryly – better laughter than tears. 'He wasn't a man, at least he wasn't human.'

'I do not understand.'

'I suppose it doesn't matter now, but you'd better not let Stanton find out or it might send him over the edge. We were never part of the British expedition, we just joined up with them before we met you. The Doctor was an alien and his ship, the TARDIS, can travel through time as well as space. I'm from about a hundred years in the future myself.' He looked at her startled expression and smiled. 'I know, it takes a bit of getting used to. Think about it while I get these readings.'

He armed himself with the appropriate instruments and went up to the navigation port opposite the heliograph sender on the half deck above. There was no sign of the Earth which would be hidden behind the narrow crescent Moon that filled most of the field below them. He could just make out the western rim of Tsiolkovskii, but the rest of the crater had already slipped across the terminator into darkness. And in the darkness was the Doctor… He shook himself and went to work. He determined the Moon's angular diameter, noted what features lay at the edge of the illuminated limb and checked the time. If he repeated the measurements an hour later he would have some idea of their speed and any lateral displacement of their course.

There were clanks from below. Looking out, he saw the solar panels were being cranked out into position one by one then adjusted to present the maximum surface area to the Sun. Stanton and his men were getting on with their job. They'd have more light soon, though he suspected their course might take them through the Moon's shadow which would delay the recharging. Still, in a few hours they would be able to start thinking about getting back on course – assuming the Vrall hadn't got them first.

He returned to Lytalia who was looking at him with bright eyes full of interest.

'Tell me more of your ship, this TARDIS,' she asked.

Turlough sat down as well as he could in free fall. 'Well, it can travel pretty well anywhere in time and space in a few minutes by dematerialising and passing through the higher dimensions. It's larger inside than out because the space inside it is folded in on itself. On the outside it looks just like a blue police box – that's an artefact from the next century. And then it…' He faltered. 'Kamelion! I'd forgotten all about him.'

'Who is Kamelion?'

'An android. He's travelling with us. He was waiting for us in the TARDIS.' He felt an unexpected pang of concern. 'He must be getting worried by now.'

'This Kamelion, can he operate the TARDIS?'

Turlough scratched his head. 'He did say he talked to it, one machine to another, sort of thing. Maybe. I've never really thought. But he'd look for the Doctor first. He should be able to leave the ship now.' He scowled. 'But how long would he take to search the whole crater? No, I don't think there's much chance of him finding us. Stupid idea.'

Lytalia brushed her fingers through his hair. 'It is not stupid. Hearing of your wonderful TARDIS gives me hope. I wish I could see it for myself.'

He clasped her hand. 'You will soon, I promise. I don't want to be stuck in this century for ever. If we can get back to Earth safely, somehow we'll convince the British authorities they should send another ship to the Moon and we'll be on it. The TARDIS will still be there.'

'I only wish my people knew this,' Lytalia said. 'We were resigned to staying on your world when we realised how primitive these ships were. But if we could travel anywhere…'

The bridge lights began to grow brighter and there was a soft hiss as air began to flow through the ventilation tubes.

'We're getting some power back at last,' Turlough said.

The bridge already looked more cheerful, or at least there were fewer shadows. 'Do you want something to eat or drink? Clean yourself up, maybe?'

Lytalia snuggled down in his coat. 'No, I just wish to rest. If you are here I feel safe.'

'OK, you do that.'

A few minutes later footsteps clanked on the ladder and Turlough opened the hatch to let Stanton's men in. They brought bread and cheese and closed beakers of water. Also, to Turlough's surprise, his backpack.

'It was floating about in the engine room getting in the way,' Stanton said. 'We left your friend's fancy tools down there. Might need them again.'

Turlough's lips pinched at the casual thoughtlessness of the remark, but he forced himself to say only, 'How long will the recharging take?'

'We've only got three mirrors left. Best part of a day to fully recharge, but in a few hours we can put on some low thrust. You worked out our course yet?'

'I've taken one set of readings. After I do the next in about forty-five minutes I should be able to make a first approximation. I suppose you didn't see anything of the Vrall?'

Stanton gave him a contemptuous look. 'If we had, you'd know about it.'

The men settled down to eat. Turlough noticed a few admiring glances at Lytalia's legs which extended gracefully from underneath the cover of his jacket. He pointedly seated himself beside her, placing his rifle in easy reach, and ate and drank. When he had finished, and after some internal debate, he took Haliwell's diary from his pack.

Very carefully, so as not to get caught again, he flipped through the pages until he came to the next entry. He read about the takeoff of the *Cygnus* and *Lynx* when the fire from the citadel got too close. Well, that was about what they'd expected. It was nice to know they'd waited until the last minute. He read on:

We made two orbits about the Moon while we recharged our batteries. Though we passed over the crater both times and observed it as well as our instruments allowed, there was no sign of our lost comrades. The floor of the crater was lost in shadow and only the central peak was illuminated by the last rays of the Sun, and that was fast diminishing. I think we could have seen the flash of the citadel's cannon from this altitude had it been still active, but even that seemed to have fallen silent, from which I assume there are no more 'enemy' targets to draw its fire.

I think we may conclude that all life in that place has been extinguished. When the Sun next touches it any remaining frozen air and water will surely be boiled away into space, leaving only the desiccated remains of that great forest and its denizens. Perhaps one day, when the mechanisms that drive that deadly cannon have failed, it may be safe for us to return and see if we can learn more about the builders of the citadel. Will it become in future years an attraction for historians and wealthy tourists, as are the great works of the ancient world on Earth? Will they speculate on the minds that shaped it, which are for ever sundered from us by the gulf of time?

I have ordered our departure from the realm of the Moon and we have just set out across the void to Earth at best speed. It is wonderful to look upon that delicate blue-and-white globe once again. All our hearts are cheered by the sight, and our only regret is that so many of our comrades cannot share it with us. Perhaps one can only appreciate the precious beauty of one's own world when one has been separated from it.

So I must turn my thoughts to our return. I cannot help wondering what society will make of the Phiadorans. That such exotic creatures will not go short of admirers is evident from the behaviour of my crew, who are clearly smitten by them. Certain oblique references transmitted by Sinclair suggest it is much the same on his ship. Well, we shall only have a short time of it, and then they will be the responsibility of others.

I must admit that I am not immune to their charms, and find the company especially of Princess Nareena both stimulating and uncomfortably distracting. The Phiadoran women have a certain forwardness in establishing personal relationships which is not seemly to the English way of doing things. At least they have accepted the substitute clothing we have made for them. It is little more than sheets stitched together, but with the judicious addition of cords tied about their waists and crossed upwards to pass over the shoulders, a simple bodice effect is created that suggests the lines of classical Greek dress, which seems appropriate for such beings.

The princess was very appreciative of our efforts. As the Moon recedes behind us she and her maidens seem increasingly anxious to set foot on the world that will be their new home, and they ply us with many questions about its geography and customs, and the likely form of reception they will receive. I have passed much of the responsibility for answering their queries on to Forrester's, admittedly most willing, shoulders, for my thoughts are straying elsewhere to more personal matters.

Emily is of course in her cabin, mourning the loss of her father. I hope she draws some slight comfort from the knowledge that his name will go down in history as one of great scientists of our age. Whilst understanding her need for solitude, I have requested a few moments with her, for there are certain matters we must discuss in private…

Turlough stopped there. He didn't want to pry into Haliwell and Emily's private life any further. At least now the sequence of events made sense. The *Draco* must have made its sudden departure while the rest of the fleet was on the other side of the Moon or had already left orbit for Earth. Haliwell didn't know they had escaped.

Turlough reached to turn another page. If he just skimmed past the personal stuff…

He hesitated, thinking of his promise to Lytalia.

What if he read on and found that Haliwell never heard of him again. Wouldn't that mean he never made it back to Earth? But then how did the Doctor get hold of the diary to put it in the time safe? That must mean things would work out. But the Doctor was dead… Turlough pinched the bridge of his nose. He was getting confused. Wait, there was still the note he'd apparently written to himself from the future… or was there?

He shook the diary but no note fell out. Surely it had been folded in half and placed inside the cover. He rummaged in his pack, but there was still no sign of it. He knew it had been there before the raid on the citadel. It couldn't just vanish into thin air...

But could it vanish into time?

The Doctor had said they were on the cusp between two different futures. Haliwell wrote that Boyes-Dennison would go down as a great scientist, but Turlough had never heard about him until a few days ago. Supposing the note came from a different timeline to the one he was now in? Perhaps he would never write it because in this reality he was destined to die soon?

Numbly he looked at the diary, wondering if it too could simply fade away. Then he thrust it into his pocket and stared at nothing as they headed into the unknown.

Chapter Twenty-Eight
A Proposal

'You wished to see me, Captain?' Emily said as Haliwell opened the door of his cabin to her knock.

He noticed her eyes were still red, but her manner was calm. 'Please come in and sit down…' He closed the door. '… And it is Richard. This is not an official matter.'

Emily stepped lightly over and pulled herself down into the single spare chair in the tiny room. Like all the furniture on the *Cygnus* it was held to the deck with magnets.

Haliwell seated himself opposite her. 'First, please know that I would not have dreamed of intruding on your grief had this not been important.'

Emily gave a small shrug. 'I cannot stay in my cabin all the way back to Earth. I think I have shed all my tears for the moment. The surgeon has told me my father's end was quick, which is some comfort. I could not bear the thought of him suffering. The only thing worse would have been for him to have been struck down by some seizure and left crippled, unable to work or think clearly. Clarity of thought was so important to him.'

'You will miss him very much, won't you?'

'For all his faults, more than you can imagine.' She sighed. 'But I will manage.'

'I know you will,' Haliwell said with feeling. 'You have such fortitude. In a way that's why I asked you to call on me.' He hesitated, choosing his words carefully. 'When we return to Earth there will be so much to do I fear we may not see each other for some time. You will be involved with concluding your father's affairs, and I with presenting my report to the Admiralty and then facing the inquiry over the loss of the *Draco*…'

'But that was not your fault.'

'Nevertheless, there must be an inquiry. And then, if the government decides to make our journey public, the attention from the press and other bodies will mean we will have no chance of meeting privately again for months, perhaps. Which is why I must say what I have to now, even though you have just suffered such a grievous loss.'

She looked at him very steadily. 'Yes, Richard?'

He reached across the small desk and clasped her hands.

'Bending on one knee is not practical under these conditions, so you must imagine the gesture. Emily, will you do me the honour of becoming my wife?'

'Oh, Richard –'

'Please hear me out. Of course I do not expect an answer immediately. Your mind can only be on your father now. All I ask is that you consider my offer. After the time we spent together, and most especially our recent mutual ordeal, I think we know each other better than most prospective couples. The adventure of marriage can hardly be more daunting than that.'

She gave a tired smile. 'But marriage is a very different kind of adventure. Our views on society, for instance, are at odds in many respects. Should we marry I would not change my opinion on such things, nor shirk from speaking my mind. Could you live with such a wife?'

'Emily, for you I will read the complete works of John Stuart Mill, take up utilitarianism… and even promote the cause of universal suffrage for women.'

'I don't think a marriage should begin by either party making sacrifices. Do you believe in the cause?'

'I believe in you. You are a wonderful example of what a woman can be. You are intelligent and level-headed and brave and resourceful. I am certain that if you had the vote, you would cast it as wisely as any man.'

'But would you allow all women, some perhaps without the qualities you are kind enough to grant me, to have a vote, as it is given rather carelessly to so many men? Equality must be presumed from the start, Richard, or there can be nothing true and lasting. That is fundamental to any relationship between men and women… or between a man and a woman.'

Haliwell hesitated uncertainly. Emily continued.

'You asked me to think on your proposal, now I do the same. Don't speak of this again until you can answer my question truthfully.' She moved to the door, then turned. 'Please remember that I will value an honest answer above all… and that whatever happens, I will always think of you as a friend.'

Chapter Twenty-Nine
Ice and Fire

The frozen forest was disintegrating about the Doctor.

Moss crunched to powder underfoot and delicate overhanging fern fronds snapped at the slightest touch. Every few minutes the thump of some forest giant toppling was transmitted through the ground. The stress of the arctic cold and the sudden fall in pressure was splitting branches already weighed down by a sheathing of rime frost. Falling boughs crashed down out of the black starlit sky into the circle of radiance cast by his lantern and smashed into fragments. Nightmarish creatures seemed to loom out of the darkness at him only to remain motionless, staring at him through sightless eyes, frozen like everything else. Once a bird-like thing, with twenty-foot wings outstretched, plunged into the ground in front of him and shattered like glass. It must have died on its perch and been dislodged by falling ice.

Through this macabre landscape he struggled, encumbered by his primitive spacesuit and with his makeshift sledge bouncing along behind him. He was making the best speed he could, but the frozen ground was treacherous and the going was desperately slow. The long bounding strides he had used before now only resulted in falls when he landed, and he could not risk damaging his suit.

He was beginning to wonder if his oxygen would last out – he was using up far more than normal to keep his metabolic activity high in order to combat the cold, especially the terrible numbing ache flowing up through his boots. If he reduced his metabolism he would move more slowly and eventually freeze, but if he kept it high he would suffocate before he reached the TARDIS. A fine paradox… perhaps a terminal one. He turned the oxygen valve down as far as he dared. His head wound began to throb again which didn't help his concentration.

After a while he noticed that everything around him seemed to be getting dimmer and for a moment, in his mentally sluggish state, he thought his sight was failing. Then he realised it was his lantern. He stopped to change its battery. Though the lantern was insulated and warmed by the heat from the arc, the cold was affecting it.

He stomped on again through the forest. At one point he had to ford the remains of a river and almost failed to reach the far bank because the water had frozen in a series of undulating shelves that were an ordeal of frustration to climb. But climb it he did, eventually, and on he went.

Gradually he became aware of a steady tremor underfoot that could not be the result of falling trees. A slight mistiness filled the air and in a minute he came upon one of the small cone-like structures that were scattered about the crater. A ruddy glow hung over its apex and rivulets of meltwater flowed away down its sides, steaming as they boiled into the thin air or froze once again into icy ripples. The ground tremor grew stronger as he approached the cone.

The Doctor knew he should ignore it, and if his mind had been clearer perhaps he would have. But he had reached a stage of exhaustion that was almost like intoxication. His scientific curiosity would not let him pass by without investigating. After several tries he managed to scramble up the slippery sides of the cone and peered over its lip into the depths. Far below he made out a red glow that pulsated in time with the ground tremors. Suddenly he understood. The vents kept the crater warm during the long lunar night through some artificial underground heat-exchange network, and perhaps even provided some illumination as well. A pity he hadn't thought to ask the Phiadorans about them. But what was going on now? He had an impression of vast subterranean forces barely held in check.

The warmth of the cone was already penetrating his suit. The rock he was lying on must be scorching hot. The unexpected wave of heat felt wonderful and he longed for more, but he knew he couldn't stay. He slithered down, picked up the sledge reins and set off again with a new sense of urgency.

'Onward, Doctor,' he told himself aloud. 'Brave heart.'

On and on through the ice forest. Time blurred. He was not sure if he'd been walking for hours or days. Had he been checking his course? He thought so. Where had he put the tracer?

He realised dimly that his breathing was becoming laboured. It took an immense effort of will to recall what that meant. Of course: change his air cylinder. He reached into the sledge for a replacement. It was empty. No cylinders, no lantern batteries.

He stood swaying slightly, trying to make sense of his discovery.

Surely he would have recalled using the last cylinder. Or had he forgotten to replace the bindings the last time he'd taken out a fresh one? Had the other cylinders fallen off without him noticing, or had he been pulling an empty sledge behind him for miles?

He swung the beam of his lantern desperately about, hoping for the glint of metal. But all he saw were trees frosted as though encased in glass.

Abandoning the sledge, he began to run, stumbling and bounding, in the direction he imagined the cliffs to be. He had to reach the crater wall eventually… unless he'd been going in circles.

At some point he fell over, tumbled, and came to rest staring up at the stars. He couldn't feel his feet any more. A lethargy was overtaking him and the pain was fading away. Sleep. All he wanted to do was sleep. His faceplate was frosting over and the stars were blurring.

Dimly he saw an impossibly long leg swing across his field of view. Another leg followed it, and he made out a dark shape settling over him.

It was one of the giant spiders! But why wasn't it frozen with everything else? Why couldn't it let him sleep!

He tried to brush it aside but his arms did not respond.

The last he saw was that the spider had Kamelion's face.

Chapter Thirty
One by One

The soft hum of the impeller drive filled the *Draco*. Turlough felt an invisible hand gently press him to the deck. For the first time in hours he had weight again, even if it was only a couple of pounds. Stanton locked the power levers and turned to the others, his aggressive self-confidence apparently renewed by his few minutes seated in the helm chair.

'Now we've got some weight under us, let's take care of our stowaway,' he said.

Turlough's observations had shown they were moving away from the Moon on a spiral trajectory, which no doubt had a proper mathematical name which he couldn't remember. He was pretty certain they had enough speed to escape the Earth–Moon system altogether if nothing was done to alter their course. Now that they had enough charge in their batteries they had turned the ship and put on a small counterthrust to begin braking and putting them on a general heading for Earth. Such approximations would have been no use to a twentieth-century rocket-powered craft that had to conserve every drop of fuel, but as long as the *Draco* had sunlight to recharge its batteries they could approach their target by increments, refining their course as they went. No doubt the dead navigator would have been far more precise in his calculations and saved them wasted time and energy, but they would get there in the end.

And while the ship braked, they would go after the Vrall.

In addition to rifles, the crewmen carried cutlasses and a couple held spiked climbing staffs that must have been intended for conventional lunar exploration and been missed when the ship was cleared. Whether they would be effective against the alien they would soon know.

Turlough was more concerned about Lytalia's health at that moment.

She was now wrapped in blankets and had taken a little food and drink, but she was increasingly lethargic and Turlough was worried that she'd picked up some infection from the clawing the Vrall had given her. If so there was nothing more he could do for her. She'd let him clean her wounds with carbolic oil, the best the ship's medicine locker could do by way of an effective disinfectant. He was over half a century too early to find even something as basic as penicillin to treat any serious infection – assuming it was compatible with her body chemistry.

Still, she was as safe on the bridge as anywhere and at least he'd be between her and the Vrall as the hunting party worked its way towards the stern of the ship. She held his hand for a moment as they prepared to depart. 'Search carefully,' she reminded him. 'Do not let it get behind you.'

They glided down the stairs while she sat by the bridge hatchway and closed it after them.

They examined each cabin on the deck below using the same method. Three men stayed out in the stairwell landing to prevent anything escaping from the room or getting past them from below, while the other three entered. Two of them used the staffs to check under bunks, prod bedding and ease open lockers, while the third held an arc lantern which he shone about the cabin to highlight anything that might be flattened against the walls or ceiling. When they were done Stanton closed the door and twisted a piece of wire about the latch. Then they moved on to the next cabin.

As each one was cleared Turlough felt the strain mounting. They knew there was something on the ship, and each empty cabin only brought the inevitable confrontation that much closer.

But wherever the Vrall was hiding it wasn't anywhere on that deck. They descended to the third deck and repeated the process. Nothing. They went down to the fourth deck. That comprised the galley, mess rooms and storeroom for food and water. Turlough took his turn holding the lantern as they checked the last. It was a time-consuming task as there were far too many potential hiding places amongst the shelves and cartons. Turlough found himself flinching at every shadow as he moved the lantern about. Gradually they worked their way back to the door. There was no sign of any intruder.

'It looks like this one's clear,' Turlough called to the men waiting on the landing.

There was a scream from outside.

Reflex jerked Turlough around, the minimal gravity turning the movement into an impossibly graceful parody of an aerial pirouette. The beam of the lantern flashed through the door and for an instant highlighted the man who had been detailed to watch the stairs down to the next deck.

A black stick-like form with skin the texture of hot tar was clinging to his back, its six rubbery limbs twined about him, the three-clawed hands on the middle pair of limbs raking at his stomach. Its thin sickle-shaped head, tapering to a sharp beak, bent back and then lashed forward with incredible force. There was a crack of bone.

Stanton had also spun round, bringing his rifle up to fire, but he was far too late.

In a fraction of a second the Vrall tensed and leapt away from its victim, its limbs bowing then snapping straight, like rubber. It was a black shimmering blur flying through the air. Stanton's shot sparked harmlessly off a stair as the Vrall bounced off one wall, then a second, its middle limbs folding flat against its body. With a final effortless thrust it plunged down the stairway to the lower decks and vanished from sight.

The man it had attacked rebounded limply from a bulkhead and fell to the deck at their feet in grotesque slow motion, his limbs still twitching, globules of blood spraying from the hole in his skull. One of his comrades blanched and crossed himself, another choked out: 'God save us, it's the devil's work! I can't take this –'

Stanton's backhand blow caught him across the side of his head. 'Shut your face – after it!'

They hauled themselves down the stairway before their courage failed them. They hit the next deck and Turlough swung the lantern quickly about, fearful of another surprise attack. But all the hatches leading off the stairwell were shut. This was the machinery deck and air plant. Plenty of places to hide, but surely the Vrall could not have passed through a hatch and closed it so quickly without making a sound.

'The engine room!' Stanton snarled.

They hauled themselves along the rails and around to the head of the next companionway. They were halfway down the stairs when all the lights in the ship went out.

The shock of the sudden change in illumination made the man ahead of Turlough grab the rails as he tried to halt his descent. Turlough cannoned into him and the arc lantern was knocked from his hand, bounced off the stairs and went out. They were plunged into complete darkness.

Turlough snatched for a grip on the handrail but couldn't find it. Somebody barged into him and they all fell in a hopeless tangle of kicking limbs, totally disorientated by the fractional pseudogravity even as its gentle pull saved them from broken bones when they struck the deck below. There were curses and cries of alarm. Stanton was shouting for somebody to find the lantern.

Turlough began scrabbling around the deck, berating himself for having left his own torch in his pack and hoping the lantern had not been damaged. In a few seconds his eyes should begin to adjust to the faint glow of the luminous body fluid still splashed about the walls, but he didn't want to wait even that long.

His questing hand brushed across a warm, slickly rubbery and quite inhuman limb. He jerked backwards in utter terror, arms flailing desperately in an attempt to fend the dreadful thing off. He actually felt a rush of air as the Vrall leapt past him. A scream cut through the darkness then descended into a bubbling moan. A rifle blazed, the muzzle-flash momentarily illuminating struggling confused figures and the Vrall locked about a man's head. There was a ring of metal as a wild cutlass blow struck some stanchion. The rifle cracked again, the bullet ricocheting dangerously off the metal walls.

Stumbling backwards from the Vrall and the shooting, Turlough fell over the heavy case of the arc lantern. He fumbled desperately for the switch and brilliant light suddenly flooded the scene.

The Vrall, caught in the act of reaching for another victim, froze for a second, perhaps dazzled by the light. Turlough turned the beam full on it and, with a yell of anger to drown his own fear, lunged forward thrusting the lantern at the thing's face.

Stanton's rifle boomed. The bullet struck the Vrall in its thin chest.

A hole appeared in the Vrall's tar-like skin even as the slightly built creature was lifted off its feet by the impact and slammed against a bulkhead. It seemed to hang there for a moment, then slithered to the floor.

'Got you!' Stanton exclaimed with brutal satisfaction.

The Vrall rose to its feet, shook itself and tensed to spring again. There was no blood on its chest and the bullet hole was already closing over.

A second man fired as Stanton was sliding the bolt to load another round into the chamber of his weapon. The Vrall was hurled backwards again. And again it climbed to its feet. With an oath the cutlass-wielding sailor swung at it before it could spring again. The blade sliced halfway through its torso and then seemed to stick. The Vrall lashed out with its clawed middle arm and the man reeled away clutching at the bloody gash on his shoulder. With another arm the Vrall tugged the blade free and tossed it aside. The gash in its side puckered and began to close.

'We can't stop it!' Turlough yelled. 'Into the engine room!'

They leapt away, piling through the hatch and heaving the heavy door closed in the Vrall's face as it sprang at them once again. They heard it thud into the other side of the door even as Stanton threw the bolts. They slumped against the metal, breathing raggedly and staring into each other's fearful eyes.

After a minute Stanton recovered enough to cross to the main switch panel and throw on the lights once again. Turlough mechanically turned off the arc lantern. His hand was trembling. If he hadn't had the luck to find it when he did, the Vrall would have killed them all.

'That thing's no animal!' Stanton spat out. 'It lured us down here, then put off the lights. What animal can do that?'

'It was taking us one by one,' Turlough said. 'Just like Lytalia said it would...' He choked. 'Lytalia! If it gets to the bridge!'

He turned to the hatch and began clawing at the bolts. Stanton caught his arm. 'Don't be a fool. Use the speaking tube if you must.'

Turlough sprang to a rubber tube labelled BRIDGE that was clipped to the wall, pulled out the stopper and yelled: 'Lytalia! Lock the hatch –'

'Blow first, so's she can hear it whistle, you fool,' Stanton said.

Turlough blew, causing the stopper at the other end to whistle like steam through a kettle cap, then waited anxiously. Of course, Lytalia would know even less about speaking tubes than he did. Would she work out what it was? He was about to blow again when the stopper at the other end of the tube was removed.

'Yes?' came her distant voice.

'Lytalia, lock the hatch down. The Vrall's in the stairwell.'

'I locked it when I heard the shooting. Are you all right?'

'We're in the engine room. I don't think it can get to us for the moment. You stay where you are until we think of something. As long as we've got control of the bridge and the engine room we can still operate the ship.'

'I shall. Be careful.'

He stoppered the tube again and looked at Stanton and the two surviving sailors, Smith and Pendle. 'I don't suppose anybody knows what we're going to do next?'

There was a depressing silence. The sailors looked dazed. Pendle was still holding his gashed shoulder. Mechanically his companion tore away his shirt sleeve and began fashioning a rough bandage.

Then Stanton spoke up. 'You're right about one thing, mate. While we stay put, between us we can still run the ship. If we can set her down safe, spike the impeller so only we can fix her, then slip out ourselves, that thing'll have to leave and we can get back aboard when it's gone.'

'But Lytalia will have to do everything on the bridge,' Turlough said.

'I'll use the tube to tell her how to fly the ship, you tell her how to figure our course.'

It might work, Turlough thought. He had to remind himself that Lytalia wasn't the primitive she appeared to be. She was probably familiar with spacecraft, as the princess had been with the saucers.

'What do we do for food and drink?' asked Smith.

'We get hungry and thirsty!' Stanton rasped back. 'But we don't let that thing take the ship away from us, agreed?'

They all nodded.

Pendle raised his head curiously. 'Something's wrong,' he said.

They looked about them anxiously. The lights were steady, the drive was humming smoothly, the meters showed the dynamo was charging the batteries...

Then Turlough realised what was missing. The faint whisper of sound from the network of pipes and vents that ran right through the ship had ceased.

The air circulation had been turned off.

Chapter Thirty-One
Questions

The Doctor lay in an uneasy sleep on the couch in the TARDIS's medical bay. Kamelion watched over him, his placid face not reflecting the concern he felt in his deeper circuits.

He had brought the Doctor back to the TARDIS with all possible speed, having metamorphed into a body form with multiple pairs of long legs to take best advantage of the low gravity and to negotiate the rough terrain. If there had been sufficient atmosphere left in the crater he would have flown like a bird.

Once inside the TARDIS, Kamelion removed the primitive environment suit the Doctor had somehow acquired and placed him on the medical couch. He activated its integral heating unit and covered the Doctor with a thermal blanket. Then he applied a medical probe to his forehead and chest.

According to the probe's readings, had the Doctor been a mere human he would already be dead. But knowing the Doctor was an inheritor of more robust genetic ancestry, Kamelion proceeded to administer the stimulant the probe's analyser indicated. Then all he could do was watch and wait.

As he did so he was troubled by a sensation of guilt.

When he had found the Doctor there had been no sign of Turlough, and he had not had the time to carry out a thorough search of the area. If Turlough still lived then he was beyond Kamelion's empathic range. The Doctor might know where to search for him – if he survived. If only Kamelion had not been delayed in starting his search he might have rescued both of them. But after the shock he had received when he had attempted to tune into their mental patterns the first time, he had been compelled to wait while his empathic circuits self-repaired and recalibrated. Then he had emerged once again into the frozen night. This time the Doctor's pattern had stood out like a beacon in the dead crater.

The Doctor stirred under his covers. His lips moved. He seemed to be trying to say something. Kamelion was not sure if that was a good sign.

Over the next few hours the Doctor's muttering became random words and phrases. Kamelion could sense his mental activity fluctuating wildly. The Doctor's body was recovering, but had his mind suffered permanent damage from oxygen starvation?

Gradually Kamelion realised certain words were being repeated. For some reason it seemed as though the Doctor was making an oblique reference to Kamelion himself.

'… mechanical servant…' the Doctor mumbled, '… why not say robot?…'

Kamelion wondered why the question should be occupying the Doctor's thoughts at such a time. It was as though a problem troubling his subconscious mind had surfaced through the confusion brought on by his ordeal. Or perhaps there was no logic to it at all. After all, the Doctor knew the most appropriate term to describe Kamelion's default body form was 'android'.

Another more or less lucid phrase emerged from the incoherent babble: '… should've understood a cry for help… understood the warden…'

The Doctor began to twist restlessly from side to side. His voice rose, shouting the rambling words aloud. Kamelion reached forward, uncertain if he should restrain him in case he injured himself.

Then the Doctor's eyes snapped open and he sat bolt upright.

'Now I know!' he said dramatically.

Chapter Thirty-Two
Vrall

The air in the engine room got thicker and staler as the hours passed.

Turlough and the three surviving mutineers lay slumped against the wall, panting heavily in an attempt to force the remaining oxygen into their lungs. Of course, there was one spacesuit with oxygen equipment left in the ship, but unfortunately it was in the lockers by the lower airlock. Turlough wondered at what point would they decide to fight the Vrall, even though they knew it was waiting for them; that it had actually turned off the air pumps to force a confrontation. Still, the air would be slightly fresher out in the stairwell. Could they open the hatch just enough to let it circulate? He thought of the Vrall's skinny body. Could they be sure it wouldn't come in at the same time?

A little earlier Turlough had come up with the brilliant idea that they could suck fresher air down the speaking tube from the bridge, where Lytalia alone would use much less. But the tube was too long for them to do this and the foul air from the engine room soon filled it. At least he'd been able to speak to Lytalia when he wished. She sounded increasingly distant, as though her injuries were sapping her strength. She offered no new suggestions for fighting the Vrall.

At some point he knew Stanton would open the hatch and face the thing that waited for them out there. And Turlough would follow him to stand by his side, murderer and mutineer though the helmsman was. Because after their encounter with the Vrall, brief though it had been, Turlough instinctively knew it was the enemy of all life. Not an animal simply following its instinct to survive, but a calculating predator without mercy, as impossible to make peace with as a Dalek. It was what the Doctor would have called irredeemably evil.

'Green was a bloody fool,' Stanton said suddenly.

Turlough blinked at him. 'So I gathered,' he said weakly.

'He'd have killed us all,' Stanton continued. 'Almost did kill all of us in the forest… I mean I was the only one who came back. Green had to complete his mission, that was all he could think of. Follow orders and to hell with us. Kill a few tars on the way, what did that matter? If we'd have stayed put and fixed the ship I could have flown us to that bloody mountain – if he'd let me fly the way I wanted to. But what did he know about it, eh?'

'Nothing,' said Turlough carefully.

'Right. He was so stupid he took both me and Tom Broady with him. Both helmsmen! Where did that leave the ship? Could he have flown it? None of the officers was half as good as me. You know why? Because there were too many levers and pedals to work. Too much like being an engine driver for them. Not for gentlemen! They wanted to keep their hands clean and give the orders. But I was really flying her. They didn't realise the feeling it gave you. That was freedom, that was. It took something special they'd never have – but they wanted to keep it for themselves anyway…' He shook his head. 'When poor Tom went, well, I had to speak my mind and tell Green what I thought. You understand?'

'I understand.'

Turlough thought he did, partly. Despite everything Stanton was loaded down with guilt over what he'd done, confused by class resentment and carried away by the power of the machine he controlled. Perhaps this sudden need to confess was brought on by his fear of imminent death.

Stanton's eyes were wide, pleading for sympathy and at the same time defiant. 'I had to do it, you see, else he'd have killed me as well. That thing… God, what a size it was… it would have squashed us both like flies. But Green wouldn't shut up. So I had to do it!'

'Do what?'

Stanton's hands were half-clenched before him, and he was staring at something Turlough could not see.

'He had to stop blabbing… so I closed his mouth. Just while it could have heard us, that's all. But when I took my hands away…

he didn't move. Just stared at me with those fool eyes of his. So I ran and ran…'

The other two sailors were gazing at Stanton in horror. They'll all crack up any minute, Turlough thought. We have to move now. Fear cleared a path through his sluggish brain.

'Listen!' he said as sharply as he could manage. 'I've thought of something. Something we can use on the Vrall.'

Stanton blinked and shook his head. Did he remember what he'd been saying? 'What? Not fire?'

'No. The fluid in the accumulators. It must be sulphuric acid. Bound to be an irritant at least.'

They goggled uncomprehendingly at him. They were not chemists or engineers. They only knew the basics of how the ship worked.

Turlough pulled himself to his feet and staggered over to the racks of accumulators, each green-tinted flask in its own padded metal-strapping case suspended on heavy springs. There had to be some means of topping them up. There was a wooden box with a stained lid bolted to the wall nearby. Unlatching it, he found half a dozen pint-sized bottles, tubes and filler cones. A label on the inside of the lid confirmed the contents. He pulled a bottle out and hefted it experimentally. He could throw this. Just as much chance as hitting the Vrall with a bullet. It would be unexpected and besides the bottle would smash, splash flying glass and droplets. At the speed the thing went it might jump through them before it could stop.

He held the bottle out for them to see. 'Worth a try,' he said. 'Anything that might sting its eyes… if it has eyes. Cause some sort of damage that would give us an edge. Well?'

The sailors looked uncertain. Stanton pulled himself to his feet.

'We do it,' he panted. 'Smithy, stay here and close the hatch behind us. All you got to do is stay put. Pendle, you'll be in the air room once we've checked it's clear. You've worked them machines before. Just start the pumps and keep them running and the hatch closed. We'll bring you some rations if we can… maybe snatch some on the way up. Me and him,' he jerked a thumb at

Turlough, 'will hold the bridge while we make for Earth at full speed. Now tell the girl we're coming and to be ready to let us in.'

A minute later they eased the hatch open. A draught of cooler fresher air poured around the crack and they breathed it in gratefully. There was no sign of the Vrall or the body of the man it had killed on the stairwell. Stanton, Turlough and Pendle slipped through the hatch and Smith closed it silently behind them.

They went straight up the stairs to the next deck. The air room hatch was open wide. Holding their bottles of acid ready, they slipped inside. Turlough knew the Vrall had to be waiting for them, knowing they would come here to start the air pumps. It had to be lurking behind a piece of machinery or a bank of gas cylinders. There were so many places it could conceal itself. With nerves stretched almost to breaking point they checked every possible hiding place.

There was no Vrall.

'It must be here but we've missed it!' Turlough said, swinging the lantern about. The beam shivered with the trembling of his hand.

'No we ain't!' Stanton insisted. 'Perhaps it's elsewhere planning some more devilry.' He turned to Pendle. 'Give us a minute before you start the pumps. Maybe we can reach the bridge before it knows what we're up to.'

Turlough and Stanton slipped out and Pendle closed the hatch behind them. They glided up the stairs, their tiptoe thrusts enough to lift them against the fractional gravity. Back-to-back they edged into the tiny galley. Stanton snatched up some packets of cheese, hard biscuits and sealed flasks of water. Then they headed for the bridge.

At the top of the final flight Turlough tapped lightly on the bridge hatch. It swung open immediately and they pulled themselves up and through, their hearts thudding with relief.

The first thing Turlough saw, jammed into a gap between two lockers, was Lytalia. She was wrapped in a blanket and her eyes were closed as though in sleep.

Turlough twisted about, swinging his bottle of acid up over his head to throw it even as he drew in his breath to shout a warning.

But it was far too late.

The Vrall slammed the hatch shut and sprang. The impact sent them tumbling backwards, the packs of food and water flasks flying loose, the bottles of acid spinning away to smash uselessly against the walls. Stanton desperately swung his rifle like a club only to have it torn from his grasp even as the whip-crack backhand lash of a skinny arm caught caught him on the jaw. Turlough thrust the heavy arc lantern into the Vrall's face and switched it on. The creature sprang backwards, its limbs curling in front of its apparently featureless sickle head. However it saw, it did not like bright light. It bounced off a bulkhead, flew upwards to rebound from the ceiling, then down to the deck, up to the wall again, picking up speed, becoming a blur. Turlough tried to keep it in the lantern beam but it was too fast.

The Vrall hurtled off the last wall and slammed into his side, knocking the lantern away and lifting him off his feet.

Wire-thick fingers cut into his flesh and he felt the incredible strength within its slender frame. For a moment its killing beak was only inches from his face. The back of his head cracked against the bulkhead, there was an explosion of stars, a sickening pain, then everything dissolved into blackness.

Turlough's head was pounding so hard his whole body seemed to be shaking in sympathy. He tried to steady himself but his hands didn't seem to respond. He forced his eyes open and his surroundings swam into focus. He was still on the bridge of the *Draco*. His hands and feet were bound. There was movement close by… He jerked his head round, sending hot needles of fire up his neck.

Stanton was lying beside him, his blood-smeared face a mask of terror and his breath coming in tiny quick gasps. The Vrall was just finishing tying a rope round his ankles.

Turlough froze, unable to take his eyes off the creature moving with such fluid grace. Was it going to be the last thing he ever saw?

But the Vrall simply stood up and drifted over to Lytalia, who was lying as he had last seen her. She was so still he had to strain his eyes to see if she was breathing. The creature stooped and pulled the blanket off her huddled form.

Turlough found his voice. 'No! Leave her alone! Don't touch...'

The words died in his throat as the Vrall lifted Lytalia with its upper set of limbs so that she hung limply in the air, arms and legs spreading a little, head lolling to one side. There was a slit running down the mid-line of her back. The Vrall's clawed middle arms reached into the slit and parted it wide. There was no spine within, just wetly reddish folds of skin and muscle and the soft shapes of internal organs contained by glistening membranes.

Then the Vrall began to climb into the shell of Lytalia's body.

Turlough screamed aloud; rage, horror, disbelief and loss all merging in one great cry of protest at the uncaring universe around him. Beside him Stanton was being physically sick.

Lytalia's body trembled and filled out as the Vrall slid further inside. Arms and legs stiffened and fingers flexed. Her head rolled for a moment then lifted erect. The Vrall's clawed middle hands were the last to vanish. They pulled the slit on her back closed from within and the faint line faded into the copper flesh.

Lytalia opened her eyes, looked around at them and smiled sweetly.

Turlough thought it was the most disgusting thing he had ever seen. He turned his head aside, screwing up his eyes, wishing like a child that the whole thing was a nightmare, wishing to be anywhere else at that moment but here.

'Turlough,' Lytalia said in gently chiding tones, 'I thought you liked me.' She stepped over, walking with lithe flicks of her toes, and knelt beside him. She took his chin in her hand and twisted his head round to face her once again. He jerked it out of her grasp. She gave him a stinging slap across the cheek that snapped his eyes open.

'That's better,' she said, 'I do so hate to be ignored.'

She looked at Stanton with mild contempt. He was pale as death and trembling, vomit staining the front of his shirt.

'I don't expect much of him, but you said you were different. A traveller in time and space. Surely you've seen enough of alien life forms to develop a more cosmopolitan attitude to different modes of existence?'

He could only gape at her dumbly. She slapped him again. 'When I ask a question I expect an answer,' she said. 'If you want to live much longer you had better remember that.'

There was only one question he needed answered.

'When…' he grated, 'did you do it… take over Lytalia? Was it in the forest… after the disc crashed? She said she fought with a night crawler – but that was you!'

Lytalia laughed lightly. 'Really, Turlough, I expected better of you. You have so much to learn about the Vrall –'

A whistle sounded from the rack of speaking tubes. 'Your friends, no doubt wondering where you are. We will talk more later, it might be amusing.'

She crossed to the hatch, opened it and climbed down the stairs.

Turlough and Stanton lay where they were, too sick with shock to think of escape. Lytalia was back in less than five minutes, a smile on her face.

'Your friends are dead,' she told Stanton brightly. 'You really are quite stupid and credulous people. I told you the Vrall took their enemies one by one. All I had to do was knock on the doors they were so carefully guarding and say I had some food and water for them. They seemed to trust my voice. I don't think your species credit females with being very capable. They turn their backs on them so easily.'

Briefly anger supplanted fear on Stanton's face. 'I'll have you for that, you murdering bitch –'

Lytalia kicked him in the stomach so that he doubled over, wheezing.

'You will do nothing of the kind, you pathetic human,' she said. She turned to Turlough. 'Now, we were talking about the nature of the Vrall, and you seemed to be suffering under a curious misconception.'

'I have nothing to say to you,' Turlough said. 'If you're going to kill me, get it over with.'

'I don't believe you really mean that,' Lytalia said. 'After the splendid fight you put up earlier. Why should you suddenly lose all that spirit now, just because you've learned the true nature of your enemy? Don't say my little deception has shocked you so much you've given up? Aren't you clinging to the faintest hope of escape or rescue, however futile?'

In truth, Turlough was too numbed to even think of such a thing. He really had given up all hope. But he was stirred enough by her words to reply listlessly: 'Is there any hope?'

'Not really,' she admitted. 'But it's no fun if we don't pretend there might be.'

From somewhere deep down a little defiance boiled up within him. 'You like to play with your prey, don't you? You like to tease and cheat and deceive, just to be that little bit crueller than the rest. That's why you were the most dangerous animals in the crater. I bet the hunters went all out to get one of your skins! Well, I hope they got a lot of them!'

She clapped her hands together in delight, as though he had paid her a compliment. 'That's better. Defiance, anger, and a little rational thought. And you're perfectly correct. We delight in deception and we prize our cruelty. Why not? It's our nature, due to an interesting combination of circumstances which I'm sure would amuse you. But ask me more about how we got where we are now, while we have the time. Things will get very busy later and you may have to die. Meanwhile I'll enjoy seeing you suffer, as you learn just how thoroughly you were deceived.'

He might as well ask her, Turlough realised wretchedly. His little speech earlier had been a stupid show of bravado. He didn't really want to die. Talk like that again and the thing in Lytalia's body might just take him at his word. But now talk might buy him time.

'You launched the ship deliberately, after killing the navigator,' he said.

'Yes. I thought we'd lost when I heard the Doctor and those other two had been disposed off, so I got us into space before they put us out of the airlock or cut the power from the engine room. I regret the Doctor's passing, I think he had an exceptional mind. Anyway, since there were still more of you than I cared to face openly, I provided a distraction.'

'You clawed your own back to make fresh wounds and prove you'd been attacked.'

'The navigator's death needed explaining – I could hardly have admitted I was simply ravenous for a little meat, could I? Then I pretended to fall ill, and I think I was most convincing. We adopt the minds and personalities of the creatures we inhabit, you see, after first destroying their free will, and this Phiadoran is quite talented in that way. Actually, I did feel tired after feeding on the navigator. We take some time to digest our meals – the real we, not this shell, I mean. We are very particular eaters in this phase of our existence. Another reason for killing one at a time. The food must be fresh.'

Stanton groaned and turned aside, wriggling and tugging until he was as far away from her as the rope permitted.

'If you are going to be sick again, I will make you regret it,' Lytalia told him simply. Stanton went rigid and swallowed hard.

Turlough could only stare into the lovely face before him and wonder how he could have missed the change when the Vrall took Lytalia over. It had to have been there, but he hadn't been able to tell! It felt as though he had betrayed her memory. Guilt piled on top of despair. 'So what now?' he asked.

'Well, originally I had intended to make for Earth in this ship, feeding as I went. But after what you told me about your TARDIS I changed my plans. We're going back to the Moon and you will show me how to operate it. That's one reason why you're still alive.' She looked at Stanton. 'And you boast you're such a fine pilot. You had better be if that cannon is still operational, you understand?'

Stanton nodded, his lip trembling. He looked a broken man.

'And now I must check our course,' she said, rising. 'A crude procedure to guide a primitive ship, but it will serve its purpose.'

She crossed to the chart table and bent over the instruments.

Turlough licked his dry lips, wishing he had something to drink and that the sick ache in his head would go away so that he could think properly. Wearily he turned to look at Stanton.

Stanton had his hands free!

He was holding a bloody sliver of glass from one of the broken acid bottles. Even as Turlough watched breathlessly, he sliced through the rope about his ankles. All the time his eyes were fixed on Lytalia's back. It was as though Turlough had ceased to exist. Free me! Turlough wanted to say, but he dared not make a sound.

Stanton got stiffly to his feet and drifted over towards Lytalia, raising the shard of glass like a dagger and bringing it down in her back.

The sheer ferocity and unexpectedness of the attack overwhelmed her for a second, sending her sprawling across the chart table. He stabbed her twice more before she twisted about, only to be struck again in the face and chest. Then she managed to double her legs up and kick out, sending Stanton flying through the air to crash against the far bulkhead.

She rose to her feet and stared in disgust at the blood flowing from her wounds, then snarled at him: 'You will regret that, little man!'

She sprang at him, but Stanton was already diving through the open hatch and down the stairway. Lytalia plunged after him. For a few seconds Turlough heard the rattle of metal steps and rails as they pulled themselves along, then there was silence.

Henry Stanton fled with death at his heels. The only reason he was not caught was that the creature was hindered by its deceptive cocoon, and to shed it would have taken valuable seconds. Perhaps it thought he would lock himself away in the engine room again. But that wasn't what he planned at all. Oh no.

He flew down the lowest stairway and through the hatchway. As he grasped a lever and threw off its locking bar Lytalia hurtled after him so fast that she rebounded from the deck. The thing inside her was so full of rage it hadn't stopped to think where it was, which was just as Henry wanted it. Lytalia tumbled upright, shook herself then reached out for him.

'Nobody tells me what to do ever again, understand?' he said.

She saw what he was holding. She read the expression on his face. She made a spring upwards for the hatch above their heads.

Henry laughed and pulled the lever.

The *Draco*'s outer airlock hatch was man-sized and located in a larger surrounding hinged flange for loading cargo. The hatch opened against internal air pressure, while the flange opened the opposite way...

A long way off, Turlough heard a slight bang followed by an ascending rushing sound that in seconds became a howling roar. His ears popped and the bridge filled with a tearing wind that caught every loose item up in its path and sucked it through the open hatch. It jerked Turlough off the deck and pulled him along until the rope fastening him to the handhold jerked tight. His skin stung and needles seemed to pierce his ears.

He swung at the end of the rope, gasping for the air that was being wrenched from his lungs. Then the howling faded away, to be replaced by the perfect silence and dark of eternity.

Chapter Thirty-Three
A Reception is Announced

The long barrel of the *Cygnus*'s heliograph pointed down through the cloud-swirled haze of Earth's atmosphere to central Scotland, while the signaller squinted along the telescope clamped to the top of the tube, scribbling rapidly on his pad. Down in Glen Marg another operator also equipped with a powerful telescope and with a Morse lamp was replying to the signal announcing their return from the Moon.

The operator on the ship signed off and handed the message slip down to Haliwell.

LOSS OF DRACO AND BOYES-DENNISON DEEPLY REGRETTED. NEWS OF YOUR SPECIAL PASSENGERS REMARKABLE. LAND AFTER SUNSET LOCAL TIME. H.M. WILL ATTEND RECEPTION. BRISTOW.

Haliwell took the message over to Princess Nareena who had been peering down at the great globe of the Earth as it rolled under them.

'Yours is a very beautiful planet, Captain,' she said. 'It reminds me of my homeworld.'

'You must miss it very much.'

'What we lost can never be replaced. But perhaps, with your kindness, we may regain something of our dignity.'

'I'm certain you will.' He showed her the message. 'We will be landing within a few hours, once we have completed our recharging orbit.'

'You could not land sooner?'

'Perhaps, but I prefer to do so with full batteries, just in case of accidents. Besides, we must wait until after sunset to avoid being seen when we descend.'

'You are still keeping this mission a secret from your people, then?'

'Those are my orders for the moment. But I think your presence will soon bring about a change in policy. Then the whole country, the entire world even, will know you are here.'

'I would like that. I want to meet all your people in time. But perhaps your rulers are correct to be cautious at first. It would not do to alarm the common people. We shall make a careful beginning at your base. You said it was situated in an unpopulated area of your country?'

'Glen Marg? Yes, it's many miles to the nearest town of any size. It won't be a grand-scale reception, I'm afraid, but I'm sure everyone will do their best to make you and your people feel welcome. And of course, our own Queen will be there to greet you in person.'

'She does me a great honour. I am certain it will be a memorable occasion.'

Haliwell found he could not share her enthusiasm. He had a far more important matter on his mind, and would exchange any number of royal occasions to have it resolved. Emily had set him a test. Should he answer with his heart or his conscience?

Chapter Thirty-Four
Out of Time

'Turlough…'

The voice came from a long way away, but it did seem familiar, if only he could remember why.

'Turlough, can you hear me?'

It was the Doctor's voice. But the Doctor was dead. And for some reason Turlough knew that he was dead also. They must be in heaven. Somehow he'd got there despite never really believing in the place. He blinked his eyes open, squinting in the soft white light. Odd that it should look like the interior of the TARDIS sickbay. He saw a familiar figure over the Doctor's shoulder. Did androids go to heaven as well?

His mind cleared and he remembered…

He tried to sit up with a jerk, instantly regretted it and sank back on to the couch again.

The Doctor gave him a beaker of some sweet-tasting fluid and Turlough downed it gratefully, realising his throat was raw.

'You're safe in the TARDIS,' the Doctor said as he drank. 'I've put us out of time, so there's no rush. I wasn't certain how long it would take you to recover, and we have certain things to do in the next few hours back in the regular continuum.'

'How did you…' Turlough tried to croak out.

'How did I survive?' the Doctor said. 'With the help of a thick skull, an inadequate Victorian spacesuit and Kamelion's tracking skills. He was also the one who brought you back in here when we materialised on the bridge of the *Draco* just as the last of the air was venting into space.'

'Thanks,' Turlough said huskily to Kamelion.

'You are welcome,' the android acknowledged.

Turlough looked back at the Doctor. 'Lytalia… she was taken over by a Vrall…'

'I know,' the Doctor said. 'And I can guess what happened on the ship. We saw the lower airlock was open. Did Stanton's mutiny claim its last victim?'

Turlough nodded, feeling sick again. Even the physical remnant of Lytalia was gone now. He'd lost everything. 'If only there'd been some way of saving the real Lytalia…'

'Turlough, listen to me.' The Doctor was looking stern. 'I know this is going to be difficult, but you must learn the truth. Whatever you felt about Lytalia, or thought she felt about you, was an illusion. You were being deceived… used. We all were.'

Turlough didn't understand. 'No. She liked me… then she was taken over in the forest –'

'Perhaps it did happen in the forest, but that was many years ago. You see, she was a Vrall when you first met her!'

Turlough pushed the Doctor away from him. 'Don't say that! She was warm and friendly, and… I'd have known if that thing was inside her!'

'Turlough, think,' the Doctor said patiently. 'Did you understand what she was calling out when you first saw her hanging off that cliff?'

'What? No, of course not. But she was speaking in her own language –'

'And when has understanding an alien language been a problem since you've been travelling in the TARDIS? You understood the warden perfectly well. What Lytalia said sounded like language, but actually made no sense. Rhythmic sounds, nothing more. You see, her Phiadoran vocabulary had already been replaced by English.'

'No! She read my mind to learn English!'

'Phiadorans are not telepathic. They already spoke English when we met them.'

'What?' Turlough felt dizzy. 'I don't understand.'

'Think back to our first audience with the princess. How did she refer to the machines that the warden controlled?'

'Uhh… "mechanical servants", I think.'

'But what would you call them?'

'Well… robots.'

'Exactly. So why, if the princess was using a language matrix derived from your mind pattern, did she not say "robot"? In fact, did you hear her or any Phiadoran use any words or phrases that belonged exclusively to the twentieth century? But "mechanical servant" is a phrase an educated Englishman of 1878 might use. Sub-Lieutenant Granby, for instance…'

The terrible logic began to penetrate Turlough's stubborn resistance.

'I must have realised something was wrong subconsciously,' the Doctor admitted, 'but it wasn't until a few hours ago that I put it together – when my consciousness was otherwise engaged. While we were tracking you down, I checked the TARDIS data base for any references to the Vrall. They're listed under various names and their origins are uncertain, but all reports agree that they can extract engrammatic information, memories if you like, from the brains of the creatures they kill. But the process is biochemical, so it would take a few hours to assimilate and replicate the information, then perhaps transmit it in encoded viral form to others of their kind. That's why they didn't make themselves known to us for so long. Until they were ready to tell us their tragic story.'

'You mean rescuing Lytalia was a set-up… and every Phiadoran we met was a Vrall!'

'I'm afraid so. The Phiadorans were marooned here once, but the Vrall took them over. Since then they've been waiting for some gullible space travellers to come along to do what they couldn't. Enter the citadel and turn off the warden's specially attuned containment fields, then take them away from here. In fact, they decided not to leave it to chance.'

'What do you mean?'

'The home-made vacuum gun we found up in the highlands. The whole story was there if I'd been able to see it! The Phiadorans said the gun had been abandoned before they arrived, but it looked more recent than that. However, there seemed no reason for them to lie, and their explanation was just about plausible.

'But I wondered from the start at the apparent coincidence of the Victorians managing to develop the impeller drive hundreds of years ahead of its time, just when there was an alien presence on the Moon waiting to be discovered. Of course, it wasn't coincidence. The Phiadoran Vrall must have known much more about Earth than they admitted. They encapsulated the knowledge of how to build the drive in the form of viral spores, a variation of the way they communicated information between themselves. They couldn't use the knowledge on the Moon because the warden would never have let them develop advanced technology, even if they had the materials. But they could build a crude "space gun" that fired small rocket projectiles, using materials found in the crater. In the Moon's low gravity it would just work. They must have fired millions of spores into space in the hope that some of them would drift to Earth and find a suitably intelligent and receptive mind, with the necessary technical resources at his disposal. Eventually, after years of trying perhaps, one spore must have found Boyes-Dennison. The rest was inevitable…'

'Haliwell and Sinclair taking the Phiadorans back to Earth!' Turlough concluded. 'But what'll happen when they get there?'

'I don't know, but from what I've read about them it's unlikely to be pleasant. I think parasitising the Phiadorans' intelligence kept the Vrall in check and disciplined in the restricted area of the crater. But if they reach Earth their base instincts might take over and they could enter an accelerated reproductive phase. Anyway, I intend to intercept them before that happens. Now, are you up to helping?'

Turlough sat up experimentally and swung his legs over the side of the couch. He felt a little heavy, but that was from being back in the TARDIS's 1 g pseudogravity field.

'Yes, I'll be fine… and thanks.'

He followed the Doctor and Kamelion through to the control room. He saw the time rotor was frozen. The scanner showed only a formless grey. They were suspended beyond space and time.

'What's your plan?' Turlough asked.

'We must inform Haliwell or Sinclair about the Vrall without alarming the Phiadorans. The Vrall will play their roles as long as they can while everything is being done for them. It's only if they land that the danger begins. But on board the ships they can be tricked into isolation and then locked away. Then I'll work out some means of transferring them to the TARDIS and we'll take them somewhere they can't trouble anybody.'

'Suppose we simply flash a Morse message to start with?' Turlough suggested. 'If we stand off a bit we can pretend we're in a ship like theirs. That's what they think we had. Even if the Phiadorans learn we're here, they've no reason to think we've found them out. Then we'll slip the important stuff in later.'

The Doctor beamed at him. 'Excellent. You've been coming up with some very astute ideas in the last few days.'

Turlough thought of the diary still in his pocket but said nothing.

The Doctor dropped them back into real space and stars appeared on the scanner. He activated the long-range detectors. 'Now, I'll just determine the fleet's coordinates,' he said. He busied himself for a minute, then a frown creased his brow.

'Something wrong?' Turlough asked.

'I can't detect the fleet in translunar space or in Earth orbit. But even assuming they took off while we were in the *Draco*, they should still be travelling… unless Haliwell increased their constant acceleration because the lunar departure used less energy…'

Words from the diary flashed before Turlough's eyes: … *at best speed*… The Doctor was looking horror-struck. 'We're too late. They've already landed!'

Chapter Thirty-Five
The Return

Commodore Bristow checked the guard of honour once again, and consulted his watch. They shouldn't be long now, he thought.

Her Majesty had arrived barely fifteen minutes earlier. He had seen her into the somewhat spartan comfort of the officers' mess and then begged leave to make a final personal round of the base. In the circumstances he could afford to leave nothing to chance.

Glen Marg was a little hollow of light and activity nestling in the barren moors. The landing field was brightly illuminated by a dozen arc lamps mounted on tall pylons, while the hooded guidance lights ringing the glen sent their invisible beams up into the sky. The night was clear and fine bar a few scudding clouds. As long as it stayed that way for another hour, perhaps the most monumental meeting in history might go smoothly.

Greeting creatures from another world – and one a princess in her own right, apparently. The idea was both staggering and daunting. If he'd heard the news from anybody but Haliwell he would scarcely have believed it. At least they were supposed to be not too outlandish in appearance and they did speak English. He just hoped the base's limited facilities would be up to the occasion. Still, if there was one service that could be entrusted with such a task, it was the navy.

A call was relayed to him from an observer. 'Sighted them, sir. Estimate at ten thousand feet.'

Bristow sent a messenger in to pass the news on to Her Majesty, then began scanning the western horizon. The ships were coming in without lights, of course, so he didn't expect to see much until they were practically overhead.

The Queen emerged into the night, well muffled against the cool air and escorted by her manservant, Brown. Bristow was not comfortable seeing her on his arm, and was well aware of all the ugly stories about their relationship. But she was apparently unconcerned about public opinion on the matter, so Brown remained. The one thing you could say for him was that his devotion was unquestioned, Bristow conceded, and that must be given its due.

'We understand they shall be with us imminently, Commodore,' the Queen said as they reached his side.

'Yes, Your Majesty. They are coming in even now…' He saw a dark shape blot out a star and pointed. 'There, Your Majesty!'

The two astral ships drifted over the glen, the lights of the base glinting off their hulls. The slight hum of their engines permeated the air as they came to a stop, hovering improbably a hundred feet up. Their landing legs extended wide and they dropped as gently as thistledown. They touched ground within a second of each other. There was a creak of metal struts, then the engine hum faded into silence.

The first ships to land on the Moon had returned.

The guard of honour marched out and took up position while a red carpet was hastily run out in line with the lower hatch of the *Cygnus*. Bristow escorted the Queen forward.

The hatch of the *Cygnus* opened and its ramp dropped to the ground in time with that of the *Lynx* a few yards away. Haliwell appeared at the head of the ramp. He blinked in the glare of the lights, took a deep breath and stepped a little stiffly down. Sinclair descended from the *Lynx* in a similar manner. They marched up to the reception party, bowed to the Queen and exchanged salutes with Bristow.

'I beg to report the return of Her Majesty's astral ships *Cygnus* and *Lynx*,' Haliwell announced formally. 'The *Draco* is missing on the Moon, presumed lost with all hands. I also regret to announce the death of Professor Boyes-Dennison.'

'Thank you, Captain,' Bristow said. 'We shall receive your full report on these matters later.'

'Though sharing the sadness over your losses we are most gratified by your own safe return, Captain,' the Queen said. 'Your ships and crews have been very much in our thoughts and prayers these last few days.'

'Your Majesty is too kind,' Haliwell acknowledged. 'Before we proceed further, I must offer the regrets of Miss Boyes-Dennison. In the circumstances she is unable to attend you at this moment.'

'We quite understand. We trust we shall meet with her at some less trying time.'

'Then may I now have the honour of presenting some most special guests we have on board?'

'I have been informed of their presence and will be most glad to receive them,' the Queen said.

Haliwell made a sign to the ships and the Phiadorans began to emerge in procession, each walking down the ramps on the arm of a crewman. After living on the Moon for so many years, they evidently needed some assistance in Earth's stronger gravity.

As the two columns of alien women came closer, Bristow found himself standing a little straighter and brushing at his moustache. A waft of some exotic perfume caught his nostrils. Haliwell's communications had not done them justice. In their thin simple dresses it was obvious they were rare beauties.

The *Cygnus*'s navigating officer, beaming unashamedly, handed Haliwell the arm of the most striking of the women, who carried herself with an unmistakable regal poise. Haliwell escorted her before the Queen.

'Your Majesty, may I present Princess Nareena of Phiador.'

The princess bowed gracefully.

'Your Highness,' Haliwell continued, 'may I present Her Britannic Majesty the Queen Empress Victoria.'

The Queen extended her hand. 'I am so pleased to meet you, Princess.'

The princess took her hand. 'Your Majesty, you can have no idea how long we have waited for this moment.' She glanced about her. 'We are all here – let us begin!'

The Queen gasped as her hand was compressed. Bristow started forward only to choke in horror. The princess's mouth had opened impossibly wide as though the top of her head was hinging backwards and a glistening black beak was emerging from between her jaws. At the same moment the rest of the

Phiadoran women turned on their escorts and brutally struck them down.

Only Brown's suspicious nature saved the Queen from the same fate.

His hand came out from under the back of his coat holding a heavy pistol which he thrust into the grotesquely distorted face of the princess and fired in one continuous motion. The shot at point-blank range blew the false head completely off the body even as it was lifted off its feet and sent crashing on to its back. Bristow saw a thin sickle head whipping to and fro over the bloody stump of a neck, a gouge down its side where the bullet had ploughed through it.

Yards away Haliwell was trying to tear another creature off Sinclair, only to be knocked aside by a backhand blow of inhuman strength. Brown's gun boomed twice and the creature was blasted off its victim, kicking and spitting.

Then to Bristow's utter horror the head on the princess's body stilled its frantic thrashing and the thing climbed shakily back on to its feet.

Brown swept the Queen bodily up in his arms. 'Run for your lives!' he bellowed.

The paralysis left Bristow. He grabbed for Sinclair's arm as Haliwell hauled the injured man to his feet and they ran him along between them. A handful of others joined them: guards, landing-field crew and men from the ships; those with guns fired back over their shoulders.

Behind them came a host from hell. The invaders were casting off the soft deceiving flesh of the Phiadorans to free the black stick-like forms beneath. They bounded forward on their six limbs with inhuman speed, many already gored with the blood of the dead that littered the field in their wake.

The survivors charged through the doors of the officers' mess and slammed them shut in the faces of their pursuers. A window shattered and a bony limb reached inside. A guard thrust his rifle through the broken pane and fired, the report almost deafening in the confined space, and the limb was snatched away. Then the defenders were piling every stick of furniture against the doors and windows and clubbing and kicking at the claws that reached hungrily through each chink to tear down their feeble defences.

Gradually the sounds of assault ceased as the last gaps in the barricades were closed. From outside came cries and sporadic firing which were silenced with frightening rapidity. Bristow fought down the palsy that suddenly seemed to afflict his limbs and surveyed the room as calmly as he could manage.

Brown, still clutching his pistol, was crouched by the Queen who was seated in the only remaining upright chair. She looked dreadfully pale but did not seem to be physically injured. For the rest there were a dozen men, some bearing superficial scratches, about half of whom were armed. As they met his gaze he saw the same pleading look in their faces; the desperate hope that this was all some nightmare.

Finally his eyes locked on to Haliwell.

'By Heaven!' Bristow said. 'What abominations have you brought us?'

Haliwell could only shake his head in bewilderment. Then a look of deeper horror came upon him, and Bristow heard him say softly: 'Oh my God… Emily!'

Emily sat quietly in her cabin on the *Cygnus*. She was grateful to avoid the formalities of the Phiadorans' presentation to the Queen. After what had passed she wanted only peace and quiet, but she was afraid, as Haliwell had surmised, that there would be little of either in the coming weeks.

The sudden bangs and shouts from outside made her look up. Were they letting off fireworks? She crossed to the porthole and looked down.

A scene of confusion and carnage met her eyes.

Dark and murderous creatures were emerging from the Phiadorans' bodies, leaping and springing on six limbs, looking like huge insects from above. A group of people were retreating into the officers' mess, Haliwell amongst them, even as the aliens swarmed over the building. She saw two of the creatures race purposefully towards the telegraph shed…

The calculation in their actions brought order back to her own numbed mind. She thrust her disbelief and horror aside, along with her sickening fear for Richard. Wherever the things came from she understood their motives – and what their next move would be.

She flung open her cabin door and raced for the stairs. There was still a skeleton crew left aboard. There was a chance…

Forrester was still staring down at the carnage below, his mind not yet adjusted to the incredible turnabout of events, when she burst on to the bridge.

'We must take off!' Emily shouted. 'We can do something as long as they don't get on to the ship.' She threw herself into the helmsman's chair. 'I need power now!'

To Forrester's credit, he did not argue but lunged for the bank of speaking tubes and roused the skeleton watch in the engine room.

'All power to the impellers immediately!' he commanded.

He blew down a second tube, but there was no response. 'I can't reach the men on the lower hatch,' he reported.

The power came on and Emily fed it into the impellers. She had helped her father design the control system and she knew she could fly as well as any man. The *Cygnus* lifted off the ground. If the lower hatch was still open she'd have to get thirty feet clear at least before they were safe. She swung the periscope around to check.

The *Lynx*, still resting on the ground below them, seemed to tremble. The portals around its lower decks flashed red and blew out. Tongues of fire licked through them and Emily realised the cylinders in its air plant had exploded. Had the creatures done it deliberately, or was it due to a mischance while fighting with the remaining crew? A part of her mind was icily detached, recognising how the Phiadorans had conspired to lure most of the crew out of the ships. But now the creatures had to take control of the ships or destroy them, because they could not allow them to leave and spread the word of their presence.

Emily gritted her teeth. She would do her best to spoil their plans. If Richard still lived they would need men and weapons to save him. Where was the nearest army base?

She heard cries from below.

Forrester had a pistol in his hand and was standing over the open hatch. He shouted something and then fired twice down the stairs. The things were on the ship! If they got to the engine room…

The power lights flickered. With its lifting coils suddenly unbalanced the *Cygnus* began to pitch over. Emily saw the craggy walls of the glen rise to meet them like a wave.

The *Cygnus* struck, tearing its hull apart and sending a shower of debris across the hillside. The crumpled remains ground their way down to the foot of the cliff and lay still.

The Vrall were masters of the glen. One found the powerhouse and smashed the generator controls, extinguishing the irritating lights. In the darkness they fed, growing larger by the minute as they gorged themselves on the dead, their beaks frothing with digestive enzymes.

A bloated Vrall fell back from the half-devoured carcass of a horse lying outside the base's stables and rolled on the ground. Its rubbery skin stretched and split down the sides of its body and a second creature pulled itself out of the back of the first. And then there were two separate stick figures the same size as the original adult Vrall. For a minute they lay still as their skins repaired the ravages of parthenogenetic division. Then they crawled back to the carcass and resumed their interrupted feeding…

Turlough watched the creatures on the TARDIS's scanner, which amplified the starlight so that every detail could be seen. Eventually he turned aside, revolted and despairing.

'They're reproducing. There'll be hundreds of them in an hour!'

'Yes, I'm afraid we're beyond any chance of reasoning with the Vrall now,' the Doctor said. His manner was icy calm, but Turlough could sense his brain working frantically behind the impassive mask of his face.

'But how do we stop them? The British army won't be up to it.'

'No, this is something quite beyond their abilities. Now there is only one option left – and it's up to us to take it.'

The Doctor lowered his head for a moment, as if in thought. When he looked up, Turlough could see a depth of resolve in his eyes which had not been there before. His fingers flew across the controls.

The TARDIS vanished from the hillside. In the glen below another swollen Vrall began to roll on the ground…

Chapter Thirty-Six
Erasure

Turlough stepped out of the TARDIS, swinging the beam of his torch about him. He stifled a gasp as it illuminated the form of a crouching giant spider. The spider did not move, leaving Turlough feeling slightly foolish.

They were in a hall of trophies. Every creature in the forest's menagerie seemed to be represented. Vast shaggy skins that could have carpeted banqueting halls hung on the walls, alternating with monstrous glassy-eyed stuffed heads, their jaws gaping in mock defiance. Skeletons of bone and chitin stood on plinths, together with whole creatures that it must have taken an army of taxidermists to prepare. And by each one was a discreet plaque giving a name, time and date, and a mounted holograph of the proud hunter standing by his kill.

'Look at this place!' Turlough said, amazed and appalled at the same time.

The Doctor looked about impatiently. 'Trophies they couldn't take home with them, perhaps. Left here for show. Not a pleasant collection, is it? Come on, we haven't any time to lose.'

With Kamelion following they ran in bounding strides along the great curving hall.

'You're sure they'll be here?' Turlough asked.

'No, but it's highly probable,' the Doctor replied, flicking the beam of his torch from side to side. 'There isn't time for me to study the citadel's energy-field generators to find out exactly what type and frequency of radiation contained the Vrall and then attempt to duplicate it. But it is logical that they kept portable weapons powerful enough to use against them. This glorified hunting lodge must have an advanced armoury. With the Vrall loose on Earth that is our only hope of stopping them.'

Turlough thought of the weapons Haliwell and Emily were

shown. 'Maybe we should look below ground,' he suggested tentatively.

'No. I think guests of this sort would not be expected to travel far to select their weapons, and the ground level of this place is clearly the most opulent. But they might still be in a separate building.'

The hall encircled the largest dome of the citadel complex and was still pressurised, though the air was chill. Through its fifty-foot-high curving windows they could look out across the frozen and now almost airless crater lit only by the ghostly starlight… and a string of red pinpoints of light along the crater rim.

Turlough had lifted his arm to point at them when the horizon erupted.

Every pinpoint spewed a fountain of liquid fire into space. Flickering crimson light cast shimmering bars through the huge windows and lit up the great hall, setting the shadows of its grisly occupants dancing. Turlough felt the floor tremble as the ground shock reached them. Glowing fragments cut impossibly high arcs in the black sky and began to rain down on the crater, even as fingers of fire started to flow sluggishly from the vents.

'The emergency system must have been building up its power reserves for this,' the Doctor said breathlessly. 'It's overloading the crater's heating vents.'

A second ring of vents a little nearer than the first blew, and they had to shield their eyes.

'They're systematically working inwards,' the Doctor said. 'The system must be programmed to eliminate every trace of this place.'

Turlough braced himself against the fresh ground tremor. 'Why not just blow the power plant? It must be some sort of matter/energy conversion system. That would wipe this place out in one go.'

'And also send out incriminating energy pulses detectable light years away. This is slower but surer. Come on, we've even less time than I thought!'

Turlough turned to resume their search and saw the volcanic

light illuminating a pair of huge doors leading into the centre of the dome. He pointed. 'Do you suppose hunters would make as much show of their weapons as they do of their kills?'

'Very possibly,' the Doctor said, bounding towards the doors. 'Glorify both the killing and the means of death. Two sides of the same coin…' He pushed against the massive doors and they swung ponderously inward. 'Ah ha!'

His torch picked out a freestanding rack containing an array of swords. Beside it were axes, then throwing nets. Similar racks and stands faded away into the gloom around them. Weapons of all shapes and sizes designed for different-shaped manipulative organs to hold and operate. The chamber under the great dome was a veritable arsenal.

Turlough ran forward, flicking his light to and fro, seeing halberds, pikes and lances. Next came throwing darts, spears, metal discs with sawtooth edges. In the next row were crossbows and small wheeled ballistas.

'These are primitive,' he said. The floor trembled again and a spear toppled from its rack. 'Where are the real guns?'

'The weapons are getting more sophisticated as we move towards the centre,' the Doctor said. 'Perhaps they're graded according to the challenge the hunters wanted to set themselves, as well as the prey they were after.'

'Well, we're not looking for anything sporting… just lethal.'

They ran down the aisle past long-barrelled muskets and pistols, then small wheeled field artillery pieces (Turlough recalled the size of some of the creatures in the trophy hall), then things that looked very much like Earthly rifles and machine guns. He skidded to a halt. The racks glittered with polished metal and plastic, formed into strange shapes that were hard to recognise as weapons.

'That's more like it – but which is the best?'

'These, I should think,' said the Doctor.

His torch was illuminating a shining rack of weapons at the very centre of the room. They were the size of heavy rifles, but with much thicker, fluted barrels.

Turlough gingerly lifted one of the guns from the rack and cradled it experimentally in his arms. It was lighter than its bulk suggested. It didn't quite fit his grasp but he could reach the trigger, which was all that mattered. A panel of small buttons was set just behind the barrel. He touched one and a tiny status-display screen came into life.

'They've still got power, but will they do the job?'

The dome rocked. Dust fell from the roof and Turlough became aware of a sound like continuous thunder reverberating up from the floor.

'Only one way to find out!' the Doctor said.

He and Kamelion snatched up two more of the guns and they ran back the way they had come.

The trophy hall was ablaze with light and Turlough could feel the heat radiating through its windows. Fountains of fire erupted just beyond the citadel ramparts, followed almost simultaneously by a ground shock that knocked them off their feet. With a shrill crack a jagged white line ran from top to bottom down the window opposite them. Kamelion pulled them upright and they bounded the last few yards to the TARDIS.

As the doors closed behind them a giant hand seemed to take hold of the ship and shake it, sending them tumbling head over heels. Then the TARDIS's internal gravity field compensated and all sense of external motion ceased. Turlough looked at the scanner but it displayed only a blazing red-and-yellow maelstrom. The Doctor worked the controls and the image stabilised to reveal a shrinking eye of fire with a brilliant dot of white at its centre.

'The final explosion blew us into space,' the Doctor said. 'I think we can say there will be nothing identifiable left of the citadel.' The entire crater was now a mass of lava flows, shimmering under a boiling cloud of dust and falling debris. 'Nothing but an unusually deep and dark-floored crater...' he added, half to himself.

At the top of its arcing trajectory the TARDIS vanished.

Chapter Thirty-Seven
Decision

The swarming Vrall tore at the makeshift barricades blocking the doors and windows of the officers' mess. There had been no firing from within for several minutes, indicating that the defenders' ammunition was exhausted, so the creatures were not even troubled by the fleeting injuries the solid projectiles inflicted. Now they could get at their food unhindered. It was the last in the glen and when that was gone they would spread out across the moors, feeding and multiplying, growing into an invincible army before the natives even realised they were there.

The last sticks of broken furniture were pulled aside and the Vrall began to force themselves through the openings. They slashed and clawed at the defenders and their pitiful improvised clubs, driving them backwards.

A scintillating green beam lashed out of the night and struck the leading Vrall. Veins of emerald fire coursed through its body and it exploded in a boiling cloud of vapour. Another beam stabbed out of the darkness and a second Vrall was blasted. A third beam struck, and a fourth.

The Vrall turned about in confusion. With their night-sensitive vision they saw two armed figures standing on the landing ground, where only moments before no living human had been.

The nearest Vrall charged them only to be cut down by a stabbing beam. For the first time the creatures felt fear. Instinct took over – when they could not fight they would hide. They scattered through the base buildings.

But they could not conceal themselves from the guns' sensors, which revealed them even when they tried to merge with their surroundings. Nor was there any escape from the beams that automatically tracked them, however rapidly they jumped and twisted. As each beam stabbed out one Vrall died. A handful fled up the track that led out of the glen, only to meet a third armed figure that rayed them down with mechanical precision, one by one…

Turlough was intoxicated by the terrible joy of the slaughter. It was a release of some primitive part of him that called for restitution of a wrong in like measure, and which thrilled at every squeeze of the trigger because it was a payment for what had been done to Lytalia. He was hardly aware of the Doctor by his side, only the stark monochromatic landscape as seen through his night-vision goggles and the leaping, scurrying things that showed on the gun's targeting display. And he found himself yelling aloud at the Vrall, calling them every obscene name he could think of as he burned the life from them. He was an avenger meting out retribution with bolts of fire, he was life and death, he was, for a terrible few moments, supreme above all things.

And then the gun's display was clear.

He continued to pull the trigger but the gun, sensing no valid target, did not fire. He spun round, dizzy on adrenaline, feeling lost and bewildered. He realised the Doctor had taken him by the shoulders and was speaking calm steady words.

'It's finished, Turlough, they're all dead. Do you hear me? You can stop firing now.'

Catching his breath, he nodded, and wiped the sweat from his brow with a trembling hand.

The Doctor walked slowly over to the remains of the officers' mess and called out: 'It's all right. They're all dead. You can come out now.' His voice was shaking with pent-up emotion.

The dim yellow light of an oil lamp shone out from a window and a head appeared cautiously. 'Doctor… is that you?' The voice was Haliwell's.

'It is, Captain. And Turlough. Sorry we didn't get here sooner, but we had a few difficulties along the way.' Almost as an afterthought he added: 'Is Her Majesty safe?'

'She is… by the grace of God and your fine efforts.'

From within the beleaguered hut came the sounds of ragged

cheering. The Doctor nodded thoughtfully and returned to Turlough.

'We're almost done here now,' he said.

'What do you mean? The Vrall are dead.'

'Yes, but now I must make sure history handles that fact properly.' He looked about the landing ground. 'Where's Kamelion?'

Turlough looked and pointed. 'There, just coming down the path... hey!' He dashed forward and took the limp figure Kamelion was carrying from the android's arms.

'From the description I heard I believe this is Miss Boyes-Dennison,' Kamelion explained. 'I found her on the upper slope of the glen. I surmise she was thrown clear of the spaceship whose wreckage lies below.'

Turlough could see that Emily's face was bloody and she had a tremendous bruise on her forehead, but she seemed to be breathing easily.

'I think you might take her to Captain Haliwell,' the Doctor said dryly. 'I'm sure he'll be glad to see her.'

An hour later some measure of order was being restored. The telegraph had been reopened and a relief party was already on its way from Balmoral. Brown remained by the Queen as she sat in the remains of the officers' mess, adamant she should not set foot outside the building again unless it was into a carriage to take her away from what he called 'this accurs'd glen'.

'Really, John,' she said when they were alone. 'I do not think you can blame the land itself for this tragedy.'

'This place was defiled by yon flying machines. Unnatural things. I said nae good would come of it.'

'You did, that is true...'

They became aware of a figure standing in the doorway. They both looked up, expecting to see Bristow or Haliwell enter. But the newcomer seemed to hang back in the shadows. The dim lamplight only sketched in his features, so they were elusive yet also tantalisingly familiar.

He said softly: 'My dear, the time is not right for the stars. This is all best forgotten.'

The Queen caught her breath even as Brown took a step back uttering a stifled oath. The accent and the stance had been unmistakable -- but it could not be!

Recovering himself, Brown rushed to the door and looked up and down the corridor. But the figure had vanished. Brown returned, shaking his head.

The Queen sat very still for some minutes calming herself and thinking intently. Then she said: 'John, please have Commodore Bristow come to me at once.'

The Doctor and Turlough waited by the foot of the track leading out of the glen. The base's electric lighting had been restored, and they had edged back into the shadows. Eventually they saw Haliwell emerge from one of the huts and look about him, as though he was searching for someone.

The Doctor called out: 'Over here, Captain.'

Haliwell ran over to them, peering uncertainly into the gloom. 'I was wondering where you had got to, Doctor. After your signal service, Her Majesty desires to meet you to express her thanks.'

'She is very kind, but I think our presence might only confuse matters. Did she have anything else to say?'

Haliwell sighed. 'She said that astral travel is to be abandoned. She believes that the nation is not yet ready to accept its consequences, and that the people might panic if they learned of the perils space held. This base is to be dismantled and the remains of the ships are to be broken up. She will personally see that the Prime Minister and the Admiralty follow the same policy. She is absolutely adamant that all plans, records and logbooks be destroyed. She even said she would amend her own private diaries. It will be as though all this never happened.' He looked about at the base and the remains of the *Cygnus* and still smouldering *Lynx*. 'But how can one forget such an incredible adventure... or the loss of so many good lives?'

'Then don't try,' the Doctor advised. 'Just don't talk about it. It's not the same thing, you know. Now, how is Miss Boyes-Dennison?'

'Recovering from that terrible knock she took, but she will be fine, I'm pleased to say.'

'That's good news.'

'But I still feel responsible for all this, for bringing those disgusting things here,' Haliwell said heavily. 'Sinclair, good fellow that he is, is claiming that he made the original agreement with the Phiadorans, but as expedition commander it was my ultimate responsibility. The peril I put the country to beggars belief!'

'Believe me, you couldn't have known what they were really like,' Turlough assured him sincerely.

'Neither of you is to blame,' the Doctor said. 'You acted from what seemed the best of motives. At least, since none of this officially ever happened there can be no official blame laid against you.'

'But I will still carry a private burden of guilt.'

'We all bear our measure of that, just don't let it consume you. Remember that even I was taken in by them, and I have had considerable experience in such matters.'

Haliwell looked at him very closely. 'Yes, I believe you have, Doctor. You seem so familiar with so many extraordinary things. I have been having a few words with Sinclair about you, and I do wonder... damn it, Doctor – what are you and where do you come from?'

The Doctor smiled. 'I like to think of myself as a citizen of the galaxy.'

'It's the best answer you're going to get,' Turlough told Haliwell.

'I see,' Haliwell said. He thought for a moment, then pulled a familiar object from his pocket. 'This is my private journal of our mission. I've brought it up-to-date as well as I can. There are some quite personal observations included within it, but I feel they are an essential part of the story and I would like them to survive. My experiences have caused me to think again on many matters. I suppose that is a consequence of journeying into the unknown. Anyway, for what it's worth, I would like to consign the journal to your care rather than have to destroy it. I know you'll be discreet.'

He handed the diary to the Doctor.

'I'll keep it safe,' the Doctor promised.

'Thank you. It will comfort me to know that some record of our adventure still exists… somewhere. Otherwise, in a hundred years who would believe any of this ever happened?'

'Who indeed? Well, goodbye, Captain.'

'You have to go so soon?'

'People to see, worlds to save, that sort of thing,' Turlough said.

They shook hands and Haliwell turned away and walked back to the base.

Kamelion emerged from the darkness behind them. 'I trust my impersonation was satisfactory, Doctor?'

'Evidently you caught the likeness of the late Prince Albert perfectly,' the Doctor said. 'The desired result has been achieved.'

They started back up the path to where they had left the TARDIS.

'So, you decided,' Turlough said. 'There'll be no more Victorian spacemen.'

'I'm afraid not. They could probably have reconstructed a lot of Professor Boyes-Dennison's work and made new ships given time, but it would be premature. Think of the political tensions that would arise when other countries found out what the British had achieved. No, the mentality of empire is not right for the exploration of space. In a hundred years or so, though Earthly society will hardly be fully mature, it will have been chastened by experience and be more ready to accept change. Then the true exploration of space can begin. In the far future of course, there will be stellar empires… but that's a different story. When I realised the timeline could be decided by a few words spoken to the Queen, I opted for continuity. This is… will be… your past.'

'Can they really cover up all this? All those lives lost?'

'No more than might be lost if a navy ship went down at sea in the course of its duty. Perhaps that's what will be said. It's close enough to the truth and far easier to believe.'

Turlough chuckled ironically. 'There was Haliwell searching for changes in mankind's appreciation of its place in the world through the experience of space travel. But he was really only looking for it amongst his own class. He didn't notice the social revolution going on in the *Draco*. Stanton had a taste of freedom and power that didn't fit in with his position in the hierarchy, and I think that helped push him over the top. You're right, they aren't ready yet.'

The Doctor had flipped to the last written page of the diary and was smiling. 'Actually, I think Haliwell has made some concession to the coming social order. These last lines are rather hastily scribbled, but listen:

'Following the dreadful experience we have just endured, this was hardly an appropriate time to raise the matter once again, but after the agony of thinking she was lost to me, I found I could not continue a moment longer without knowing. I told Emily that in all honesty I did not yet agree with her aspirations for womankind, but that I remained willing to be convinced otherwise by reason and example – if she would be my teacher. Then I put my own proposal to her once again. To my greatest joy, Emily said yes.'

Epilogue

They were back in the TARDIS sliding through the infinity of hyperspace once again.

The Doctor looked at Turlough's morose expression. 'You're not begrudging Haliwell and Emily their chance of happiness, I hope?'

'No, good luck to them. But I can't get Lytalia out of my mind. What would have happened if we'd landed on the Moon before the Vrall took her over? I suppose I'll never know.'

The Doctor sighed. 'I was wondering whether to tell you this. I came across some facts about the Phiadorans in the data base while searching for information on the Vrall. Perhaps you should read it for yourself.'

He called up the file. Lines of text scrolled across the screen.

The Phiadoran Clan Matriarchy. Dominated the Phiadoran Directorate systems from 611,072.26 (Galactic Time Index) to 611,548.91 GTI. Members of this exclusively female oligarchy used a range of methods to suppress political opponents and civil dissenters, including deception, bribery, covert surveillance, kidnapping and assassination. They are also believed to have possessed genetically engineered and enhanced pheromone glands, which were used to influence the judgement of susceptible species, particularly males. The Matriarchy was overthrown in the Sarmon revolution which brought about the disintegration of the Directorate. The fate of the clan members ruling Phiador at the time of the revolution is unknown...

'...until now,' Turlough concluded, feeling sickened. 'It was all a lie!'

'Most of it. I don't think the presence of the Vrall had much effect on the Phiadorans' personalities, just gave them a different objective. You may recall instances where their innate natures were barely under check. Nareena insisting she should pilot a saucer, for instance, and the effect they had on Haliwell when he first met them.'

'Enough!' Turlough said. He took a deep breath. 'It was never love. Lytalia was just using me, encouraging me to play the hero so she could get off the Moon. I was taken in completely. Sounds like the Vrall and the Phiadorans deserved each other.'

'Perhaps evil met its twin on the Moon. I wouldn't be surprised if the clan hadn't set up the hunting park themselves long ago. How ironic that they were then exiled there.'

'What'll happen to the place now... what's left of it?'

'In October 1959, the Russian unmanned probe Lunik 3 went round the Moon and took the first pictures of the far side. One of the most notable features was a deep and unusually dark-floored crater basin which they named Tsiolkovskii, after a Russian teacher who wrote a famous early paper on rocket travel. I don't think anybody will suspect the purpose it once served until some deep excavations are made there. But that's a problem for another century.'

The Doctor looked at the diary Haliwell had given him.

'Now I think I'd better put this in the time safe and set those retroactive coordinates. Once it's sealed away, you can put the one you've got in the library.'

Turlough's hand went guiltily to his pocket. 'You knew I had the original! How?'

The Doctor pulled out a grubby strip of paper from his own pocket. 'Because I found the note you had written spilling out of your pack after the saucer crashed.'

'I thought that had vanished into time, or something! I wondered if I might go next!'

'You might have done if you hadn't been lucky. It was very foolish of you.'

'Don't worry, I won't be looking into my own future again. It's too much strain trying to get everything to work out properly.'

'Yes, I sometimes feel the same,' the Doctor said dryly. 'You'd better write out a fresh note to put in the diary. The same wording as before – unless you feel tempted to give your earlier self some hint about what's to come?'

'No way! He'll have to go through it just like I did.'

'Good, I wouldn't advise making any changes just now.'

Turlough found a slip of paper and wrote his cryptic message. The Doctor placed the diary in the time safe, set the lock and closed the roundel. 'And that is the last temporal loose end tied up,' he declared.

'You know,' Turlough said, 'a few days ago I was trying to make some sense of my life. We met Haliwell's expedition and I thought: at least they've got a purpose, even if it is just to extend their empire. And then I met Lytalia and thought that maybe she and I… Anyway, after everything that's happened, I still don't know where I'm going.'

'But perhaps,' the Doctor suggested, 'you're now a little better equipped to get there?'

'Oh, I've learnt a few things… like never trust a pretty face.'

'That's too cynical. Just learn to look deep. What really counts always lies beneath the skin.' He smiled. 'Now, where shall we go next?'

Turlough shrugged. 'I still feel cold thinking about that crater. What about somewhere a bit warmer?'

'I'll see what I can do,' the Doctor said.

About the Author

Christopher Bulis admits to being old enough to have watched *Doctor Who* live from the very first episode. Since then he has acquired a degree in architecture and also worked in the fields of art and design before turning to writing. Unaccountably, he has failed to pursue careers in the SAS, gold prospecting or white-water rafting, which traditionally make these biographies much more interesting to read. Unlike a rather more famous fantasy author, he has never kept carnivorous plants. (PS: Since the above appeared in the back of *More Short Trips*, Chris has moved house and… no, sorry, that's as exciting as it gets.)

PRESENTING

DOCTOR WHO

AN ALL-NEW AUDIO DRAMA

Big Finish Productions is proud to present all-new *Doctor Who* adventures on audio!

Featuring original music and sound-effects, these full-cast plays are available on double cassette in high street stores, and on limited-edition double CD from all good specialist stores, or via mail order.

Available from September 2000
THE FIRES OF VULCAN

A four-part story by Steve Lyons.
Starring **Sylvester McCoy** as the Doctor
and **Bonnie Langford** as Mel.

Two thousand years ago, a cataclysmic volcanic eruption wiped the Roman city of Pompeii from the face of the Earth. It also buried the Doctor's TARDIS...

Arriving in Pompeii one day before the disaster, the Doctor and Mel find themselves separated from their ship and entangled in local politics. With time running out, they fight to escape from the shadow of Mount Vesuvius. But how can they succeed when history itself is working against them?

If you wish to order the CD version, please photocopy this form or provide all the details on paper. Delivery within 28 days of release.
Send to: PO Box 1127, Maidenhead, Berkshire. SL6 3LN.
Big Finish Hotline 01628 828283.

Please send me   [ ] copies of *The Fires of Vulcan*
each @ £13.99 (£15.50 non-UK orders) Prices inclusive of postage and packing.
Payment can be accepted by credit card or by personal cheques, payable to Big Finish Productions Ltd.
Name...
Address...
....
Postcode...
VISA/Mastercard number
....
Expiry date...
Signature...

Other stories featuring the Seventh Doctor still available include:
THE GENOCIDE MACHINE   THE FEARMONGER

For more details visit our website at
http://www.doctorwho.co.uk